**THERE IS THE LAW,
AND THERE IS JUSTICE.
THE TWO ARE NOT ALWAYS
THE SAME . . .**

"GRITTY . . . ATMOSPHERIC."
Pittsburgh Post-Gazette

"ROUGHHOUSE ACTION AND
CRACKLING DIALOGUE."
Seattle Post-Intelligencer

"DARKER, RICHER . . .
A THOUGHTFUL THRILLER."
Ft. Lauderdale Sun-Sentinel

"G.M. FORD IS MUST READING."
Harlan Coben

Resounding praise for

G.M. FORD

and

BLACK RIVER

"Another two-fisted shot from the hard-boiled school of crime fiction . . . Ford demonstrates an adroit hand with roughhouse action and crackling dialogue and gonzo humor . . . ***Black River*** zips along with relentless drive, a Dodge Charger of a novel."

Seattle Post-Intelligence

"G.M. Ford has decided to get serious . . . Seattle takes on more interesting shades from Corso's darker perspective."

New York Times Book Review

"Beach Book of the Week."

People

"Ford serves up great dollops of intrigue, danger, and edge-of-the-seat suspense . . . What more could a mystery fan want?"

Booklist

"Corso is a terrific, unpredictable character worth spending time with."

Albany Times-Union

"The best writer of Seattle-based crime fiction these days is . . . G.M. Ford."
Seattle Magazine

"***Black River*** overflows with a well-conceived plot, true villains, and an anti-hero whose focus never strays. Ford invests a subtlety in ***Black River*** that makes the story seem deceptively simple. It's not . . . A briskly moving plot that never falters . . . Ford delivers a thoughtful thriller."
Ft. Lauderdale Sun-Sentinel

"Pace, plot, pitch, prose: all precisely as they should be in a model modern mystery . . . Corso's terrific."
Kirkus Reviews (* Starred Review *)

"Gritty . . . atmospheric . . . Balagula is a well-rounded villain . . . Ford tells an engaging story with several clever twists. Plot is clearly his forte."
Pittsburgh Post-Gazette

"Frank Corso is irresistible, part Sam Spade, part Hunter S. Thompson . . . You're in the hands of a superior storyteller."
Martha C. Lawrence

"Welcome back, Mr. Corso—and Mr. Ford."
Publishers Weekly (* Starred Review *)

"G.M. Ford . . . may be the best-kept secret in mystery novels . . . He's at the top of his genre and that's as good as it gets."
Dennis Lehane

"Ford is a stylish and supremely confident writer. His depiction of Seattle is masterful, his scenes of violence deft and chillingly convincing . . . Corso may . . . develop into one of the more interesting and durable series heroes around."
St. Petersburg Times

"The Raymond Chandler of Seattle."
San Antonio Express-News

"[Ford] continues to create some of the most colorful major and minor characters in mystery fiction."
Milwaukee Journal Sentinel

"Corso is definitely Ford's hottest character to date."
Toronto Globe and Mail

"Ford is wham-bang, straight-laced, no fooling around . . . I admit that I've never been a huge fan of series mysteries . . . [***Black River***] may just keep me coming back."
Denver Post

Also by G. M. Ford

FURY

The Leo Waterman Series

THE DEADER THE BETTER
LAST DITCH
SLOW BURN
THE BUM'S RUSH
CAST IN STONE
WHO IN HELL IS WANDA FUCA?

BLACK RIVER

G. M. FORD

AVON BOOKS
An Imprint of HarperCollins*Publishers*

This is a work of fiction. Names, characters, places, and incidents are products of the author's imagination or are used fictitiously and are not to be construed as real. Any resemblance to actual events, locales, organizations, or persons, living or dead, is entirely coincidental.

AVON BOOKS
An Imprint of HarperCollins*Publishers*
10 East 53rd Street
New York, New York 10022-5299

ISBN: 0-380-81621-0
www.avonmystery.com

First Avon Books paperback printing: July 2003
First William Morrow hardcover printing: July 2002

Printed in the U.S.A.

10 9 8 7 6 5 4 3 2 1

To Bill Farley—
master of all things mysterious
and bookseller extraordinaire

In the country of the blind, the one-eyed man is king.

—H. G. WELLS

BLACK RIVER

1

Wednesday, July 26 5:23 a.m.

Like nearly everyone born in the tin shacks that line the banks of the Río Cauto, Gerardo Limón was short, dark, and bandy-legged. A textbook *cholo*, Limón was less than a generation removed from the jungle and thus denied even the pretense of having measurable quantities of European blood, a deprivation of the soul which, for all his adult life, had burned in his chest like a candle. That his partner, Ramón Javier, was tall, elegant, and obviously of Spanish descent merely added fuel to the flame.

Gerardo shouldered his way into the orange coveralls and then buckled the leather tool belt about his waist. A sticky valve in the truck's engine ticked in the near darkness. Twenty yards away, Ramón spaced a trio of orange traffic cones across the mouth of the driveway leading to the back of the Briarwood Garden Apartments.

The kill zone was perfect. The driveway had two nearly blind turns. This end of the building had no windows. To the north, half a mile of marsh separated the apartments from the Speedy Auto Parts outlet up the road.

"You wanna pitch or catch?" Gerardo asked.

"Who was up last?" Ramón wanted to know.

"We turned two, remember?"

Last time out, they'd encountered an unexpected visitor and had to play an impromptu doubleheader. Ramón's thin lips twisted into a smile as he recalled the last time they'd worn these uniforms. As he settled the tool belt on his hips, he wondered how many times they'd run their "utility repairmen" number. Certainly dozens. He'd lost count years ago.

Ramón Javier liked to think he might have become a doctor, or a jazz musician, or maybe even a baseball player if things had been different. If his family had made it to Miami the first time. If they hadn't been dragged back to that stinking island and treated like pig shit for five years.

Ramón settled the yellow hard hat onto his head and checked the load in the .22 automatic, screwed the CAC22 suppressor carefully onto the barrel, and then slipped the weapon through the loop in the tool belt generally reserved for the hammer.

He checked his watch. "Three minutes, " he said. "What will it be?"

"Whatever you want," Gerardo said. "I don't care."

"Don't forget, we got orders to lose the truck," Ramón said.

Gerardo shrugged. "You pitch. I'll catch."

Wednesday, July 26 5:24 a.m.

The kitchen floor squeaked as he made his way over to the refrigerator. He removed a brown paper sack, set it on the counter, and checked inside. Two sandwiches: olive loaf and American cheese on white. A little salt, a little pepper, and just a dab of Miracle Whip. Satisfied, he grabbed the plastic water bottle from the refrigerator, stuffed it into the pocket of his jacket, and headed for the door.

Overhead, the Milky Way was little more than a smear across the sky. Too many lights, too many people, too much smog for the stars. He used his key to open the truck door. The '79 Toyota pickup, once bright yellow, had oxidized to a shade more reminiscent of uncleaned teeth.

The engine started at the first turn of the key. He smiled as he raced the motor and fiddled with the radio. The ON-OFF knob was going. You had to catch it just right, and even then, first time you hit a bump, it would switch itself off, and you had to start all over again.

He caught two bars of music. Chopin, he thought, when the light in the cab flickered. As he sat up, a movement caught his eye. He looked to his left, thinking it was that sorry ass troll who lived in the basement. Guy never slept. Never washed either.

Wasn't him, though. No, it was old hangdog himself. Standing there with his hands clasped behind his back, staring in the truck window like he's the messenger of doom or something.

He rolled down the window. "You want something?" he inquired.

"How do you live with yourself?" the guy asked. "Have you no shame?"

He raced the engine three times and then spoke. "Don't you ever give it up, man? It's over. What can I say? Shit happens."

Given a second chance, the driver probably would have chosen his words more carefully. As last words go, *shit happens* left a great deal to be desired. Those three syllables were, however, the last mortal utterance to pass his lips, because, at that point, old hangdog pulled a gun out from behind his back and shot the driver four times in the face.

As he stood next to the truck, trying to absorb the gravity of his act, the truck radio suddenly began to play classical music, scattering his thoughts like leaves. He looked uncomprehendingly at the weapon in his hand; then he lobbed it through the window into the driver's lap and slowly walked away.

Wednesday, July 26 5:26 a.m.

"What was that?" Ramón asked.

"Shhh." Gerardo held a finger to his lips.

The pulsing yellow light circled them in the darkness.

"Sounded like shots to me," Ramón whispered.

Gerardo slipped the gun from his tool belt and held it close along his right leg as he worked his way along the side of the building all the way to the back, where he could see out into the parking lot. He peered around the corner and then came running back.

"He's sitting there warming up the truck, just like always."

"Musta been backfires," said Ramón, without believing it.

They'd been following him for a week. Memorizing his schedule. Getting to know his habits. Gerardo checked his watch. "One minute," he whispered.

Whatever his other failings, and the quality of his life suggested they were many, their victim was always on time. Left his cruddy apartment just before five-thirty each morning. Warmed up his truck for three minutes and then left for work in time to arrive at five minutes to six. The only time he'd varied from his schedule was Friday night, when he'd stopped for gas and groceries on the way home.

Gerardo's thick lips began to tremble as he stared at his watch and counted time. "Thirty seconds," he whispered. "Twenty-nine . . ."

Wednesday, July 26 5:31 a.m.

He signed his confession, checked his watch, and then dialed nine-one-one. "There has been a killing at the Briarwood Garden Apartments. Twenty-six-eleven Marginal Way South," he said. "In the back parking lot. I'll meet the officers there."

"Let me have your—"

He hung up on the dispatcher. Then he smoothed his confession out on the counter and read it over. It began: *This morning, July 26, 2000, I killed a man who deserved to die. For this act I am prepared to suffer whatever consequences society sees fit to impose upon me.* It was followed by his signature. He'd thought of explaining his crime but felt certain they wouldn't understand. They knew so little of honor.

The more he looked at the word *consequences*, the more convinced he became it was spelled incorrectly. To be thought a killer was one thing; to be thought ignorant was another.

Wednesday, July 26 5:34 a.m.

"He's late," Gerardo said.

This time it was Ramón who scurried up to the corner of the building and peeked around. In the ghostly overhead light, he could see the mark sitting behind the wheel, hear the sounds of music and the engine running. He wondered if perhaps the driver had fallen asleep at the wheel. Something about the situation didn't feel right.

When he looked around, Gerardo had doused the emergency light and was throwing the traffic cones into the truck. He hurried along the side of the building.

"He's still sitting there," he whispered to Gerardo. "Maybe we should wait a few more minutes."

Gerardo's face was grim. "Something's wrong," he said. "Get in."

Ramón hopped into the passenger side just as the truck sprung to life.

"You play center," Gerardo said. "I'll play third."

They'd done it so many times before, nothing more needed to be said. Gerardo gunned the truck up the narrow drive, swung left around the parking lot, and slid to a stop with the bed of their pickup blocking the mark's. Both men leaped from the truck and ran to their respective positions, Ramón out onto the grass in front of the truck, where he assumed the combat position, holding his silenced automatic in two hands, pointing directly at the dark windshield, Gerardo a half pace to the rear of the driver's-side window, where by the mere extension of his arm he could place the end of the suppressor behind the victim's ear.

"What the fuck is this?" Gerardo said.

When Gerardo returned his weapon to his belt and leaned down to peer in the window, Ramón hustled across the grass to his side. The mark sat open-mouthed. Four separate rivers of blood ran down over his face and disappeared into his collar. He'd been shot twice high on the forehead, once in the right eye and once again just to the left of the nose.

"Somebody shot him," Gerardo offered, in that literal manner of his that drove Ramón crazy.

"No shit," Ramón said. He pointed down at the .22 target pistol in the dead man's lap. "Shooter dropped the piece," he said.

"What the fuck are we gonna do? *We* was supposed to shoot the guy. What kinda fuck would do something like this?" Gerardo demanded.

"Lemme think, will ya?"

Ramón looked around the parking lot. Nothing. Apparently nobody had heard the noise. "We gotta finish this thing," he said after a minute. "Just like the plan."

"But we didn't pop him."

"Don't matter," Ramón said quickly. "We still gotta finish." He checked the area again. Still nothing. "We finish . . . just like it was us who offed him."

"It ain't right," Gerardo said. "We was supposed to do it."

Ramón knew the muley look. He pointed the silenced automatic through the window and shot the lifeless corpse twice in the side. The body toppled over in the seat.

"There . . . we shot him," he said. "You feel better now?"

Gerardo didn't answer. Just stared sullenly off into space.

"Go ahead," Ramón said. "Give him a couple."

Gerardo shook his head. "It's not right," he said again.

"Go on," Ramón coaxed.

Gerardo hesitated for a moment, gave a small shrug, leaned into the cab, and shot the body three times in rapid succession.

Ramón began to move. "I'll drive his truck. You follow behind. We do it just like we planned."

"What if—"

Ramón cut him off. "You gonna go back and tell the man we struck out?" he asked. "You gonna tell him how we was sitting on our thumbs out front while somebody else was earning our money for us?" They both knew the answer was no. In their present position, failure was not an option.

Ramón pulled open the driver's door and used his foot to push the body down onto the passenger-side floorboards. "Let's go," he said. "Nice and easy like always."

Gerardo hustled over to their truck and moved it forward, allowing his partner to back out into the lot. He began to sweat, as he followed the flickering taillights down the drive, around the corner, and into the street, where they drove north at forty miles an hour.

A mile down the road from the Briarwood Garden Apartments, flashing lights appeared in the distance, blue and white. Both men tensed at the wheel, watching the lights grow closer, until a pair of white police cruisers came roaring by in the opposite direction. Both men smiled with relief and watched their rearview mirrors as the lights disappeared into the darkness.

Wednesday, July 26 5:41 a.m.

The swirling light was captured in the iris of a single orange eye. Then, a moment later, the static crack of a radio scratched the air, and the heron began rushing forward through the water, curling its long neck for flight, beating indignant wings against the cold night air. He watched as the great bird forced itself upward into the black sky and then pulled his confession from his jacket pocket and read it once again. He stayed in the shadows as he made his way toward the pulsing blue-and-white lights ahead. At the final corner, he stopped. Everything was as he had imagined it would be—a pair of police cruisers sat in the middle of the lot, doors open, light banks blazing; four policemen stood in a knot in front of the cars, the harsh glare of their headlights turning their legs to gold—everything but the truck and the body.

The yellow truck was gone. He leaned back against the building to steady himself. Then he looked again. Still gone. He blinked his eyes in disbelief and then, afraid he might have fallen asleep, checked his watch. Five forty-two. Eleven minutes since he'd called nine-one-one. No way the pervert had lived and driven off. No way the cops had towed him off so quickly. His pulse throbbed in his temples and his knees were weak. He'd never been more confused in his life. Without willing it so, he began to move. As if in a trance, he pocketed his confession and hurried back the way he'd come.

2

Tuesday, October 17 9:43 a.m.

He could hear the blood. Above the rush of the traffic and the whisper of the breeze, the rhythm of a thousand hearts came to his ears with a sound not unlike the rush of wings. Between the towering buildings, he could see whitecaps rushing across Elliott Bay and the dark shores of Bainbridge Island floating in the distance, but of the impending crowd there was only the sound.

It wasn't until he reached the corner of Seventh and Madison that the assembled multitude came into view. The entire block was surrounded by orange police barricades. Mounted officers cantered back and forth between the crowd and the federal courthouse. The helmeted blue line stood shoulder to shoulder, batons at the ready. A dozen satellite trucks squatted in the street, aiming their wide white eyes at the sky.

Corso stopped for a moment and looked up at the clouds, grateful for a break in the relentless rain. Overhead, a swirling sky held the promise of more, and the air was heavy with water. Fall had arrived as a silver river, slanting down from the sky, day after day, for weeks on end. Even a brief respite from the deluge lessened the gloom.

Taking a deep breath, Corso shuddered inside his overcoat, before crossing Seventh Avenue and starting over the freeway bridge. Ahead, the crowd rippled like a snake. He stopped on the corner. Shouted questions pulled his gaze to the left, where an ocean of photographers suddenly raised their cameras above their heads and began snapping away. Atop the satellite trucks, cameramen scrambled to their feet and began squinting through viewfinders.

Two men and a woman were striding south on Sixth Avenue: the federal prosecution team. Corso's mind began to flip through the pages of their dossiers, as he watched them stroll up the street. The guy in the rumpled trench coat was Raymond Butler. He was the gofer, the research guy. An AGO lifer, Butler went all the way back to Balagula's first trial in San Francisco, before they understood what kind of animal they were dealing with. They found out the hard way when their star witnesses, a pair of construction superintendents named Joshua Harmon and Brian Swanson, disappeared from a Vallejo motel and were subsequently found floating in San Pablo Bay, alongside the pair of Alameda County sheriff's deputies who'd been assigned to guard them. This turn of events left the judge in the first trial no choice but to declare a mistrial. The public outcry for justice prompted the feds to seek a change of venue: north to Seattle where, they hoped, a second trial could be conducted beyond the reach of Balagula's tentacles.

The guy without the overcoat was Warren Klein,

current golden boy of the U.S. Attorney General's Office. A real Horatio Alger story. A poor boy who graduated fourth in his class at Yale, deemed too rough around the edges for major law firms, he signed on with the AG's office and hit it big when a string of successful organized crime prosecutions down in Miami propelled him from relative obscurity to the lead position in what figured to be the most public trial since O. J. Simpson. Off the record, his colleagues found him cold and conniving and, behind his back, whispered that his appointment as lead counsel had surely put him in over his head. Corso's sources thought otherwise. Word on the street was that Klein had something up his sleeve. Rumor had it that he'd turned a witness, somebody who could tie Nicholas Balagula directly to the Fairmont Hospital collapse. If it was true, rough edges or not, Warren Klein was about to enjoy the lifestyle of the rich and famous.

On the inside, closest to the narrow boxwood hedge, was Renee Rogers, lead prosecutor in the last trial. Once the best and brightest, her star had dimmed considerably when, last year in Seattle, Balagula's second trial had ended in a hung jury. That the trial had been held amid the tightest security in state history, and had also been among its most costly, had further fueled the fire of public outrage when an anonymous sequestered jury had failed to agree on what every legal pundit in the country had assumed to be an open-and-shut case. The likelihood of jury tampering and persistent whispers of a drinking problem had carried away any chance for Rogers's further advancement with the AG's office. This time around, she was in the second chair and rumored to be shopping the private sector.

Lost in thought, Corso watched the paparazzi move along the sidewalk like a meal going down a python. A sudden click of heels pulled his attention to his side. The name tag said Sunny Kerrigan. The logo on the camera and the hand-held microphone read KING 5 News. He'd seen her before. She was the second-banana weekend anchor.

"Mr. Corso," she said, "could we have a few minutes of your time?" The cameraman took a step forward. She pushed the mike up at Corso's face. He stepped around her and started across the street. She trotted along at his heels like a terrier.

"Is it true, Mr. Corso, that you're acting as a consultant to the prosecution, and this is why you're the only spectator allowed in the courtroom?"

Corso lengthened his stride and veered off to the left. He was halfway across the street when she hustled around him and tried to block his path. "Could you tell us, Mr. Corso, whether or not—"

He sidestepped her again, slapped the camera out of his face, and kept moving. "Hey," the cameraman whined, as he fought to balance the camera on his shoulder. "No need for that."

"Mr. Corso . . ." she began.

Whatever she had to say was drowned out by a roar from the crowd. At the south end of the block, the police lines parted, allowing a black Lincoln Town Car to roll along the face of the building. The air was suddenly filled with the click of lenses and the whir of automatic winders. The crowd surged along with the car, creeping down the block as the Lincoln moved slowly along. Kerrigan shot him a disgusted look before she and the cameraman hurried off and disappeared into the melee. Corso breathed a sigh of relief.

He picked up his pace, moving the opposite way, toward the area just deserted by the crowd. He walked along the helmeted line of cops until he spotted a sergeant standing behind a barrier. He held up the laminated ID card. The sergeant stepped up, reached between a pair of officers, and plucked the card from Corso's fingers. He looked from Corso to the card and back. "Okay," he said, after a moment.

The barrier was pulled aside and Corso stepped through.

"Quite the spectacle," Corso offered.

"It's crap," the sergeant said. "California ought to clean up its own mess instead of sending it up north to us."

He had a point. This had all started three years ago when, following a minor seismic tremor, the west wall of the newly completed Fairmont Hospital in Hayward, California, had collapsed, killing sixty-three people, forty-one of them children. Subsequent investigation revealed the structure had been built amid a web of extortion, falsified bids, and assorted frauds, including substandard concrete, nonexistent earthquake protection, and fabricated inspection records. They also found that all roads, however tenuous and well disguised, led to one Nicholas Balagula, a former Russian gangster who had, over the past decade, carved out a substantial U.S. criminal empire beneath the noses of the California authorities. As the bulk of the hospital's financing was provided by a federal grant, the case was deemed to be within the federal jurisdiction and assigned to the federal prosecutor's office.

"Oughta just take that Balagula guy out and shoot him," the sergeant said.

"I'm with you there."

Forty yards north, the crowd now filled the entire northbound lane of Sixth Avenue. The Lincoln's taillights blinked twice and then went out, as it stopped in front of the rear entrance to the courthouse. Both rear doors popped open.

First out was Bruce Elkins, Balagula's attorney. He carried an aluminum briefcase in one hand and a brown overcoat in the other. He was a short barrel-chested specimen who, these days, favored Armani suits and hundred-dollar custom-made shirts. On two separate occasions, he had attempted to resign from the case. The courts, however, mindful of a defendant's right to the counsel of his choice, had respectfully disagreed.

Next out was Mikhail Ivanov, Nicholas Balagula's longtime right-hand man. He was a nondescript man of sixty-three with a full head of gray hair and an unreadable face as bland and blank as a cabbage. In the last fifty years, Ivanov had helped Balagula cut an unparalleled criminal swath across three continents, picking up scraps as Balagula amassed a personal fortune rumored to be in the hundreds of millions of dollars. Faithful as a dog, on two occasions with the law closing in he'd saved his boss by stepping forward and confessing to the crimes. He'd served seven years on the first occasion and four the next. These days, he billed himself as Balagula's financial planner. Sources said he'd been squirreling money away lately, in foreign banks. Looked like he might be about ready to retire.

Ivanov turned in a full circle to survey the scene and then leaned down and spoke into the car.

Nicholas Balagula emerged from the limo at a lope. His shaven head reflected the dozens of flashbulbs that were firing all over the street. For court, Balagula dressed strictly off the rack, wearing a blue Sears, Roebuck suit that made him look every inch the beleaguered building supply dealer his attorney painted him to be. He acknowledged the snarling crowd with a small wave. The air was filled with shouts of his name and the whirring of cameras as he hurried across the sidewalk and disappeared through the doors, with Mikhail Ivanov bringing up the rear.

Elkins had bellied up to the barricades to work the media. For the past week, during jury selection, he'd been a fixture on the evening news, claiming that the seating of an anonymous jury behind a one-way Plexiglas screen was a clear violation of his client's right to face his accusers and that bringing his client to court a third time was little more than vengeful retribution by a defeated and embarrassed prosecution, whom, as everyone knew, he was going to best for a third and final time.

"Frank!" a woman's voice called.

Corso turned toward the sound. Six feet tall without the big Doc Martens, Meg Dougherty was striding along in front of the cops. One camera dangled from her neck, another was slung over her shoulder. Everything black: clothes, hair, nails, everything—a cross between Morticia Addams and Betty Paige in a full-length black velvet cape.

"What a zoo," she said, with a grimace. She stopped a pace away from the line of cops. "You suppose you boys could step aside for a minute, so a girl could give a guy a hug?"

Corso glanced over at the sergeant, who pursed his lips in thought.

"She stays outside the barrier," he said.

Dougherty nodded okay. The sergeant checked the crowd and said, "Give the lady a little room." The two cops directly in front of her stepped out into the street.

Corso and Dougherty stepped into the breach and shared a hug, a hug long enough and hard enough to embarrass them both and send them reeling away from each other like opposite poles of a magnet. Corso brushed at his coat, while she tugged her sleeves back down over the tattooed words and leaves and tendrils that spiraled their way around her arms.

"There seems to be a barrier between us," he joked.

"There always was, Frank."

They hugged again, and he remembered the smell of her, something like vanilla and cinnamon. After a moment, they stepped back and stood in silence, taking each other in.

"How're things going?" he asked.

"Same old," she said. "And you?"

"Busy."

"I saw you on television the other night."

He shrugged. "Got a new publicist. She's a real go-getter."

She gestured up the street. "Way too many bodies for me," she said. "I never had much taste for full-contact photography."

"What else are you working on?" Corso asked.

"The usual. Freelancing for anybody with the cash.

Trying to put a new show together." She offered a wan smile. "Always hoping to come up with that one big story that will put me over the top and turn me into the next Frank Corso."

He opened his mouth to protest, but she kept on talking.

"You seen the papers?"

He shook his head. She checked her watch.

"So you haven't heard what they found buried in the bridge footing?"

"What?"

"A truck."

"I've missed you," he said, out of the blue.

She shifted her weight and looked up at the steel-wool sky. Up the street, Bruce Elkins had abandoned the crowd and smiled his way inside.

"Me too," Dougherty said finally.

"I think of you a lot. Maybe we could—"

"Don't," she said. "We agreed . . . remember?"

"Way I recall it was more like *you* agreed."

"Whatever," she snapped.

Corso's lips tightened. He turned away.

She winced and put a hand on his arm. "I didn't mean it like that . . . like it sounded." When he didn't respond, she stepped in closer and lowered her voice. "It was too much for me, Corso. It felt like beating my head against a brick wall."

He looked at her over his shoulder. "At least it wasn't boring."

"What it *was* was exhausting. I always felt I was on the outside looking in." She waved a hand in the air. "You're like a stone. I shared myself with you, Frank." She slashed the air again. "Willingly . . . blissfully . . .

and seven months later I didn't know any more about you than I did when I started."

She stepped around in front of him and took his face in her hands.

"Besides . . ."

The cop on Corso's right turned his face away, as if embarrassed to be listening.

Corso cleared his throat. "Maybe we should do a nice platonic dinner or something. Catch up on old times and all that."

"Besides," she said again, louder this time, "I've got a boyfriend. It's been over a year, Frank."

Corso's pale eyes flickered.

"People pair up. That's what happens here on earth. It's how we keep the planet populated."

"I didn't say anything," Corso protested. "Did I say anything?"

"You didn't have to. Besides . . . he'd go crazy if I went without him. I've told him all about you."

Corso made a rude noise with his lips. "I know you. You've been rubbing his nose in my famous-author status, haven't you?"

She laughed. "Only when he really deserves it. He's read all your books. He says you're a passable stylist."

Corso's face arranged itself into something between a sneer and a smile.

"He's super jealous of you, but at the same time, another part of him really wants to meet the famous author I used to hang with." She bopped Corso lightly in the arm. "You know how childish guys are."

"Sure . . . bring him along. We'll all be chums."

"You'll like him."

"No I won't, but bring him along anyway," Corso said.

Again she laughed that deep laugh of hers and poked him in the chest with a long black fingernail. "This gonna be one of those bullshit I'll-have-my-people-call-your-people things, or are we really gonna get together?"

To help Corso make up his mind, she reached inside the cape and came out with a small black leather notebook. She stood pencil poised, a determined expression on her face.

Corso heaved a sigh. "How about Saturday night at the Coastal Kitchen?" he said. "Like around seven or so."

She wrote it down with a flourish and looked up. "You'll be pleasant."

"Don't worry. I'll make nice to the boyfriend."

"You could bring somebody. Maybe that would—"

He was already shaking his head. She sighed.

"You've gone back to being a hermit, haven't you?"

Corso shrugged. "You know me. I'm relationship-challenged."

"It would really help if you didn't hate everybody."

"I don't—" he began.

"Uh-oh," Dougherty said, "I think your cover's blown."

Sunny Kerrigan and her cameraman were leading a knot of media types down the street in their direction. "Shit," Corso muttered.

Dougherty stepped back from the barrier. The cops closed ranks. She got up on tiptoe and yelled over their heads, "Saturday! Seven!"

Corso nodded and turned away. He could hear the Kerrigan woman talking into her microphone. "This is Sunny Kerrigan, KING Five News, reporting live from the first day of the Nicholas Balagula trial, where reclusive author Frank Corso . . ."

He pulled his collar up around his ears and hunched his shoulders as he started up the street. That night, news footage would show a headless apparition in a black overcoat pulling open the courthouse door and disappearing inside.

Tuesday, October 17 10:05 a.m.

Renee Rogers flicked her eyes toward the stairs just in time to see Corso mount the last three steps to the mezzanine. He was even better looking in person than he was on TV, she decided: six-three or -four, somewhere in the vicinity of forty, wearing a black silk shirt and jeans under what must have been a three-thousand-dollar cashmere overcoat. A man of extremes, she thought, as he strode across the marble floor in her direction. Probably what got him in so much trouble, way back when.

While he didn't exactly swagger, his walk was ripe with attitude. Something in his movements suggested he didn't much care what other people thought. She wondered what he was covering up with all the physical bravado.

He walked across the marble floor and stopped by her side. He held out his hand and said, "Frank Corso."

She took his hand in hers and was surprised at how rough it was and how small her own hand seemed in comparison. "Renee Rogers," she said.

Over his shoulder, she watched Klein and Butler come out of the men's room together. Klein's narrow eyes widened for a moment when he caught sight of Corso. He straightened his vest and came quickly across the floor in their direction.

Renee Rogers had a good idea what was coming. When Klein had received the memo stating that an exception to the no-spectators rule was being made for a writer named Frank Corso, he'd gone ballistic. While a quick reprimand from the AG herself had closed his mouth, it hadn't had any effect on his anger.

He pulled up by Corso's right elbow. Corso again offered his hand. Klein didn't so much as look at it. Instead, he stepped between Corso and Rogers, as close to nose-to-nose with Corso as a guy eight inches shorter could get.

"I don't know what kind of strings your publisher pulled to get you in here, but whatever it was doesn't carry any weight with me."

"He went to college with the Attorney General," Corso offered.

"And those Ivy League types do stick together, don't they?"

"You should know," Corso said.

Klein's neck was beginning to redden. "I went to Yale on a scholarship. I didn't have a rich set of parents picking up the tab. I bussed dishes and swept floors."

"Well, then, you'll have skills you can fall back on if you lose this case, won't you, Mr. Klein."

Klein did a bad job of suppressing a smirk. "Not gonna happen, smart guy. I've got that SOB dead to rights, and I'm not gonna let you or anybody else get between me and putting Nicholas Balagula behind bars. He may have subverted the justice system on other people's watches, but he's not going to do it on mine."

Over Klein's shoulder, Corso saw Renee Rogers's face blanch at the words. Raymond Butler looked down at the floor and adjusted his tie.

"The only thing that would make me happier than seeing Balagula in prison would be seeing him in the electric chair, which as far as I'm concerned is where he belongs," Corso said.

Klein threw him a barracuda smile. "Then you've got a front-row seat for the game." He reached out and tapped Corso on the chest with his index finger, three times. "But a seat in the front row is all you've got. "

Corso eased his hands from his pockets.

"It's all I want," he said.

Renee Rogers felt the crackle in the air. Klein reached toward Corso again.

"Don't," Corso said quietly.

Klein's extended finger stopped in midair, about an inch from Corso's chest. The lawyer narrowed his eyes as he looked up. "Are you threatening me?"

"Perish the thought," said Corso. "I'm merely expressing my heartfelt desire not to be touched again." Smiling now. "I mean—after all—who knows where that finger has been?"

Raymond Butler hid his mouth with his hand and turned away. Renee Rogers was openly amused. Warren Klein looked from one to the other, nodded, as if the moment had confirmed something he already knew, and strode off. Butler threw Rogers a grin and followed along in Klein's wake.

"Don't mind Warren," Renee Rogers said. "He's a

bit overwrought. His shining moment has come at last, and he doesn't quite know what to do with it."

"I hope he's right about his case," Corso said.

"He's got Balagula by the balls for the Fairmont Hospital collapse. One of his investigators turned a witness who can link Mr. B to both the faulty concrete and the falsified core samples."

Corso gave a low whistle. "Pity *you* didn't have the guy last time."

She rolled her eyes. "The guy was a suspect. Ray talked to him half a dozen times. Claimed Harmon and Swanson were lying about him being part of the conspiracy." She waved an angry hand. "And, of course, they were no longer around for rebuttal."

"Then out of the blue . . ."

"Klein sends somebody around in my tracks, and all of a sudden this same yokel says he can put Balagula in the room when the core sample scam was discussed."

"Why the change of heart?"

"He says the thought of all those dead children started wearing on him. That he was never going to be right again unless he told the truth." She caught the bitterness flowing into her voice and clamped her mouth shut.

Corso watched her jaw muscles flex and flutter. "Maybe it *is* better to be lucky than good," he offered.

She made a face. "Wouldn't have mattered. Balagula'd already compromised the jury." She arched an eyebrow at Corso. "As you so well know."

"*I* got lucky," Corso said.

She held his gaze. "What you've got, Mr. Corso, are very good sources."

"Gosh and golly," Corso said, with a smile.

"It's not funny," she insisted. "It's not right that some guy who writes true-crime books should be able to come up with better and more accurate information than the Attorney General's Office."

"Narrative nonfiction," he corrected.

"I'll never forget when my secretary handed me that *TIME* magazine article you wrote. If I'd had a gun and known where to find you, I'd be in prison today."

Enraged by the hung jury, Corso had made it his business to find out how fourteen nameless, faceless citizens had been identified and then compromised. Fourteen souls culled from a pool of over five thousand King County voters. Jurors were interviewed from behind screens. No questions that might reveal identity were permitted. In the end, neither the feds nor the defense had known the names of those who were chosen. Twelve jurors and two alternates were selected and immediately sequestered for the duration of the trial in a downtown hotel under the tightest security imaginable, and still Balagula had managed to get to somebody. Only question was how.

Weeks later, while reviewing the trial transcript, Corso came upon the precise moment when he believed the Balagula camp got its hands on the master jury list. Right at the end of the first week, everything changed. Overnight, Elkins switched his defensive strategy from an aggressive attempt to discredit and deny to a strategy of stalling for time. He flooded the judge with motions. Claimed to be ill. Claimed Balagula was ill. All in all, he managed to add what Corso figured was three weeks to the trial, a delay that turned out to be more than enough time for the defense to work its magic.

The Balagula camp first took the list of five thousand names to Berkley Marketing, a boiler-room telemarketing firm operating out of a leaky warehouse in South Seattle. Paid them to make voice contact with every person on the list. In only three days Berkley had reduced the list to thirty-three persons whose whereabouts could not, in one manner or another, be verified.

They then sent the names of the thirty-three possibles to Allied Investigations, an enormous nationwide security agency, who pounded the pavement for a week and reduced the number of missing persons to sixteen.

Next up was Henderson, Bates & May, a law firm specializing in "jury profiling." In addition to consulting with well-known mental health professionals looking for weak personalities, they also pried into everyone's financial history through a mortgage bank they owned named Fresno Guarantee Trust, in hopes of finding a weak link, which quite obviously they had managed to do.

The trail wasn't hard to follow, because none of the parties had broken the law and were, at least at the outset, cooperative. When the feds turned up the heat, and it became apparent that they were into something sticky, Berkley Marketing and Allied Investigations revealed the jobs had arrived by fax and the money by mail, leaving only Henderson, Bates & May as a possible source of information. Unfortunately, attempts by the AGO to lay hands on the "juror profiles" created by Henderson, Bates & May were rebuffed by HB&M on the grounds of attorney-client privilege, an assertion that was upheld in several higher courts.

"You ever find out where he got the jury list?" Corso asked.

She grimaced. "Ray's pretty sure it was a secretary in the county clerk's office, but we can't prove it."

"What's to stop them from doing it again?"

"Absolutely nothing. All we can do is make the jury pool as large as possible, keep them anonymous, and sequester them out of his reach. There's nothing we can do about leaks at the state and county level."

"Be a good idea if this was over in a hurry," Corso said.

"That's Warren's plan." She made a dismissive gesture with her hand. "That's why it's a single indictment. Only the Fairmont. Sixty-three counts of murder two."

"Chancy."

"And unpopular," Rogers added. "The good people of Alameda County want somebody to pay for their deputies."

"What if he wiggles out again?"

"Then he walks. There's no way we can possibly try him again for anything. We don't get him this time, we don't get him at all."

"And if you get him?"

"Then he gets life plus twenty-five and everybody's happy".

"Rogers," Klein called from the far end of the mezzanine. He tapped his watch with his forefinger.

"He sure likes to tap things, doesn't he?" Corso said.

She smiled. "Gotta go. Nice meeting you, Mr. Corso."

Corso assured her that the pleasure was his. She could feel his eyes on her as she walked away and disappeared down the stairs.

Tuesday, October 17 3:41 p.m.

"Your Honor, I must again protest."

"That's what you get paid for, Mr. Elkins. Protest away."

Bruce Elkins spread his arms and then dropped them, allowing his hands to slap against his sides in a show of disgusted resignation. "I don't see how we can possibly go on with this proceeding, when Mr. Balagula is being denied his most basic . . . his most fundamental . . . constitutional rights."

"What rights would those be?"

"His right to face his accusers. His right to make eye contact with the very people who will decide his fate."

Judge Fulton Howell waved his gavel in the air. "As you well know, Mr. Elkins, The Fourth Circuit Court of Appeals has recently disagreed with you. They have ruled that the extenuating circumstances surrounding this trial warrant extraordinary measures to ensure the integrity of the judicial process. The matter is not open to discussion. Please proceed with your case."

"With all due respect, Your Honor—"

The judge waved him off. "As we discussed at length this morning, Mr. Elkins, the court will not be party to any unnecessary delays. Either proceed with your case or I will appoint another attorney to represent your client."

Elkins had been at it for over three hours, claiming that every piece of the prosecution's case was, in some manner or another, a breach of his client's rights and, as such, should not be introduced as evidence. He was prospecting for reversible error, forcing the judge to rule on so many motions that some higher court somewhere would be bound to disagree with at least one of the rulings and thus create grounds for appeal.

Elkins was good. Animated and theatrical, he accepted the stream of negative rulings from the bench with a show of profound disappointment, like a kid on Christmas morning who finds there's nothing under the tree with his name on it and tries to be brave. What Elkins knew for sure was that, one-way glass or no, after a while the jury was going to start feeling sorry for him.

Nicholas Balagula watched it all with an expression of bemused detachment. A man of the people in a cheap suit and a Timex watch, he sat sipping from a glass of ice water, which he periodically refilled from the government-issue plastic pitcher on the defense table.

"Proceed, Mr. Elkins," the judge said again.

Elkins returned to the defense table, where he extracted a document from one of the brown file folders that littered the top of the table. He held the piece of paper at arm's length and by a single corner, as if it were septic.

"Surely, Your Honor will agree that last-minute additions to the witness list must be considered prejudicial to the defense." Judge Fulton Howell's face said he didn't agree to any such thing. Undaunted, Elkins waved the document and began to play to the jury box. "After twice having failed to prove my client guilty of so much as a misdemeanor, after nearly three years of litigation and the squandering of untold millions in public funds"—he spun quickly, waving the document in the direction of the prosecutors—"these people would have us believe they can suddenly produce a witness whose testimony is sufficiently compelling as to permit his last-minute inclusion on their witness list. Sufficiently earth-shattering as to justify the blatant disregard for the most basic rules of evidence and discovery."

Klein was on his feet now. "Your Honor—"

Elkins raised his voice and kept talking. "As if the malicious and mean-spirited persecution of Mr. Balagula were not travesty enough—"

"That's enough, Mr. Elkins," the judge said.

"As if the emotional damage and financial ruin visited upon Mr. Balagula and his family were not a blot on our system of justice—"

"Your Honor!" Klein again.

The judge's jowls shook as he banged the gavel three times.

"That's quite enough, Mr. Elkins," he said.

Now Elkins looked contrite. Caught with his hand in the cookie jar. He used his manicured fingernails to flick the document in his hand. "Victor Lebow is a disgruntled employee, Your Honor. A man with a grudge. A man with a score to settle." He raised a finger and played to the crowd. "A man, I might add, who was facing the very real possibility of spending the foreseeable future in a federal penitentiary, until . . ." He paused for effect, his face a mask of righteous indignation.

"Your Honor," Klein pleaded.

". . . until these people agreed to give Mr. Lebow total and complete immunity from prosecution, in return for his testimony against Mr. Balagula."

Klein's face was red. "If I may," he began.

"A man who"—Elkins walked to the rail and confronted the invisible jury, invisible behind the one-way screen—". . . a man who is being paid for his testimony."

Judge Fulton Howell leaned forward in the seat, resting his forearms on the bench. He heaved a sigh and waved his gavel at the jury box. "The jury will disregard Mr. Elkins's outburst." He got to his feet and checked his watch with an air of sadness and then pointed the little hammer at Elkins and Klein. "Mr. Elkins, Mr. Klein: in my chambers." He checked his watch and sighed again. "Court is adjourned until ten o'clock tomorrow morning." *Bang!*

Corso watched as Klein and Elkins followed the judge through the door behind the bench. To the right, Raymond Butler pulled a cell phone from his coat pocket and wandered over to the wall. Renee Rogers began sorting papers and putting them back in their proper folders. When he swiveled his head the other way, Corso saw Nicholas Balagula and Mikhail Ivanov whispering together and staring intently in his direction.

* * *

"It's no wonder they believe in God," Nicholas Balagula said. He looked around the courtroom with thinly disguised contempt. "What else but divine intervention can explain how such fools as these could have prospered?"

Mikhail Ivanov leaned closer, hoping his proximity would encourage Balagula to keep his voice down, but it was not to be.

"How else can they justify this silly legal system?" Balagula waved a hand in anger. "It is for children and fools. It punishes only those foolish enough to put themselves at its mercy."

"They have more people in prison than the rest of the world combined," Ivanov reminded him. He could feel the eyes of the jury on them.

"They have the coloreds and the poor in prison." Balagula shook his big head, as if in disbelief. "In Russia, we lock people up for their politics. Here, they lock you up for your class. For your culture." He looked Ivanov in the eye. "Marx was right."

Desperate for a change of subject, Ivanov nodded toward the far side of the room. "Our Mr. Corso is in attendance again." Few subjects got so predictable a rise out of Nico as did the subject of Frank Corso. Despite years of glaring media coverage, Nico rarely took offense at anything generated by the media storm. *The dogs of capitalism,* he called them, and neither read the papers nor watched the news. Mr. Corso, however, was another matter. Anything written about him by Mr. Corso he wanted to see immediately.

"He looks like some . . . some hippie."

"Don't be fooled, Nico," Mikhail Ivanov whispered. "He's a most dangerous man."

Nicholas Balagula curled his thick rubbery lips. "And we are not?"

Ivanov sighed. All too often lately, Nico seemed to feel as if he were invincible. As if the pair of hard-won mistrials had somehow guaranteed his future infallibility.

"That's not the point, and you know it," he said. "What's the point of baiting the bear unnecessarily?"

"He's been nipping at our heels for years. Harrying us. All those stories and articles. I want to take his measure for a moment." He hunched his shoulders and spread his big hands. "A little talk. That's all."

"A little talk is often a dangerous thing."

Nicholas Balagula emitted a short dry laugh. "If danger was what I had in mind, Mikhail, I'd send Gerardo and Ramón, and then our nosy Mr. Frank Corso would know what danger is all about."

Ivanov opened his mouth to object, but it was too late. Nico was already on his feet, already stepping out from behind the defense table and walking across the silent courtroom. His hands swung at his sides as he strolled toward the lone spectator at the other end of the room.

Behind his stone face, Ivanov inwardly grimaced and then began moving in the same direction, vowing, as he walked, that when this was over and they were both finally free and clear, he would retire to his villa in Nice. Maybe take a mistress. Perhaps a woman with children, upon whom he could dote in his old age.

At the far end of the room, Raymond Butler stopped talking and pressed the phone hard against his chest. Renee Rogers stood statue-still as Nicholas Balagula walked past the prosecution table and then began to veer toward the rail . . . toward Corso.

Balagula stopped at the rail, six feet from the chair in which Corso sat.

"You would be Mr. Frank Corso," he said.

Corso got slowly to his feet. He was four inches taller than Balagula but gave away at least fifty pounds to the older man. "Yes," he said. "I would be."

"You've been making quite a hobby out of me," Balagula said.

"In your case, I like to think of it as a job," Corso replied.

The pair of bailiffs who flanked the judge's bench began to move toward the men.

"I am but a poor émigré to your country. I have—"

Corso cut him off. "In your country you were a murdering piece of shit, and now you're a murdering piece of shit here."

Balagula pressed his thighs against the rail and leaned toward Corso. "I have used better men than you as if they were women," he said.

Corso smiled, took a step forward, and leaned down into Balagula's face. "And afterward, they sent flowers. Right?"

"You should learn to mind your own business."

"Like those babies in Fairmont Hospital?"

Mikhail Ivanov stepped between the men. He used his arms to push Balagula back a step. "The car is ready," he said. "We must go."

Balagula kept his gaze locked on Corso as the bailiffs stepped into the gap between the two men. "We'll meet again, Mr. Corso. I'm sure of it."

"In hell," Corso said, as Ivanov steered his boss through the hinged gate and toward the doors. No one moved until the door closed behind the pair.

A massive sigh from Renee Rogers pulled Corso's attention from the door. "You do have a way with people," she said, as she snapped her briefcase shut. Against the far wall, Ray Butler leaned, chatting into the phone, oblivious to the confrontation. "After twenty-odd years of marriage and three kids, Ray and his wife Junie just bought their first house. In Bethesda. They're like teenagers all over again."

"Must be nice," Corso said without meaning it.

She inclined her head toward the pair of bailiffs. "These gentlemen have kindly agreed to escort me out through the parking garage. I'm told we can avoid the media that way. Would you care to join me?"

Corso stared up the aisle toward the door. "Sure," he said, without looking her way.

Stopping at the top of the aisle, Nicholas Balagula looked back at Corso and the prosecution team. His color was deeper than usual. Ivanov could tell that his friend's encounter with Corso had left him feeling peevish and unfulfilled, and thus Ivanov had an inkling of what was to come next.

"Tonight," was all Balagula said.

"I've had to make alternative arrangements," Ivanov said.

"Oh?"

"Our customary provider has refused to continue."

"There are others, I'm sure."

"He objects to the condition in which the goods were returned."

"Surely there can be no shortage."

Ivanov shrugged. "Your tastes are difficult."

"Tonight," Nicholas Balagula said again.

5

Tuesday, October 17 4:09 p.m.

She pulled the olive from the red plastic sword, popped it into her mouth, and chewed slowly. "So, what is it about the Nicholas Balagula saga that so captures your attention, Mr. Corso?" she asked, when she'd finished.

"What do you mean?"

They sat on opposite sides of a scarred oak table, four blocks west of the courthouse. Twenty years ago, Vito's had been the favored watering hole of Seattle's movers and shakers. These days it was just another remnant waiting for the wrecking ball. Seattle at the millennium. If it wasn't glitzy, it was gone.

Renee Rogers downed the final swallows of her second Bombay Sapphire martini and wiped her full lips with her cocktail napkin. "You've been following this case from the beginning." She ate the other olive and gestured to the bartender for another drink. "I remember you sitting in the first row of the balcony during the San Francisco trial. I'd see you up there every day and wonder who you were."

"Balagula offends my sense of the natural order of things."

"How so?"

Corso thought it over. "I guess there's a part of me that believes something corny like *What goes around comes around.* That things are intended to be a certain way, and if you deviate too far you suffer the consequences."

"A moral order."

"Something more organic. More like a river, maybe," Corso said. "One of those rustbelt rivers where they poured so many toxins into the water it finally caught fire. And then—you know—all they had to do was to stop the dumping, and a couple of years later it went right back to being a river again. Nothing Balagula touches is ever the same again. It's like he spreads pestilence or something." He made a face. "Sounds stupid when I say it out loud."

"I understand," she said. "I know the type. I've spent the last seventeen years putting them behind bars."

"Not guys like him. Most people kill because they don't see any way out, or in the heat of passion, or because they've got a blood lust. Balagula's used murder as a business strategy from the beginning, even when the stakes were small."

"Since the day he arrived."

"All the way back to when he first surfaced in Brighton Beach fifteen years ago, claiming to be a wholesale jeweler. Next thing you know, the four biggest wholesale jewelers in Brooklyn go missing within the same six-month period and Balagula ends up with all their business."

When she smiled, he could see the lines in the corners of her gray eyes. He wondered if the color was natural or contact lenses.

"Do I detect a streak of self-righteousness in the famous writer?" she asked.

"My mama used to say I had enough moral indignation for a dozen preachers." Corso took a sip of beer and checked his watch.

"I understand you're a year late with the book."

Corso raised an eyebrow. "A book needs an ending."

She leaned back in the chair, rested the base of the martini glass against her sternum, and shook her head sadly. "The end to this one's been a long time coming." She sighed.

"I'm pretty sure my publisher would agree."

"You've got enough clout to make them wait."

"It's not about clout," Corso said. "It's not about the quality of your work or the love of words. It's about money, pure and simple. If you're making them money, they'll put up with you. If you're not, you go back to your day job."

She winced. "I always looked at publishing as something romantic." She waved the martini glass in the air. "Something almost mystical," she said.

"And I used to think truth and justice would just naturally prevail," Corso said, with a shrug. A silence settled around them as he poured the remains of the Tsingtao into his beer glass. "Who knew?" he added.

The bartender appeared at her elbow with another martini. She waited for him to leave and then picked up the glass. "Here's to shattered illusions."

Corso raised his glass. She took a sip, reached over and clicked his glass with hers, and took another sip. "This is my last case for the AGO," she said.

"So I hear."

"I've got seventeen years in."

"Life goes on. You're a survivor."

She offered a wry smile. "Coming from you, I'll take that as a compliment."

Corso laughed. "I've certainly had my ups and downs."

"About ten million of them, as I recall."

"The paper settled for six million and change."

"How'd you do it?"

"Do what?"

"Go on."

"I'm like one of those Thomas Hardy characters. I just keep on keeping on."

"Seriously," she said. "I haven't worked in the private sector since I had a job at a root-beer stand. I'm damaged goods."

Corso chuckled. "And now you find yourself sitting across the table from one of the most notorious pieces of damaged goods on the planet, and you figure you might as well get a little advice on plague dispersal."

She wrinkled her nose and laughed into her glass. "Something like that."

"You got any offers?"

"A few."

"I had exactly *one*. One publisher with a failing family newspaper who decided she was so desperate to save the paper that she'd hire the Typhoid Mary of the newspaper business just for the publicity."

"And?"

"And one thing led to another. We hit a couple of big stories. The paper righted itself. I wrote a book. Turned out to be a big seller. So I wrote another one." He shrugged. "Life went on."

"Did you feel exonerated?"

"You mean like, 'You had me down and look at me now'?"

"Yes."

He shook his head. "It's too arbitrary for that."

"Arbitrary how?"

Corso thought it over. "My whole life was aimed at being a reporter. Not just a reporter but the best reporter. I was going to win a Pulitzer. I was going to win the Nobel Prize. As far as I was concerned , it was my destiny." He looked down at the table and then up at Renee Rogers. "You understand what I'm saying? That was my path. The rest of this"—he waved a hand—"everything that's happened since is just me stumbling around the woods. It's not like I planned any of it. It just happened. It's arbitrary."

"You see the *Post Intelligencer* yesterday?"

"No. Why?"

"They did a big story on you: RECLUSIVE LOCAL WRITER SURFACES. About how you were going to be the only spectator allowed in the courtroom. About you getting fired by the *New York Times* for fabricating a story, about the lawsuit and the settlement, how you've since become a bestselling author and all that." She ate another olive and took a sip of the martini. "They said you'd never told your version of the *New York Times* story. They said you have a standing offer from Barbara Walters. Is that true?"

"Yeah."

"Why's that? Most everybody wants to tell their side of the story."

"Because nobody in their right mind would believe me if I did."

"Try me."

"No, thanks."

"No fair," she teased. "You know my story. How I let a guy with a history of jury tampering compromise a jury of mine."

"You show me yours, I'll show you mine?"

Her eyes held a wicked gleam. "Something like that," she said.

Corso heaved a sigh. "I got hustled," he said. "I got overconfident and started reading my own press clippings about how I was destined for a Pulitzer. Next thing I knew, I was hot on the trail of a guy a lot like Balagula, and everything was going my way. Witnesses were coming out of the woodwork to sign depositions. Everything was falling into place for what was going to be the exposé of the century. The biggest story since Watergate."

"And that didn't ring any bells with you?"

"I was so full of myself, it seemed like it was my destiny."

She nodded. "I remember the feeling," she said sadly. "I was absolutely certain that nobody could get to my jury." She sat and watched as he rolled his glass between the palms of his hands. Finally she asked, "Why is it newspapers have trouble printing your name without the word *reclusive* as part of the package?"

"I've had my fifteen minutes. It's somebody else's turn."

Corso downed the rest of his beer. The cold liquid did nothing to stem the dryness of his throat.

"I gotta go," he said. "Time and deadlines wait for no man." He reached into his pocket, but she waved him off. “I’ve got it covered,” she said, with a smile. “Look at it as your tax dollars at work.”

“Thanks,” Corso offered. “I’ll see you tomorrow.”

He got to his feet and retrieved his coat from the rack by the door. He could feel her eyes moving over him like ants as he shrugged his way into the coat and stepped out through the stained-glass doors.

Outside, the promise of rain had been kept. Huge silver raindrops exploded on impact with the asphalt. Cars sloshed down Fifth Avenue, swept along inside silver canopies of mist. Corso pulled the coat tight around his neck and began walking uphill.

6

Tuesday, October 17 4:13 p.m.

Half his index finger was missing. Water dripped from the squared-off tip as he pointed toward the far end of the lot at a pair of buildings, barely visible through the rain.

Fifty-something with a narrow face that hadn't seen a razor in a week, he wore rubber boots and a sewer suit, the ensemble topped off by a drooping army camouflage hat.

"Building on the right!" he shouted above the din. "Name's Ball, Joe Ball. He's the foreman. If anybody can help you, he's the guy."

"Thanks!" Meg Dougherty yelled out the car window.

When he nodded you're-welcome a river ran from the brim of his floppy hat, splashing down onto the ground at his feet. He shook his head.

"Been around here twenty years!" he shouted. "Don't ever remember it raining any more than lately."

"Me neither." Shattered raindrops wet Dougherty's left cheek. She had her finger on the window handle but hesitated.

"Not this hard, this long!"

"It's almost biblical," she agreed.

He smiled, revealing a set of tombstone teeth, tilted and oddly spaced along his gums.

"That's what my old woman says," he said. "Says the Day of Judgment is at hand. Says we're all gonna pay for our sins this time around."

"I sure hope not," was all she could come up with.

He showed his teeth again. "You and me both, lady," he said. He turned and walked to a battered Chevy pickup, where he offered a final wave and climbed in.

Dougherty rolled up the window, pulled the shift into drive, and started bouncing down the gravel track toward the buildings in the distance.

The raindrops were huge, pounding the little car's sheet metal as she drove the quarter mile. The flailing wipers barely broke even. From fifty yards, she could finally make out the buildings. A pair of old-fashioned Quonset huts, EVERGREEN EQUIPMENT painted on the front of each. A black sign on the door of the right-hand building read OFFICE. NO ADMITTANCE.

Dougherty parked the Toyota parallel to the front of the building, as close to the office door as possible. She shut off the engine, pulled the hood of her cape over her head, and then sat for a moment, working up the courage to step out into the torrent. With a sigh, she elbowed the door open, stepped out, and made a dash for the office.

The office was old and hot and empty. In the right front corner of the space, a gas-fired stove poured too much heat into the room. Behind the scarred counter, an orange NO SMOKING sign loomed over a pair of gray metal desks, whose tops were awash in a rainbow of paperwork. The walls were covered with yellowed posters. Several had come partially loose and curled at the edges: CATERPILLAR, PETERBILT, BRUNSWICK BEARINGS. An Arcadia Machine Shop calendar featuring a spectacularly endowed blonde wearing little more than a surprised expression and a red polka-dot thong. At the back of the room, another door stood ajar.

"Hello!" she called. She waited and then called again, louder this time. Nothing. The spring-loaded gate squealed as Dougherty pushed through. "Hello," she called a third time. Still nothing. And then, from somewhere in the bowels of the building, she heard a noise. Not words, more like a squeal. A dog, maybe.

She walked behind the desks and pulled the rear door open. Big as an airplane hanger, the building smelled of old grease and cheap cigars. The walls were lined with workbenches and tool cribs. The floor was littered with machinery in various stages of repair. Along the far wall sat a road grader, its blade removed and lying next to the huge tires. A pair of dump trucks were parked bumper to bumper in the center of the space. Across the way, a rusted bulldozer lay in pieces, its parts scattered about the floor like the skeleton of some ancient beast.

The noise reached her ears again, high-pitched and unintelligible. She waited a moment for her eyes to adjust to the gloom and then began to pick her way forward, moving toward the sound, stepping carefully around the debris on the floor. Skirting the dump trucks, she opened her mouth to call, then heard the word and swallowed it.

"Please," someone blubbered. "Please."

She stood still. The fear and desperation were palpable. She could feel the tension on her skin, as she steadied herself on a filthy fender and took another step forward. She was close now. She heard a hiccup and then a sniffle.

She peeked around a pile of oil drums. He was in his mid-forties. Bald. Kneeling in the middle of the floor, twenty yards away, his hands clasped in silent prayer. His lips quivered as he mouthed some silent litany. And the tears. His cheeks were wet with tears. "For God's sake, man, I got three kids," he whined.

"Shoulda thoughta that before," another voice said.

"Before you fucked up your end," yet another voice added.

The kneeling man waved his folded hands in front of his body like he was ringing a bell. "How was I supposed—"

"You take money to bury a truck, the truck better stay buried."

"You fuck up, you become a loose end," the second voice said.

"We leave loose ends, we become loose ends," said the third.

"Please," the guy chanted. "Please."

"Shut up."

"No way I coulda—"

Dougherty heard a single flat report. Saw the kneeling man rock backward. Watched as his clasped hands came undone and his arms spread like wings. She gasped as the small red flower bloomed in his right eye and a single rivulet of blood ran down across his face. She stood transfixed as he fell over onto his side, his lips silent now, his single lifeless eye staring down at the floor.

She clamped a hand over her mouth and began to backpedal.

"Strike him out," the second voice said.

She heard a grunt and two more silenced shots. As she spun on her toes and began to run, her arm hit something and sent it spinning off into space. She didn't wait for it to land.

7

Tuesday, October 17 4:16 p.m.

Ramón Javier stepped forward, placed the silencer against the back of the victim's head, and pulled the trigger twice. The head rocked back and forth as if saying *no* to the floor. Satisfied, Ramón pulled a handkerchief from his pocket and began to wipe the weapon clean when he heard the sounds. The sound of metal hitting the floor and then the unmistakable scrape of a shoe.

They moved in unison. Ramón held the automatic up by his right ear and started moving toward the noise. Gerardo required no prompting. He ran for the car.

Ramón eased along the oil drums, keeping himself covered in case the intruder was armed. He squatted and peeked around the corner. Got just enough of a look to see it was a woman, before the shadow disappeared behind the truck.

He abandoned his caution now and broke into a full sprint; his long legs propelling him forward into the gloom. By the time he reached the center of the room, he realized he'd been too careful; she was halfway to the office door.

Have to take her on the fly, he thought. No problem.

He began sidestepping to his left, looking for a better angle of fire. Detached and calm, he waited for her shadow to appear in the halo of the office door. He could hear the slap of her boots on the floor. He smiled as he raised the gun. And suddenly there she was, awash in the office lights, wearing some sort of black cape. He saw her face, the wide eyes as she glanced over her shoulder into the darkness, the deep-red lipstick. He sighted down the barrel. Exhaled.

And then his left foot came down on something metal and irregular, and with a pop his ankle rolled beneath him, sending bolts of agony shooting up and down his lower leg. The pain sent him lurching forward, hopping on his good foot. Ahead in the gloom, the office door slammed the wall and then ricocheted itself closed again. He cursed himself and hobbled after the retreating shadow.

Reduced to quarter speed, he gimped the distance and threw open the office door. His ankle was on fire as he hobbled around the counter. The exterior door flapped in the wind, its metal blind clanking to and fro. Above the roar of the wind and rain, he heard an engine start. He cursed again and limped out the door, silenced automatic held with both hands.

Five yards to his left, a peeling blue Toyota fishtailed in the muddy gravel, its rear end swinging out of control as the tires fought for traction. Ramón could barely make out the shape of the driver through the fogged rear window. He aimed and squeezed off a shot. The rear window shattered and disappeared. He could see the back of her head clearly now, the black hair bouncing as she fought the wheel, trying to keep the careening little car on a straight line.

Bitch don't get lucky twice, he thought to himself.

He aimed carefully. The little car was going nowhere, its tires spinning in the mud. Fifteen feet to the back of her head. He smiled, exhaled, and began the slow pull of the trigger, just as the rear end of the car swung back to the left. Suddenly finding firmer ground, the spinning tires spewed a hail of mud and gravel back into his face, choking him, blinding him, sending his silenced shot sailing off into space.

Ramón wiped his face with his sleeve and then choked as he spit out a small rock. Again, he pawed at the debris on his face but managed only to spread the glop around. His right eye was filled with mud, his left a mere slit. Mouth awash in grit, he was still trying to clear his vision when Gerardo slid the Mercedes to a stop.

"Come on, man!" Gerardo screamed. "Come on!"

Ramón limped around the front of the car and threw himself into the passenger seat. Gerardo tromped on the accelerator, rocketing the car forward, slamming the passenger door, forcing Ramón to brace himself with his bad foot. He groaned in pain.

Gerardo held the accelerator to the floor. The Toyota was fifty yards ahead, speeding toward the gate, throwing up a rooster tail of mud in its wake.

"We gotta get her," Ramón said through clenched teeth. "No matter what."

The Toyota became airborne as it bounced out the gate. The Mercedes had already made up half the distance. Ahead, a half mile of access easement connected the construction yard with the collection of warehouses and loading docks that ran along the east side of Western Avenue. Nothing needed to be said. They had to get her before she made it out to the traffic on Western.

The Mercedes only needed the first two hundred yards to close the remaining gap. Gerardo's mouth hung open as they roared up to the Toyota's rear end. Ramón braced himself on the dashboard as Gerardo drove the front bumper into the rear of the speeding Toyota, sending the little car careening left and right. For a moment it looked as if she would lose control and either roll the car or slide down into the marsh, where they could easily finish her off. Instead, the Toyota swung wide and then suddenly righted itself for a final dash to the warehouses ahead.

Ramón leaned out the window, tried to steady his arm on the mirror, and fired two shots. Nothing. He cursed the rocking of the car.

"Get her," he said, as much to himself as to Gerardo. "Get her."

The Mercedes was fifteen yards behind and gaining fast when she crimped the wheel and tried to turn the Toyota left at full speed. They watched in anticipation as the Toyota began first to slide sideways into the building, then as the car began to raise two wheels to the sky. Through the filthy windshield, Ramón caught a glimpse of the undercarriage as the car began to roll. Gerardo stood on the brakes, sliding the Mercedes around the corner in a controlled power slide. Both men felt certain they had her now. Gerardo babied the gas pedal, ready to move in close. Ramón switched the gun to his left hand and put his right on the door handle, ready to jump out and finish the game.

Suddenly, a feather of sparks appeared. Instead of flopping over on its side, the Toyota's roof hit the cinder-block wall, sending the little car bouncing back onto its wheels, careening down the narrow alley like a drunk.

Again, Gerardo floored the Mercedes. The big car roared forward, throwing Ramón back into the seat. Ramón pushed himself forward. He stuck his head out the window, just as the Toyota turned right at the end of the building, bounced off a fence, and disappeared from view. The rain stung Ramón's cheeks, as Gerardo slid the car between the building and the fence. And then the world went red and blue.

A Nationwide moving van was backed up to a loading dock, its massive red-and-blue trailer completely blocking the way. Ramón could see her eyes in the rearview mirror, which explained why she never hit the brakes.

The Toyota plowed into the trailer at full speed. Gerardo stood on the brakes. Ramón braced himself on the window frame and watched as the nose of the little car ducked under the trailer, as suddenly, yet seemingly in slow motion, the Toyota's windshield exploded and the car's top began to peel back like a soup can.

Gerardo spun the Mercedes in a complete circle, leaving them pointing back the way they'd come. He looked over at Ramón. White spittle had collected at the corners of his mouth. "Go finish her," he said. "Strike her out."

Ramón felt a slight discomfort in his ankle as he jogged toward the Toyota but couldn't, at that moment, remember what had happened to cause the pain. The remains of the car steamed in the downpour. Somewhere in the wreckage an electric fan still whirred. The windshield was dust. The top had been peeled completely back onto the trunk, leaving only the shattered body of the car wedged beneath the trailer.

He was no more than a dozen feet from the rear of the car when he heard voices. On the far side of the truck, somebody said, "Holy shit."

"Robby, call nine-one-one!" shouted another.

Ramón began to backpedal. When a pair of legs hurried toward the front of the truck, he turned and hustled back to the Mercedes.

Gerardo wasted no time getting them back around the corner.

"You finish her?" he asked.

"No," Ramón said. "We got tourists."

Gerardo stopped the car and looked over at his partner, who, for one of the few times in their twenty years together, looked shaken.

"She hadda be dead," he offered.

"Took the top of her head clean off," Ramón said.

"You seen it?"

"Yeah."

A long silence ensued. Finally, Gerardo spoke. "What now?"

"We better clean up our other mess," Ramón said.

Gerardo dropped the Mercedes into DRIVE and started rolling.

8

Tuesday, October 17 9:11 p.m.

The rain fell in volleys, arching in from the south like silver arrows, blurring the windows and hammering the hull with a fury. The gimbaled ceiling lamp squeaked as *Saltheart* rocked back and forth. A fender groaned as the boat mashed it against the dock.

The sounds pulled Corso's attention from his keyboard. He got to his feet and stretched. Although he'd lived aboard for years and seldom noticed the boat's movements, tonight he could feel the rocking. As the wind buffeted the boat about the slip, he yawned, walked forward into the galley, and dumped his cold coffee into the sink.

He poured himself a fresh cup, doctoring it with a little cream and a spoonful of sugar. He looked up again just as the alarm buzzer went off. The last twenty feet of C dock were covered with bright green Astroturf, ostensibly to provide better traction but in reality to hide a web of pressure-sensitive alarm wires that warned Corso of the approach of visitors.

They were leaning into the wind, using a quivering

umbrella like a battering ram. Even in semidarkness, through rain-sheeted windows, he had no doubt about these two. These two were cops. He grabbed his yellow raincoat from its hook and stepped out on deck.

Outside, the wind and rain roared. The air was alive with the sounds of slapping waves, groaning timbers, and the *tink-tink* of a hundred loose halyards, flapping all over the marina. At the top of the swaying masts, the anemometers whirled themselves blurry in the gale.

They stood shoulder to shoulder on the dock, sharing the umbrella: the new breed of cops, a pair of stockbrokers with thick necks, squinting in the tempest. The one on the left sported a helmet of sandy hair that trembled in the breeze. The other guy wore a black wool cabbie's hat. They were both about thirty and accustomed to walking in people's front doors without an invitation. Standing as they were, six and a half feet below Corso's boots, they found themselves in an unaccustomed position of weakness, and Corso could sense it made them uncomfortable. He smiled. From waterline to deck, *Saltheart* had nearly six feet of freeboard. Without the boarding stairs, there was no getting on deck gracefully. It was strictly assholes and elbows and hoping like hell you didn't fall between the boat and the dock, where you'd be trapped and, on a night like this, would either drown in the frigid water or be ground to jelly between the fiberglass hull and the concrete dock.

"You Frank Corso?" Hair Helmet asked.

"Depends on who wants to know."

The question sent them digging around in their coats. Coming up with a pair of Seattle Police Department IDs. They held the IDs at arm's length. Corso leaned down over the rail. Detectives First Class Troy—the hair—Hamer and Roger—the hat—Sorenstam.

"What's this about?" Corso asked.

"Margaret Dougherty," Hamer said.

"Meg?"

"Yeah," said the other cop.

"What about Meg?"

They exchanged a look. Hamer hunched his shoulders against the wind and gestured toward the boat. "You think maybe we could—"

"What about Meg?" Corso insisted.

"She crashed her car over by Western Avenue," Sorenstam said.

"Into a Nationwide van," added Hamer.

"She okay?"

"We're investigating the accident," Sorenstam said.

"Is she okay?" Corso said, louder and slower.

"Why don't we step inside and—" Hamer tried again.

"What's going on?" Corso said.

"If you don't mind, Mr. Corso—"

"I mind."

"She's up at Harborview."

Sorenstam made a sad face and waggled a hand. "Docs say it's touch and go."

Corso felt his insides go cold. Felt so much like somebody's palm was pressing on his chest that he actually looked down, as if to remove the offending hand.

He sighed, folded back the hinged section of rail, lifted the stainless steel boarding ladder from its place on the side of the pilothouse, and turned and hooked the steps over the bulwarks. "Come on aboard," he said.

Corso led them in through the port door. Sorenstam thoughtfully left the umbrella on deck before stepping inside and looking around.

"Nice," he said. "Nice setup you've got here."

"It suits me," Corso said.

"Helluva view of the city," said Hamer, as he began to unbutton his overcoat.

Corso held up a hand. "Whoa, don't get too comfortable. I'm going up to Harborview. You've got between now and when the cab gets here."

He grabbed his cell phone from the navigation table, dialed nine, and pushed the talk button. After a moment, he recited his phone number, then his name and address. He left the phone turned on and set it back on the table.

"Car in the shop?" Hamer asked.

"Don't own one," Corso said.

"Not a black Mercedes?"

Corso stuffed his wallet into his right rear pants pocket. "I own a one-third interest in a Subaru Outback. Coupla other people here on the dock and I bought it together. Parking's a pain in the ass and none of us needs a car full time, so we went in together."

"Pretty unusual," Hamer commented. "Famous guy with a lotta money like you doesn't own a car of his own."

Corso pulled his overcoat from the narrow closet. "Guess I'm just an unusual guy," he said. "What's this about a black Mercedes? Was it involved?"

"We're at an early stage of our investigation. We—"

Corso cut him off. "You guys want to stop jacking me around here or what?"

The phone rang. The electronic voice said the cab was waiting.

He shrugged his way into the coat. Stuck the phone in the pocket. They stood stone-faced as Corso grabbed a Mariners baseball cap from a hook over the door, pulled his ponytail out through the hole in the back, and settled the cap on his head.

He slid the door open. Gestured with his hand. "After you," he said.

Corso followed the pair down the steps and onto the dock. Hamer stepped forward. Got right up in Corso's face. "I'd think a real friend of Miss Dougherty's would be more anxious to help bring this matter to a close."

"I'd think a couple of cops would have better things to do on a night like this than blow smoke up my ass."

"And what's that supposed to mean?" asked Sorenstam.

"I'm supposed to believe a couple of dicks are down here on a night like this over a traffic accident?" He gave an exaggerated shrug. "What? Things have gotten so slow they're assigning traffic cases to detectives? Is that it?"

Sorenstam reached in his pocket. Pulled out a black leather notebook and flipped it open: *Corso. Sat. 7 pm. Coastal.* Dougherty's handwriting.

"There's this," Sorenstam said.

Hamer moved even closer, crowding Corso now. "And a witness who says he saw a black Mercedes on the scene. Says he saw a guy with a gun get in the Mercedes and drive off. He says the guy was tall and dark. Had a ponytail."

"Now you add that to coupla fresh bullet holes in the

trunk of her car," his partner said. "And you've got pause to wonder."

"Pause to wonder," Hamer repeated.

Sorenstam read Corso's mind. "Car was a rust bucket," he said. "The holes are clean as a baby's ass."

"And that brings you down here to me?"

"You've got two priors." Sorenstam said it like he was sorry it was true. "Assault one and assault with intent."

"Against members of the press," Hamer added.

"Meg's a friend."

"Her diary says it was more than friends."

"We had a thing going for a while."

"She dump you?" Hamer asked.

"It was mutual," Corso said. "Until this morning, I hadn't seen her in six or seven months."

They tried to stonewall it, but Corso could see the surprise in their eyes.

"This morning?" Hamer said.

"Around noon. Maybe a little before."

"Where was this?"

"The federal courthouse."

"So you two just ran into one another?"

Corso shrugged. "We were both doing what we do."

They looked blank.

"The Balagula trial," Corso said. "I'm writing a book about it. She was there taking pictures. We ran into each other."

"Just coincidence, huh?" sneered Hamer.

"After all these months," his partner added.

Corso opened his mouth to speak, changed his mind, and turned and walked away instead. At the far end of the dock, a pair of mallard ducks quacked angrily as they paddled around in the flotsam and jetsam driven ashore by the storm. Corso pulled open the gate and started up the ramp toward the parking lot. Above the bluster, he could hear the cops jogging along behind as he strode to the top.

Corso was one stride onto the asphalt when Sorenstam stepped in front of him, forcing him to come to an abrupt stop. "Happened around four o'clock," Sorenstam said. He was so close, Corso could smell his breath mints. He looked over his shoulder. Hamer was tailgating him hard. Corso took a deep breath.

"Let me make this easy on you fellas. At four o'clock this afternoon, I was having drinks with a federal prosecutor named Renee Rogers."

"Where was this?"

"Vito's on Madison."

The cab's headlights appeared behind a crystal curtain of rain.

"She's staying at the Madison Renaissance," Corso said. "Give her a jingle." He sidestepped out from between the cops and walked away.

9

Tuesday, October 17 9:29 p.m.

When Corso slipped through the door, there were three of them in the room with her.

Dougherty lay on her back, tilted halfway up in bed, her head bandaged up like the Mummy. Her black cape hung from a hook on the wall, like some nocturnal flier wounded and brought to ground. There must have been half a dozen tubes coming out of her. Corso winced at the sight.

Standing with her back to the bathroom door, chewing on a knuckle, was a girl of about sixteen, wearing a white uniform and a red-and-white striped apron. Next to the bed stood a pair of orderlies, a yoke of late twenty-somethings, losers spending their boogie nights emptying bedpans. One of them, a redheaded guy already sporting a nice case of male pattern baldness, stood with his hands in his pants pockets, squinting down at the bed, where his partner lifted the side of Dougherty's hospital gown with the tip of a pen.

"Take a look at this shit," he whispered to Redhead. "It's filthy."

Corso felt his despair turn livid. He crossed the room in four long strides, grabbed Redhead by the collar, and jerked him off his feet, sending him sliding backward across the room on his butt. Another step, and Corso grabbed a double handful of the other guy's kinky black hair and lifted him to the tips of his toes.

The guy screeched like an owl as Corso slid him across the linoleum and slammed him face first into the back of the door. By the time Corso dragged him back and pulled open the door, the guy's knees had gone slack and the screeching had turned into little more than a wet gurgle. With his left hand still in the guy's hair, Corso grabbed him by the belt and lofted him out into the hall on a fly. When the door swung shut, a red stain decorated the inside.

Corso pointed at Redhead and the candy striper. "This is no freak show," he said. "I see anything like that going on again, and it's you motherfuckers who're gonna need intensive care. You hear me?"

Between gulps, Redhead managed a tentative nod. Candy Striper was now sobbing and gnawing on her entire fist.

"Get the fuck out of here," Corso said.

They kept their eyes locked on Corso and their backs against the wall as they sidestepped their way out the door.

Corso walked to Dougherty's side. Her eyes were still beneath the lids. The way the bandage clung to her head told him they'd shaved off her hair. Yellow fluid had leaked from her skull, staining the top of the bandage. He touched her cheek with the back of his fingers and then tried to settle the hospital gown around her body. Dissatisfied, he lifted a blue cotton blanket from the foot of the bed, shook it out full-sized, and covered her with it.

As he stared down at her, the door burst open: big black security guard waving a can of pepper spray, followed by a nurse. She swam her way around the guard and stood with her hands on her hips. She wore a forest-green cardigan over her crisp white uniform. Her plastic name tag read RACHEL TAYLOR, DIRECTOR OF NURSING SERVICES.

She was about forty. Trim, with a round face and a big pair of liquid brown eyes. Probably a runner, Corso thought. Her face was flushed, her anger a pair of red patches on her cheeks.

"Leave this room immediately," she said. "This woman is in critical condition. Your presence here is endangering her life."

"Not until I get some assurances."

"You assaulted one of my people," she said. "The police are on the way."

"But it's all right with you that your *people* debased and humiliated this woman. That works for you, does it, honey?"

"Which of my people would that be?"

"Those two morons and the candy striper."

"What are you talking about?" she demanded.

Corso told her. It didn't take long, but by the time he'd finished, Nurse Rachel Taylor's face had lost the ruddy glow of anger and taken on an ashen cast.

She opened her mouth and then closed it. Something in his manner told her it was true. She turned and spoke out into the hall. "Morgan, ask Dr. Hayes to fix Robert's face, pronto. Then I want to see the three of you in my office. You wait until I get there. You hear me?"

She turned back to the room and looked up at the security guard. "It's okay, Quincy. You can go. See if you can't call off the posse."

Quincy wasn't happy. He fixed Corso with what he imagined to be his most baleful stare. Something in Corso's eyes made him nervous. "You sure?" he asked, without moving his hooded eyes from Corso. She said she was sure, and, with a great show of reluctance, Quincy left the room, one halfhearted step at a time.

"I'm afraid I owe you an apology," she said. "That sort of unprofessional behavior has never been tolerated by this institution. I can assure you that those involved will no longer be affiliated with this hospital."

Corso nodded and walked over to Dougherty's side. "She'd hate being dressed this way," he said. He looked back over his shoulder at the nurse. "You have anything we could cover her up with?"

"Like what?"

"Like something with legs and sleeves."

She thought it over. "Scrubs," she said, after a minute. "There's long-sleeved scrubs."

"That'd be great."

"I'll call down for some."

"She'd really appreciate it," Corso said.

"I'll take care of it," the woman said. Something in her tone told Corso she didn't think modesty was going to make any difference.

They stood in silence, the question floating in the air between them.

"How bad is it?" Corso finally asked.

"Hard to tell."

Again, silence settled over the room.

"Prognosis?"

She folded her hands. "The protocol for an injury such as this is to offer neither hope nor despair. There's simply no way of telling."

"Why's that?"

"Anything could happen. She could sit up tomorrow afternoon and ask for ice cream, or she could never sit up again. There's just no way of telling."

"Anything I can do?"

"You religious?" she asked.

"No."

She shrugged. "Then I guess you're doing everything you can."

She stood and watched as Corso stared out the window, out over Pioneer Square and the mouth of the Duwamish River toward the lights of West Seattle in the distance.

"The brain itself shows no visible signs of damage, but there is quite a bit of swelling."

"Which means?"

"Which means if the swelling continues, they'll have to relieve the pressure by cutting a hole in her skull."

When he looked out the window again, she asked, "Did you know her well?"

"Yeah . . . for a while."

"Did she have the tattoos then?"

"Yeah."

He knew what she was going to ask before she worked up the courage. "Why would anyone . . . ?" she began.

"She didn't volunteer," Corso said. "Somebody did it to her."

He heard her breath catch. "Oh," she said. "She's the one who—that guy—he doped her up and . . ."

Corso nodded. "Yeah. She's the one."

A few years back, Meg Dougherty had been a successful young photo artist. Already had a couple of hot local shows and was beginning to attract a national following, she was dating a trendy Seattle tattoo artist; guy who kinda looked like Billy Idol. They were *the* trendy couple. You'd see them all the time in the alternative press: big loopy smiles and sunglasses at night, that kind of thing.

Unfortunately, while she'd been developing photos, he'd been developing a cocaine habit. When she told him she wanted to break it off, he seemed to take it well. They agreed to have a farewell dinner together. She drank half a glass of wine and—*bam*—the lights went out. She woke up thirty-six hours later in Providence Hospital: in shock, nearly without vital signs, and tattooed from head to toe with an array of images, designs, and slogans designed to render her body permanently obscene.

She spent a month in the hospital and, over the past couple of years, had endured endless sessions of laser surgery and dermabrasion to remove the Maori swirl designs from her face and the graphic red lettering from the palms of her hands. The rest of the artwork she was pretty much resigned to living with.

Corso turned from the window and faced her. "You'll see to it they leave her alone. That her privacy will be respected."

"You have my word, Mr.—"

"And get her those scrubs."

"Consider it done."

He reached inside his overcoat and came out with a business card. His name and cell phone number. "If there's any problem, any change in her condition . . ."

"I'll personally let you know." She glanced down at the card and furrowed her brow. She stared at the card for a long moment and then figured it out. "You're the writer," she said.

When she looked up, Corso was gone.

Tuesday, October 17 11:22 p.m.

Mikhail Ivanov had once read in the *San Francisco Chronicle* that he had killed over forty men with his own hands. He knew this to be an exaggeration. Although he had never kept count, he felt sure the actual figure would be no more than half that number.

Numbers aside, Mikhail Ivanov harbored few regrets. In his mind, he'd merely done what he did best. He had no head for business. Nico took care of that. Even as a child, Nico had had an extraordinary eye for profit. Where others saw a trickle of coins, Nico saw a torrent of cash. It was as if he had been born with an eye for advantage. As Ivanov saw it, taking care of the details had merely been his part of the business arrangement.

Of the many tasks he had performed over the years, only one left him feeling cold in the bowels. Perhaps, as Nico often suggested, he was a prude at heart. Little more than a foolish American Bible Belter. Or perhaps, as he had begun to think in recent years, some things were fundamentally against the laws of nature and, as such, had an uncanny way of connecting violators to the universal darkness of the soul.

Either way, dealing with flesh peddlers made his skin crawl. Tonight's specimen had come not with recommendation but with a warning. They said he carried a knife and was prepared to use it at the slightest provocation. Faced with the angry withdrawal of their normal source, Ivanov had no choice.

Standing side by side in the hotel corridor, they looked like father and son. The man was past forty, with the thin face of a penitent and a pair of narrow eyes that never stopped moving. "You the Russian?" he asked.

Ivanov said he was and pulled the door open, allowing them to enter. The boy wore a red raincoat and matching boots. He was probably twelve or thirteen but small for his age. He had been shaved and scraped to make him look ten, but Nico would be neither fooled nor pleased. Ivanov sighed. "Okay," he said.

The man took the boy by the elbows and set him in the chair closest to the door. He took off the boots and then stood him on the carpet. Starting at the bottom, he unfastened the six black clasps holding the coat closed. He folded the coat and laid it on the seat of the chair and put the boots on top.

The boy now wore nothing but a rhinestone dog collar and a pair of black vinyl underpants. Ivanov inclined his head toward the adjoining door in the far wall and then walked soundlessly across the room and knocked. After a guttural sound from within, he opened the door and ushered the boy inside and closed the door.

The man stood with his hands in his pockets until

Ivanov pulled out a roll of bills and began to count. "Anything he breaks, he pays for," the man said.

Ivanov kept counting.

"I heard some ugly shit," the guy said.

Ivanov continued to count.

10

Wednesday, October 18 8:34 a.m.

Mikhail Ivanov stood in the doorway and watched the flesh peddler. He'd pushed the elevator button three times now, and still it hadn't arrived. He kept glancing from Ivanov to the boy and back. He whispered something to the boy but got no response.

From inside the suite, the sound of the shower hissed in Mikhail Ivanov's ears. He wondered how many showers it would take before he himself felt clean again. Before the stench of perversity managed to work its way out his pores, so he could wash it down the drain once and for all. He sighed.

A muted *ding* announced that, at last, the elevator car arrived. The flesh peddler stepped inside. The boy hesitated, looked back down the hall at Ivanov. His small face was knotted like a fist. A hand reached out and pulled him out of sight.

Ivanov turned away. He closed the door and walked back into the suite. His stomach churned. Standing in the middle of the room, he breathed deeply and thought of his house in Nice. Of the bright blue

Mediterranean visible from every window. Of the smells of sand and sea. And of how, before long, he would be free of all this.

Wednesday, October 18 1:24 p.m.

Warren Klein started with an artist's rendering of Fairmont Hospital, one of those idyllic airbrushed liknesses that appear prior to construction and make the viewer feel as if, illness notwithstanding, he'd like to move right in.

"This is what the public was promised," Klein intoned. "A modern state-of-the-art facility of which the community could be proud. A facility whose pediatric surgical expertise could be expected to be a model for future facilities nationwide."

Elkins began to rise. Judge Howell waved him back into his seat.

Klein used an old-fashioned pointer to indicate a section of text at the bottom of the page. "Ladies and gentlemen of the jury, I call your attention to this section of promotional copy at the bottom of the picture." He turned toward the black glass jury box. "You have been provided with a copy marked PEOPLE'S EXHIBIT ELEVEN."

The sounds of the jury shifting in their seats and the rustling of paper filled the air in the nearly silent courtroom. Klein waited for a moment and then began to read. "The design of Fairmont Hospital will include next-generation construction criteria virtually guaranteed to prevent collapse or serious damage in the event of seismic activity."

Klein let the tip of the pointer fall to the floor with a click. "Ladies and gentlemen of the jury, the state will show that Fairmont Hospital, which sat less than ten miles from the San Andreas Fault, was in fact constructed without the slightest regard for either seismic activity or human safety."

Elkins was on his feet now. "Your Honor, please. . . ."

Klein raised his voice. "In one of the most seismically volatile areas in the world, this man"—he aimed the pointer at the defense table—"this man, Nicholas Balagula, in order to line his own pockets, falsified both construction and inspection records, putting the lives of nearly four hundred people at constant risk—"

The judge banged the gavel. "Mr. Klein."

"—and eventually leading to the untimely deaths of sixty-three people, forty-one of whom were children." Klein stood stiff and still, the pointer aimed at the defense table, allowing the gravity of his words to sink into the invisible jurors.

Satisfied that he'd made his point, Klein reached toward the easel.

Elkins looked wounded. "If the court please."

"Yes, Mr. Elkins," the judge said.

"I wish to renew my objection to any further inflammatory images. As you know, I have—"

The judge cut him off. "As *you* know, Mr. Elkins, *I* have already ruled on the matter of the photographs."

"Yes, Your Honor, but I'm afraid I must take exception to—"

"Your exception is noted, Mr. Elkins." The judge turned his attention to Klein. "Proceed."

Once again, Klein addressed the jury directly.

"Ladies and gentlemen of the jury, before I proceed, I feel an obligation to prepare you for what is to follow. The images you are about to see are, to say the least"—he pretended to search for a word—"harrowing," he said finally. "I apologize for their graphic nature and for any undue discomfort which they may cause you." He was pacing now, working his way from one end of the jury box to the other. "But I can assure you that any pain or discomfort you may experience will pale in comparison to the suffering of the loved ones of those who perished and is virtually insignificant when compared with the final moments of the sixty-three unfortunate souls who died in the collapse of Fairmont Hospital."

He walked over to the prosecution table and handed the pointer to Raymond Butler. As he made his way back toward the easel, the room crackled with tension. He gestured toward the idyllic rendering of the hospital. "This is what the good people of Alameda County, California, were promised." In a single motion he pulled the picture from the easel and leaned it, face in, against the jury box. "This is what they got," he said, in a loud voice.

A ground-angle shot, three feet by four feet, in living color, the crumbled rear wall of the hospital slightly out of focus in the background. A sea of broken concrete, ribbons of twisted electrical wire, and a single strip of filthy gauze all pulled the eye toward the bottom of the picture, where—poking up from beneath the rubble—was a leg and tiny foot, soft and pink and fat, the ankle encircled by a blue-and-white beaded anklet that read MICHAEL.

From inside the jury box came a hiccup, quickly followed by a sob. Someone moaned. Rogers and Butler looked away. The judge's face was ashen. The bailiff at the far end leaned into the jury box and then walked over and whispered in Judge Howell's ear.

The judge's lips were pressed tight as he banged the gavel. "The jury has requested a recess. Court will reconvene at two-thirty this afternoon."

Warren Klein beamed as he sauntered over to the prosecution table.

"For Christ's sake, Warren, cover that picture up," Renee Rogers whispered.

His smile was replaced by astonishment. "Why would I want to do that?" he asked. "I want them to—"

"You've made your point, Warren. Leaving it uncovered is overkill."

"She's right," Butler added. "There's a thin line between getting the jury's attention and offending them."

"What a pair of shrinking violets," Klein scoffed. "No wonder you couldn't put him away." He looked over at the Balagula contingent. "With an animal like that, you've got to fight fire with fire."

Renee Rogers opened her mouth to argue, changed her mind, and instead pushed past Klein, walked over to the easel, and covered the picture. Klein followed her, his neck getting progressively redder as he crossed the room.

His whisper could be heard all over the courtroom. "Are you forgetting who's in charge here?" he demanded.

"With you reminding everyone, Warren, one could hardly forget."

She stood her ground. Klein stepped in, nose to

nose. "I'm going to put that little foot right up Balagula's ass," he said. "You just watch me." He curled his lips into a sneer, turned, and walked back to the table, where he gathered his notes into his briefcase. "Lunch?" he inquired.

When Rogers and Butler looked at him like he was crazy, he laughed out loud.

"No wonder he kicked your ass," he said. "Neither of you has the stomach for the job." He strode from the room, swinging his briefcase and whistling.

Renee Rogers wandered over to Corso. "Warren's looking for lunch company."

Corso shook his head sadly. "I'll have to take a rain check," he said. "Dead babies tend to put me off my feed."

"I could use a drink," she said.

"Or ten," Corso added.

"Afterward. Vito's."

"I can't today. I've got something I want to run down."

She raised an eyebrow. "Something to do with Seattle PD calling me to make sure we were together yesterday afternoon?"

Corso told her about Dougherty.

"How is she now?"

"I called before I came down this morning, and they said her condition was unchanged."

She put her hand on his arm. "I've got a terrific urge to say something stupid. Like how she's going to be all right or how it will surely work out for the best."

Corso nodded his thanks. Her hand was warm and vaguely comforting.

"Why would anybody want to kill a photographer?"

"I don't know," Corso said, "but I'm damn sure going to find out."

* * *

Nicholas Balagula watched the drama taking place at the prosecution table.

"It appears our Mr. Corso has become a member of the inner circle."

"Miss Rogers and Mr. Butler probably wish to assure themselves of sympathetic treatment in his book," Mikhail Ivanov said. "These Americans thrive on celebrity."

"I think he's in her pants," Balagula said.

Their conversation was interrupted by Bruce Elkins, who leaned down between Ivanov and Balagula. "Do you two think you could look like maybe some of this affects you somehow? It would help me considerably if you didn't sit there looking at pictures of dead children like you were taking a walk in the park. The jury notices things like that, don't think they don't."

"Of course you're right—" Ivanov began.

Balagula cut him off. "You take care of your end," he said to his lawyer, "and the rest will take care of itself."

Elkins shook his head. "One of these days, Nico. One of these days your arrogance is going to come back to haunt us all."

"Not today," Balagula said with a smile.

Elkins stood still. "Is there something I should know here?" he demanded.

"Like what?" Ivanov asked.

"You tell me," Elkins said. "I have no intention of

being party to anything unethical. Am I making myself understood?"

But Nicholas had Balagula turned away and was now staring intently at the prosecution table.

Mikhail Ivanov watched in silence as Elkins gathered his belongings and headed out the front door for his daily dance with the media. "He's right, you know," he said, after a moment. "Arrogance is a dangerous thing."

Nicholas Balagula ignored him. "Have Gerardo and Ramón follow our Mr. Corso. Let's find out where our nosy writer friend goes to roost."

"Whatever for?"

"Because I said so," Balagula said. He turned his hooded eyes toward Ivanov. "That's all the reason you need, is it not?"

Ivanov could feel the burning in his cheeks. "I'll take care of it," he said.

He walked to the door and peeked out. Not because he was interested in what Elkins had to say but so Nico would not be able to see his face.

11

Wednesday, October 18 3:52 p.m.

Corso kicked a rolled newspaper aside, stepped over the threshold into the apartment, and closed the door behind himself. He stood for a moment in the narrow entry hall, staring down at the silver key in the palm of his hand. He heaved a sigh. When Dougherty hadn't bothered to ask for her key back, he'd figured it was because she'd changed the lock. That's what he would have done. The fact that the key still worked saddened him and left him feeling hollow and cold.

He pocketed the key and walked down the green carpet runner into the living room. Everything was as he remembered—the burgundy oriental rug and the bright green couch, the nest of rosewood Chinese tables, the framed posters. All of it—except for the photographs. The places that had once held pictures of him . . . of them . . . now showed a sandy-haired guy with a close-cropped beard and glasses, laughing, lounging, leaning his head against her shoulder.

He turned away from the photographs and pulled

open the mahogany door to what had once been a walk-in closet: an eight-by-eight space that Dougherty, before the advent of digital photography, had used as a darkroom and that now served as her makeshift office. At the back, a built-in desk held her computer. A trio of battered file cabinets lined the left wall. Overhead, a pair of shelves overflowed with books and magazines.

The cops had been through her files, leaving the drawers open and the folders scattered about like leaves. A black-and-white picture of himself lay on top of the pile: standing on a rock at the apex of Stuart Island, the entrance to Roach Harbor barely visible in the distance. He reached out and turned it over. She'd written *Frank Corso, Stuart Island, 11/9/99*. Must have been what sent the cops scurrying to his door.

He sat in her chair and ran his hands along the armrests. He remembered the week on the island. No phone, no electricity, no nothing . . . except each other. Walking in the woods and digging clams down on the beach. Watching darkness fall from the deck and then retiring inside. And the nights filled with low moans among the rustle of the trees and the ragged songs of the night birds.

Corso got to his feet. Ran one hand over his face and another through his hair. A voice in his head was getting louder, telling him to get to work, to stop spacing out and start looking for something that might give him a clue as to why somebody would want to do her harm. He gathered the folders that littered the desktop and tapped everything back inside before returning them to the file cabinet.

The cops had her little black notebook, but that was just what she used when she was out on a shoot. At home, she kept track of her life in a series of six-by-eight journals she bought from Urban Outfitters. Her idea books, she called them.

She went through two or three a year and never threw them out. The entire top shelf above the desk was filled with old journals, purple, red, blue, and green. Like the files, they were a mess. The brick she used as a bookend had been moved. A dozen journals lay sprawled on their sides. He stood them up, put the brick back in place, and eased out the purple book on the far right. Inside the front cover she'd written *1/00–7/00 Post-Corso Journal Number Two*. His fingers felt thick and stiff as he thumbed through the pages. It was awash in her bold, looped handwriting. It also was full, which meant she'd started another.

He went through the office slowly, looking for her current journal, cleaning up as he went along. There were only three possibilities: either she had it with her in the car and the cops had it, or the cops had taken it when they went through the apartment, or it was still here someplace. Took him five minutes to satisfy himself that it wasn't in the office.

Finally, he sat down in her chair again and pushed the button on the keyboard of her candy-colored iMac. A symphonic tone filled the little space. He waited for the computer to boot, then went directly to Adobe PhotoShop. Clicked his way to MY PHOTOS and surveyed the field of labeled and dated folders. Near the right margin, a folder read MAGNOLIA BRIDGE 10/17/00. He double-clicked the icon. She'd taken thirty-two pictures of the construction site. He opened a picture of the truck still embedded in the hill, zoomed in twice on the license plate, and found it too mud-encrusted to read. Five pictures later, the fire hoses had cleaned the plate enough for Corso to be able to make it out: Washington plate 982-DDG. He pulled his notebook from his pocket, wrote the number down, and then picked up the phone and dialed.

"Licensing," a man's gruff voice said.

"Ellen Gardner, please," Corso said.

"Hang on," the guy said.

A putrid instrumental version of Bob Marley's "Three Little Birds" forced Corso to hold the phone away from his ear. Halfway through the second chorus, the music stopped. "Gardner."

"It's Frank."

"And what can we do for you today, Mr. Jones?"

"Washington plate: Nine-eight-two-DDG."

"Five minutes."

"Different number." He recited from memory. "Ring it once and hang up. I'll call you back."

"Why certainly, sir. You have a nice day too." *Click.*

Nine minutes later, having searched the tiny kitchen, he stood in the doorway to the bedroom, unable to force his foot across the threshold, bracing himself against the doorjamb with both hands, like Samson about to bring down the temple, when the phone rang once and then went silent. With a sigh, he propelled himself forward into the room, like a ski racer pulling himself out the gate.

The black-and-gold bedspread was dented where she'd been sitting. He stood by the side of the bed and dialed the phone. This time, Gardner answered.

"It's me."

"Registered to Donald Barth. Twenty-six-eleven Marginal Way South, Renton, Washington. Nine-eight-one-oh-nine. Mr. Barth is employed by the Meridian School District in the maintenance department."

"The check's in the mail."

"Why, thank you, sir," she drawled.

Corso pulled open the drawer in the nightstand, and there it was. Shiny black, with a bright blue elastic holding it shut. He pulled the elastic aside and opened the book to where her pen was stored. The final page of the journal read *Consolidated, Rough and Ready, Baker Brothers, Evergreen, Matson and Mayer.* He read the list several times. Backward, then forward. The names sounded vaguely familiar, but he couldn't put them in context.

He leafed back another page. Times. The bridge. *D/L 2:30.* Then another. *Airport—David—Tues. American 1244.* Nothing. He went back a full week, but nothing among the notations suggested anything that could have led to such dire consequences.

He returned the journal to the nightstand and walked back out into the living room. In his mind, he retraced his steps through the apartment. Looking for something he might have missed or misinterpreted. Nothing came to mind.

He was still deep in thought when the lock clicked and the door swung open. The sandy-haired guy in the pictures, reading the newspaper headlines, briefcase slung over one shoulder, dragging a wheeled suitcase along behind like a stubborn puppy. He stopped in his tracks at the sight of Corso and lowered the paper to his side.

"What are you . . . ?" he began, before a glimmer of recognition swept through his eyes. "You're—"

"Frank Corso. You must be David."

David gave no sign that he'd heard. Instead he slid his luggage into the hall leading to the bathroom and threw the paper on top.

"How'd you get in?" he demanded.

He couldn't have been much more than thirty: five-ten, slim. His beard was redder than his hair, but not as red as his face. He repeated his question.

"Meg's been hurt," Corso said.

"What—just because you're this famous writer, you think you can walk around other people's apartments without an invitation?" He pointed toward the door. "Get the hell out of here, right now."

"Listen," Corso started.

The younger man cocked a fist and took a quick step forward. Corso straight-armed him to a halt.

"Take it easy," he said quietly. "She's in Harborview Hospital. She was—"

He didn't get a chance to give him the particulars. Without warning, the kid telegraphed a looping overhead right at Corso's chin. Corso moved his head. As the punch came whistling by, Corso grabbed the kid's arm and used his forward motion to send him staggering out into the living room. Now Corso had his back to the yawning door. "Take it easy, man," Corso said. "She needs you to have a calm head here. She's—"

This time the kid rushed him, head down, his arms grasping like horns, in an all-out tackle. Again, Corso sidestepped like a matador. This time, however, he sent a short right hand the kid's way, clipping him alongside the jaw as he rushed past, sending him lurching head first into the door across the hall. The hall echoed with a hollow boom. David lay still at the base of the door.

Corso reached down and touched the guy's throat. His pulse was fast and heavy. With a sigh, he stepped into Dougherty's apartment and began to pull the door closed. That's when he spotted the series of pictures on the front page of the *Seattle Times*.

Upper left was a picture of an embankment, washed away by the rain. Halfway down the embankment, the front end of an automobile poked its nose out of the dirt. The next picture showed a fire truck using its high-pressure hoses to loosen the hill's grip on the vehicle. The third picture captured the very moment when the buried truck came loose from the hill and began its freefall to the ground below. He turned the page sideways. Picture credit read: M. DOUGHERTY.

The squeak of a door pulled Corso's attention from the page. Across the hall, a bald-headed guy had his door open on a chain. His eyes moved back and forth between Corso and the body on his doorsill. David groaned and rolled over on his back.

"Whenever Junior wakes up, tell him Meg's up at Harborview. Room One-oh-nine in the Intensive Care Unit. Okay?"

The guy gave a minuscule nod and quickly closed the door. Corso refolded the paper and took it with him as he walked down the hall and out into the street.

Outside, the trees swayed in the wind and the sky was flecked with blowing leaves.

Corso turned left out the door and started up Republican Street toward the Subaru. At the far end of the block, a halo of exhaust swirled around a dirty black Mercedes, obscuring a pair of low-rider silhouettes.

12

Wednesday, October 18 4:41 p.m.

"Things are a goddamn mess is what they are."

He was about fifty, wire-thin, with an Adam's apple the size of a Ping-Pong ball. His narrow, unshaven face was twisted into a sullen mask. "We got every damn piece of equipment we own down at the bridge site. We got the city offerin' to pay us double-time to keep workin' all night, and the boss ain't no-goddamn-where to be found."

Corso unbuttoned his coat and slipped it from his shoulders. The office was like a sauna. "Gone home?" he asked.

"Hell, no. His missus ain't seen him since yesterday morning. Poor woman's near outa her mind. Called the cops last night when he didn't make it to supper. Cops come and rousted me out at a quarter to three. Got my old woman over there sittin' with her till we got some idea what in hell's going on."

"What do the cops say?"

He slashed the air with his hand. "Those dumb shits don't know nothin' more than what I tol' 'em. Wanna know if he's got a woman somewhere. I tol' 'em half a dozen times: Joe Ball's a family man. Just bought him a house a few months back. Ain't got no floozie stashed someplace. Joe Ball ain't here at seven sharp they's somethin' big-time wrong, mister. And you can take that to the bank."

"When'd *you* see him last?" Corso asked.

The guy heaved a sigh. "Tell you the same thing I tol' them. Last time I laid eyes on Joe was about three-thirty yesterday. Right in this here office. I'd been out at the site for fourteen hours. Joe was here when I come back and punched out." He turned a palm toward the leaden sky. "Tol' me he'd see me in the mornin'."

"He was alone?"

" 'Ceptin' for the girl who come later."

"Girl?"

"I was up by the guard shack fixin' to go home. She come by just as I was packin' up. Said she was a reporter. Doin' a story on the bridge repairs. Wanted to know about the equipment we had down at the job site. I sent her down here to see Joe."

"Black hair?" Corso used his finger to draw a line across his forehead. "Cut straight across like this?"

The guy nodded. "That's the one."

For the third time in the past hour, Corso failed to suppress a shudder. He'd experienced the first when, fifteen minutes after leaving Dougherty's apartment, he finally got around to scanning the fourth photograph.

She'd used a long lens to zoom in on the macabre figure sitting behind the wheel of the buried truck. The fire hose had cleaned the windshield enough to reveal the ivory grin of the decomposed body that sat slouched in the driver's seat, his head thrown back as if sharing some cosmic joke with the sky.

The news copy told how construction crews attempting to repair a washout of the foundations supporting the Magnolia Bridge had come upon the yellow Toyota pickup buried a dozen feet down into the hill.

According to the *Seattle Times*, police were speculating that the truck must have been buried some three months earlier, when torrential rains had first threatened the bridge, necessitating an emergency repair operation of equally monumental proportions.

It wasn't the massive sinkhole or the remnant driver that sent a cold chill running down Corso's spine like a frozen ball bearing. It was the cement truck and the logo. Two intertwined *R*s: ROUGH AND READY CONCRETE.

He'd slid the Subaru to the curb, hurried over to the pay phone on the corner of Fifteenth and Republican, and thumbed his way through the frayed yellow pages to Construction Equipment. Like he figured, they were all there: Consolidated Trucking, Rough and Ready Concrete, Baker Brothers Cranes, Evergreen Equipment, Matson and Mayer Pile Driving. Shudder number one.

A quick perusal of the company's addresses revealed that Evergreen Equipment was located on a piece of reclaimed marshland adjacent to Western Avenue. Right where the cops said she'd crashed. He remembered what she'd said about chasing the story that would put her over the top and shuddered for a second time.

The guy leaned over and rested his hands on the

Subaru's window frame. Half his right index finger was missing. He eyed Corso suspiciously. "You know somethin' about this, mister?" Before Corso could answer, he went on. " 'Cause Joe's old woman would be most appreciative iffen you could shed a little light on what's goin' on here. I know she surely would." The guy leaned farther in the window. He smelled of mildew. "Girl ain't missin' too, is she?"

Corso shook his head and told him about her crash. About the witnesses who said she was being pursued by a black Mercedes, and about how he'd surmised that Dougherty was chasing the story of how the truck got buried in the hillside. The guy shifted his weight from foot to foot and rubbed his chin as Corso spoke.

"You think Joe comin' up missing and the girl's accident are related?" he asked, when Corso finished.

"I wouldn't jump to any conclusions, if I were you," Corso said.

The guy thought it over. "I don't like it," he said finally. "You can set your watch by Joe Ball. Him not bein' here at a time like this . . . and then the girl . . . I don't like it."

"That makes two of us, buddy," Corso said. He dug around in his pocket. Came out with a business card. "Anything comes up you think I ought to know about, give me a call. Okay?"

"I don't like it," the guy said again.

Wednesday, October 18 4:59 p.m.

"I don't like it," Gerardo said. "What the fuck's he doing down here, anyway? Boss says he's just some nosy writer dude. He got nothin' to do with this shit."

"Take it easy. We just gonna do what we was told," Ramón said. "We gonna stay on him and find out where he lives."

Although his voice was calm, Ramón was worried too. Ever since they'd found the guy dead in his truck, nothing had gone quite as planned. Somebody'd offed the mark before they got the chance. The truck had become unburied. The girl walked in on them while they were cleaning up. Tourists showed up and prevented them from making sure she was dead. Nothing but loose ends and sloppy work.

"We gonna tell the boss where he went?" Gerardo demanded.

"We tell 'em that, we gotta tell 'em about the girl."

Gerardo thought it over. "Maybe we shoulda told 'em the guy was dead when we got there. Maybe then none of this other shit woulda happened."

"I don't think so," Ramón said. "We tell 'em we lied about the hit, they's gonna be somebody tailing *our* asses."

"I don't like it," Gerardo said again. "Maybe we oughta just pop this writer guy's ass and be done with it."

"Here he comes," Ramón said.

The green Subaru wagon was rolling down the access road, heading back out onto Western Avenue. Ramón waited until the car turned right at the farthest warehouse and disappeared from view, then dropped the Mercedes into DRIVE and took his foot off the brake. "Let's see where he goes next," he said, as much to himself as to Gerardo.

13

Wednesday, October 18 6:44 p.m.

"We have no vacancy," the guy said. "We have a vacancy, I put a sign out in the street. Apartments here never vacant long."

Southeast Asian. Couldn't have been much over five feet tall, standing ramrod straight in the door of his apartment. Mid-sixties. Close-cropped hair and a pair of black eyes that could stare a hole in a brick.

"I didn't come about an apartment," Corso said. "I came about a former tenant named Donald Barth."

"Ah," the man said. "Quite sad. The police came yesterday."

"Mr. . . . ?"

"Pov," he said quickly. "Nhim Pov. I am the manager here."

Nhim Pov stepped out onto the tiny concrete porch and closed the door behind himself. "What about Mr. Barth?" he asked. "What business of yours is his unfortunate death?"

"I'm a writer," Corso said. "And I'm trying to figure out what it was about his life that induced somebody to shoot him nine times and then bury him and his truck in the side of a hill."

"I told the police. Mr. Barth was very quiet, a very private man. I know nothing personal about him whatsoever."

"How long did he live here?"

"Five years, I think. I come here as manager three years ago. Mr. Barth was married then. Then last year this time she left, and he live here by himself."

"He have any problems with any of his neighbors?"

"He make trouble, he would not be living here still." He offered a small smile. "I run what you Americans call a tight ship, Mr. Corso. People who make difficulties do not get their leases renewed."

"He pay his rent on time?"

Again the little man smiled. "Same answer. The county has a long waiting list. People can no longer afford to live around here. They get old. They have no money. Where else can they go?"

Nhim Pov was right. The emerald city had become so glitzy that a little two-bedroom fixer-upper was the better part of three hundred grand. A decent apartment was a thousand dollars a month. It had gotten so the people who made the city work could no longer afford to live there. Not just blue-collar folk, either. Across the lake in trendy Bellevue, the new mayor, who was bringing down a cool hundred and fifty thousand a year, applied for and was granted another hundred grand as a housing allowance, because Bellevue has an ordinance that says the mayor has to live within the city limits, and without the extra stipend he couldn't afford to do so.

"When did you first realize that Mr. Barth wasn't coming back?"

"A few weeks after he left," he said. "Mr. Barth always paid his rent on the first of the month. Always. So I look in the parking lot and see his truck is gone. I have no need to go in and make sure he is okay, right? I think maybe he is away somewhere. Maybe have an emergency." He waved a hand around. "Some of these people very old. If I don't hear from them I call. They don't answer, I knock on the door. Sometimes they're sick. Sometimes they're dead."

"So after a couple of weeks, you start to wonder."

"I go in his apartment." He shrugged. "Everything is just as he left it, I guess. I never been in there before."

"Then?"

"Then I wait for the rest of the month. When he still doesn't come, I move his furniture out to the shed, clean up the apartment, and rent it to Mr. Leng."

"You still have his stuff?"

"What else am I to do with a man's life, sell it?"

"Lotta people would."

"Many people have no honor."

"Could I look through his belongings?"

"Police already been all through it."

"Just a short look. I won't take long."

Nhim Pov thought it over and then suddenly stepped back inside his apartment. Through the crack in the door, Corso could see a print of Buddha on the far wall and a small shrine set up in the corner.

In a moment, Mr. Pov was back on the porch, holding a set of brass keys in one hand and a dictionary in the other. "What is this word *induce* you said before?" he asked Corso.

"Did I?"

"You say you wanted to find out what would *induce* somebody to kill Mr. Barth and bury the body."

"It means to lead or move, by persuasion or influence."

Pov found the word in his dictionary. His lips moved slightly as he read the words. "So then . . . the force comes from without," he said.

"Yes," Corso said. "You're quite a student of the language, Mr. Pov."

"Nice of you to say," he said. "I have worked hard on my English."

"You're quite good."

The little man beamed. "Thank you." He bowed at the waist. "From a writer, I take that as highest honor."

He slipped a red felt bookmark into the page and set the dictionary on the floor inside his front door. He closed the door, tried the knob to make sure it was locked, and then turned to Corso. "Now, Mr.—" he began.

"Corso. Frank Corso."

Nhim Pov was smiling now. "Mr. Corso, you have kindly *induced* me to show you the remains of Mr. Barth's belongings."

Corso followed the little man down the sidewalk and then across the wet grass between buildings. They emerged onto a grassed-over area running along the edge of the marsh. Nihm Pov stopped and pointed out over the water. "At night . . . sometimes . . . the moon and the water—they remind me of my homeland."

"It's what's left of the Black River," Corso said.

"Oh." He looked up at Corso. "How so what's left?"

Corso walked over to the edge of the water. "The

Black River used to be the major drainage for Lake Washington. All these little creeks running in, feeding the lake, and the Black River draining it out into the Cedar River and then the White and the Green, until they all got together as the Duwamish and emptied into Puget Sound."

"What happened?"

"People just couldn't leave things alone. When they dug the Lake Washington Ship Canal, they lowered the water level of Lake Washington by nine feet and suddenly the Black River was gone." Out in the middle of the marsh, several dozen ducks bobbed about on the rippled surface, asleep, heads tucked under their wings. "Except that the Black River wouldn't die," Corso continued. "It went underground." He swept his hand around. "It pops up as marshes and seepage all over this part of the county. They can't build on it, so they've turned it into bird sanctuaries."

"It is a river's nature to remain a river," Nhim Pov said.

"Yes," Corso agreed. "It is."

"That is the beauty of America, is it not?" Pov said, as they turned away from the water.

"What's that?"

"That a man such as myself can arrive on these shores and create a life for himself and his family without having to give up his beliefs and customs."

"How long have you been here?"

"Ten years."

"From?"

"I came from Thailand, where I was in a refugee camp for nine years."

"From where originally?"

"I am Cambodian. I am in America now, but I will always be Cambodian. Like this Black River, I will always be what I am."

They rounded the corner of the final building. A line of half a dozen sheds stood along a row of trees. Nhim Pov strode over to the nearest shed, slipped a key into a shiny silver lock, and slid the door aside. He stepped inside, reached up, and pulled an unseen cord. A single bulb illuminated the interior with weak yellow light.

Nhim Pov stepped back outside and gestured with his head. Corso stepped inside. The air smelled of fresh earth and mildew. Donald Barth's possessions had been piled on either side of a narrow central aisle. Corso walked to the back wall without touching anything and then turned and walked halfway back.

In the center of the couch a Dole pineapple box held half a dozen framed photographs. Probably the stuff he had hanging on the wall, Corso figured. An old photo of a woman in a patched housedress, her narrow expressionless eyes squinting into the sun: maybe his mother. Another of a thin young man wearing a set of marine dress blues.

A crude wooden frame held an oval picture of a handsome couple, smiling and holding hands on an arched garden bridge. He was a good-looking fellow, with a thick head of dark hair and a noticeable cleft in his chin. She was younger, a pretty girl with a small mouth and even features. Corso held the picture up. "This Mr. Barth?" he asked.

Nhim Pov nodded. "And Mrs. Barth."

Corso leaned the picture against the side of a box and picked up another. Inside a black metal frame, a young boy of seven or eight sat in the sand wearing a green bathing suit. Laughing in the gentle surf, with what looked a lot like the Santa Monica Pier in the background.

Corso pulled the picture of the couple on the bridge from the box again and held it up next to the picture of the boy. The resemblance was unmistakable. Corso showed the picture to Pov.

"His son," Pov said.

Corso was about to put both pictures back in the box when he noticed the disparity in the color of the paper. Although decades newer, the picture taken on the bridge was yellowed and brittle looking.

Corso returned the boy's picture to the box. He turned the photo of the couple over. A rectangular piece of cardboard was held in place by six wire nails.

He looked over at Mr. Pov. "Mind if I take this apart?" he asked.

"As long as you put it back," the man said.

Corso set the frame face down on the couch. He rummaged in his pants pocket and came out with a handful of change, from which he extracted a dime. He used the dime to pry the nails up, then used his index finger to bend them back and out of the way, until he could lift the piece of cardboard free and set it aside.

He scratched one corner of the picture loose and peeled the whole thing up off the glass. It was a wedding invitation, framed in such a way as to allow only the picture to be visible. Below the picture, it read: *Marie Ellen Hall and Donald J. Barth invite you to share the joy of their coming nuptials.* WHERE: *Blessed Sacrament Church, 5041 9th Avenue NE, Seattle, Washington, 98107.* WHEN: *Saturday April 3rd, 1993. Reception to follow in the Parish Hall.* RSVP: *206-324-0098.*

"Be all right if I took this with me?" Corso asked Pov. "I'll bring it back as soon as I'm finished."

Pov nodded. "Okay," he said.

Corso spent another twenty minutes going through the remains of Donald Barth's life. "I guess that's it," he said finally, dusting his hands together.

Mr. Pov pulled the chain on the light and they walked outside together. Overhead a full moon ducked in and out of a starless steel-wool sky. Mr. Pov slid the door closed and snapped the padlock back in place.

"A philosopher once said that a man's true worth is not measured by the extent of his possessions but by the paucity of his needs," Corso said.

"Ah," Pov said. "What is this *paucity*?"

Corso told him and then spelled it.

"If such is true, then Mr. Barth was a wealthy man indeed."

Corso thanked Mr. Pov for his help. The men shook hands and parted company. Nhim Pov turned left, toward his apartment, and Corso went right, toward the hissing purple lights of the parking lot.

* * *

Gerardo was outraged. "What the hell's he doin' here for a damn hour, anyway? He don't got nothing to do with this. Every place we go, this guy's pokin' his nose in our business."

"He's got some connection going for himself."

"What connection is that?"

"Between the girl and the guy in the truck."

Gerardo scowled. "Like what?"

"Damned if I know," Ramón said.

"Maybe he knows the Ball guy buried the truck for us."

"How would he know that? He's just supposed to be some nosy-ass writer who's always talkin' shit about the boss."

"Here he comes," Gerardo said, pointing out through the darkened window. As they sat in the gloom, the Subaru rolled out from behind the Briarwood Garden Apartments and bounced into the street. Gerardo started the Mercedes's engine. He waited until Corso was halfway up the block before turning on the lights and following.

"We maybe better figure out where this guy fits into the picture," Ramón said, as they followed the Subaru up the freeway entrance ramp.

"Soon," Gerardo agreed. "Real soon."

14

Wednesday, October 18 9:03 p.m.

"Stop," Ramón said.

Half a block up Ninth Avenue, Harborview Hospital rose into the night sky like a stone rocket ship on a launching pad. Gerardo and Ramón watched as Corso stopped at the gate, plucked a ticket from the automatic dispenser, and wheeled the Subaru out of sight.

Gerardo pulled the car to the curb in a tow-away zone. "You goin' in?"

"Yeah."

"What for?"

"I dunno. I got a feeling."

"What kinda feeling?"

Ramón checked his watch. "He's gotta be visitin' somebody."

"Like who?"

"That's what I'm gonna find out."

"You want in the trunk?"

"I'm just goin' to look."

A hospital security guard left the entrance and began limping their way.

"Rent-a-pig gonna tell us to move," Gerardo said.

Ramón popped the door and stepped out into the street. "Take it around the block," he said. "I'll catch up with you in a bit."

The guard was still coming. "Oughta blow his fat ass up," Gerardo groused, but Ramón didn't hear. Ramón was already jogging up the sidewalk, cutting through a flower bed to the corner of the building, where he stood and watched as Corso crossed the parking lot and entered the back door of the hospital. Ramón hopped over the shrubbery and stood on the sidewalk, watching Corso stride down the shining hallway.

Wednesday, October 18 9:29 p.m.

The room was quiet, the burnished metal stillness broken only by the underlying hum of machinery somewhere deep in the building. Nurse Rachel Taylor leaned over Dougherty's bed, adjusting the flow of an overhead IV. Tonight's cardigan was bright red. Corso cleared his throat. The woman looked back over her shoulder, smiled, and held up a finger. A minute turned to two before the woman walked across the room to Corso's side.

"Don't you ever go home?" Corso asked.

"Not according to my daughter," Rachel Taylor said, with a sigh. "To hear Melissa tell it, my insistence that we remain fed and clothed amounts to abandonment."

"How old?"

"Fourteen."

"Great age for girls," Corso offered.

"Yeah . . . if you don't mind their brains being controlled from outer space."

Corso walked to the side of the bed and looked down. Dougherty lay on her back. Yesterday's stained bandage had been replaced, but she was still little more than an inanimate maze of tubes and wires, stiff and unmoving beneath the crisp white covers.

"How's she doing?" Corso whispered.

"Her vital signs are better, but the brain swelling is worse."

"What now?"

She took Corso by the arm and moved him toward the door. "Come on," she said. Corso followed her out into the hall. "I hate to talk about comatose patients as if they're not there," she explained. "I always have this feeling that on some deeper level they may be listening." Corso nodded his understanding.

"What next?" he asked.

She wrinkled her nose. "Next we iron out a couple of administrative matters."

"Such as?"

"I had a very unhappy financial administrator down here this evening."

"And?"

"And he wants to move Miss Dougherty up to Providence Hospital."

"Why would he want to do that?"

"Because we're chock-full of patients and Providence is only sixty percent full, and because neither Miss Dougherty nor the young man with whom she lives has any kind of health insurance."

Corso trapped the words in his throat. What started as a profane protest came out as little more than a low growl. He closed his eyes for a moment and rubbed the bridge of his nose with his thumb and forefinger. In the darkness behind his eyelids, he could see the endless halls of the veterans' hospital where his father had coughed out his last breath. Where he and his mother and his brother and sister had traveled every Tuesday night for seven years to pay homage to a man they barely knew—a man who left whatever decency he might once have possessed lying in the bottom of a frozen Korean foxhole and came home with little more than an unquenchable thirst and an ungovernable temper. Corso's nose stung with the smell of stale urine along the maze of scuffed hallways. He could see the ghosts sitting outside their rooms in the late evening, mouths agape, stubbled black-tooth chins resting on stained gowns. The burned and the legless, the lame and the disjointed, the shakers, the droolers, and the goners, all lined up along the halls like sentinels.

When he opened his eyes, the nurse held up a moderating hand. "It's standard procedure," she said. "Providence is a full-service—"

Corso cut her off. "Providence is a dump. I want her to stay here."

"If she stays here, she's going to have to move to a semiprivate room."

"A ward."

"There are no"—she made quotation marks in the air with her fingers—"*wards* anymore. The most patients we have in a single room is four."

"She wouldn't like being in a room with other people."

Rachel Taylor made a resigned face. "Sometimes, Mr. Corso—"

"I'll take care of the bill," Corso said suddenly.

The nurse took a step back, looking at Corso as if for the first time. "Do you have any idea how much money we're talking about here?"

"No," he said, "and I don't care. Whatever it is, I'll take care of it."

"Her present bill alone . . . You're serious, aren't you?"

"I don't have many friends," he said. "I can't afford to lose any."

The sadness in his eyes told her he wasn't kidding. "You have to work it out with the business office."

"How do I do that?" he asked.

She took him by the elbow. "Come down to the nurses' station, and I'll get you started on the paperwork," she said. Before he could move, she gripped his arm tighter. "If you don't mind me saying it, Mr. Corso, she's a very lucky woman to have a friend like you."

Corso grunted and started down the hall.

* * *

Ramón was backed into a service alcove, a collapsible wheelchair on either side of him, as he peeked down the hall toward the red-sweater nurse and the nosy-writer man. He'd watched as they came out of the room together. Watched as they talked and then disappeared down a hall to the left. He checked the area. Nothing. Nobody. He stepped out and started down the hall. His shoes squeaked with every step as he made his way down the gleaming corridor. Still nobody in sight as he used his right hand to push open the door of Room 109.

In the green glow of the life-support machines, he could make out a single heavily bandaged figure lying propped halfway up in bed. As he started to step into the room, he glanced to his left and caught sight of a long black cape hanging on the wall. His breath suddenly lay frozen in his chest. He could feel the bile rising in his stomach. His mouth tasted like sheet metal.

He stood, one foot in the room, the other still in the corridor, when a voice said, "Excuse me." Startled, Ramón turned quickly toward the sound. A thick little Japanese guy, looked like a doctor: all in blue, stethoscope flopped up over one shoulder, wearing a fruity-looking shower-cap thing.

"Wrong room," Ramón said with a smile.

"You better check in at the nurses' station," he said. "This is the ICU. We can't have you wandering around in here."

Ramón pulled his foot out of the door and then pointed down the hall to his right.

The guy nodded. "Right down there," he said.

"Thanks."

Ramón kept the smile plastered to his face as he sauntered along. Fifty feet ahead the bright lights of the nurses' station washed across the dim corridor. He checked back over his shoulder. The nosy Jap doctor man was back at the corner checking up on him. He could hear voices ahead.

The red-sweater nurse looked up. "Can I help you?"

"Loooking por maternity," Ramón said, with a thick Cuban accent.

The nurse straightened up and came rustling out from behind the desk. "You're lost," she said. "Maternity's on the ninth floor. Come with me."

As she took Ramón by the elbow, the writer man looked up and made a flicker of eye contact. Ramón didn't like what he saw. Something hard. Something sure. Not the usual tourist bravado. The guy was a player.

Unnerved, he stumbled slightly as he walked up the hall toward the pair of elevators along the left wall. She pushed the UP button, and immediately the silver door on the left slid open with a *bing*. Ramón kept smiling as she shepherded him inside and then reached in and pushed 9. "There you go," Nursie said.

Ramón resisted the urge to stop the elevator. To get off and hurry back to the street. No. Just be cool. Nursie seemed like the kind of bitch gonna stand there and make sure the car went to 9. Ramón did not wish to be remembered.

Hospital elevators are built for comfort, not for speed. A full five minutes passed before Ramón stepped back out onto Ninth Avenue. A thick icy drizzle hissed on the awning above his head. Gerardo and the car were nowhere in sight. To the north, the lights of a red-and-white fire department aid car tore circles in the darkness, as the crew rushed a gurney into the emergency room. Ramón jammed his hands into his pants pockets, nodded at the security guard, and hustled north, toward the puddles of darkness beneath skeletal oak trees.

He was half a block past the oaks when Gerardo swung the Mercedes around the corner of Ninth and Madison and began coming his way. He heard the door locks pop as the car slid to a stop in front of him and then heard the noise again as he slid into the seat.

"What now?" Gerardo asked.

The radio was on the Spanish-language channel, Música del Mundo. A soft samba spilled from the speakers. "I don't know," Ramón said.

For a moment, Gerardo stopped breathing. He squinted at Ramón in the darkness. Turned the radio off. Something was bad wrong. Ramón always knew what to do next. Gerardo swallowed some air and waited.

"We got problems," Ramón said.

"Like?"

"Like that girl who crashed her car is still alive. In the hospital. That's who he's visiting in there."

"What's the writer guy got to do with her?"

"I haven't got a fuckin' clue," Ramón said. "It's like he's got the eye on us or something."

Gerardo scowled. Lifted his hands from the wheel. "You said you seen her head come clean off."

"I did," Ramón said with a shrug. "Musta not been bad as it looked."

"That's not good. She seen us both."

"No shit," said Ramón. He slipped into his seat belt. "Let's get outa here."

"What about the writer guy?"

"Fuck him," said Ramón. "We gotta decide what to do, man. Things are gettin' outa hand here."

15

Thursday, October 19 9:29 a.m.

His name was Crispin, Edward J. Or at least that's what the name tag said. HARBORVIEW MEDICAL CENTER, PATIENT SERVICES REPRESENTATIVE. "I'm telling you, Mr.—"

"Corso."

"We quite literally don't have a room for her."

"Find one."

"You don't understand," he huffed. "We've already pushed her surgery back to Saturday morning in hopes that a room would free up." He shrugged. "As we speak, I still don't have a single post-op room available. Not one." He got to his feet and put a chubby hand on Corso's shoulder. "Providence can operate this afternoon. They've got plenty of space. She'll be quite happy with the service there."

Corso's eyes were cast to the side, staring down at the dimpled knuckles gripping his shoulder. Edward J. Crispin got the message and retrieved his hand. Thus chastened, he pulled his collection of chins down onto his chest and went all official.

"The space issue notwithstanding, Mr. Corso, and as much as it pains me to be forced to deal with such pedestrian issues as finances at a time like this"—he reached down and thumbed open a bright green folder; his overworked cardiovascular system had painted a bright red spot on each of his cheeks—"as of this morning, not including today"—he peeked down at his desk—"the charges for services total seventy-one thousand three hundred sixty-five dollars and thirty-three cents." He flicked the folder shut. "Plus tax."

Corso dropped a Visa card onto the folder. "Pay the bill," he said. "Start a tab for further charges."

Crispin made a rude noise with his lips. "If you do the math, sir, you'll find that liability possibilities could run"—he pursed his lips—"halfway to seven figures." He gave the figure a moment to sink in. "With all due respect, Mr. Corso, credit limits don't go that high."

"Why don't you run the card and see," Corso suggested.

Edward J. compressed his lips and jabbed a finger at the phone. "Alice, come in here for a moment, please." Almost immediately, the white louvered door behind him opened. She was maybe twenty. A mouth breather, wearing a white blouse under a blue denim jumper. Her black wiry hair was held at bay by a pair of tortoiseshell hair clips. "Yes, Mr. Crispin."

He passed her the folder and the credit card and then leaned over and whispered in her ear. He waited until the door clicked closed before turning his attention back to Corso.

"You don't have to do this, you know. It's not like we're going to put her out in the street. Anyone and everyone who comes to us gets the very best we have to offer, regardless of their ability to pay, but we do try, in cases such as this, to spread the liability around a bit, if you catch my drift. Providence is a fully accredited hospital. It's—"

"I want her to stay here."

He was about to start back on his spiel when his phone buzzed. He picked up the receiver and listened. "If you'll excuse me for a moment," he said, before disappearing through the door. Corso could hear the hiss of whispers but couldn't pick up the words.

Another minute and Crispin reappeared. He leaned over and set the card and an invoice in front of Corso. With a flourish, he pulled a pen from his coat pocket. "If you'd just sign at the X, Mr. Corso."

Corso signed his name. "You'll keep her where she is until you have a room for her."

Crispin did something midway between a shrug and a nod. "We'll put something together," he said tentatively. He busied himself with tearing off the perforated strips and handing Corso a copy of the bill. "We'll make it work," he said.

"That's the spirit," Corso said, as he left the room.

Corso took the stairs. He jogged one flight up to ground level, then wormed his way through the lobby congestion and out the main exit onto Ninth Avenue. A gray sky swirled overhead as he stretched his long legs out, crossing Ninth diagonally, swiveling through the traffic until he eased up onto the opposite sidewalk and began moving steadily north.

Three blocks up, at Madison, he turned left down the steep hill. The breeze from the sound carried smells of salt and seaweed. Half a block down, the Madison

Renaissance Hotel slid into view, its colorful flags stiff in the breeze. Another block and the federal courthouse slipped out from behind the Sorrento Hotel, its bleak plebeian facade black against the roiling gray sky.

The media horde had fallen into its feeding rhythm. This morning, Warren Klein held court at the back door. A knot of reporters jockeyed for position along the police barriers, as Corso crossed the freeway and approached the melee from the rear.

As Klein stepped up to the microphones, the clouds suddenly split, bathing the back of the courthouse in soft fall sunshine. Renee Rogers and Raymond Butler stood leaning against the building, squinting into the glare.

Corso could hear questions being shouted as he showed his ID to the nearest cop and ducked under the barrier. Klein's face was scrunched into a knot, and he was shading his eyes with his hand.

"Provided we're not faced with any undue delays—and I must say that, thus far in the trial, Judge Howell is moving the proceeding along with great dispatch—I'd hazard a guess that we'll have the case in the hands of the jury by the middle of next week."

Corso slid along the wall until he was rubbing shoulders with Renee Rogers.

"Warren's gonna look like a mole on TV," Rogers whispered.

"Not real media savvy, is he?" Corso said.

"He's hired a media consultant," Butler said. "To help polish his image, he says."

Corso couldn't hear the question, but whatever it was it got Klein started on his daily spiel about how it was an open-and-shut case. He was going to set up a foundation of extortion and negligence. He was going to prove Nicholas Balagula's connection to a maze of companies responsible for the construction of Fairmont Hospital, and, most important, he would tie Nicholas Balagula directly to the plan to fake core sample results and other test data.

Renee Rogers leaned over and whispered in Corso's ear, "You may be getting some company in the courtroom." Corso raised an eyebrow. "Both Seattle newspapers are suing for the right to be present at the trial. The Second Circuit Court is going to take it up this afternoon."

"And?"

"And recent decisions have been coming down on the side of the media."

"Klein doesn't seem worried."

"Warren thinks the sunshine was arranged," Butler said.

They shared a quiet laugh. Corso closed his eyes and languished, the warmth of the sun melting on his cheeks.

"You find out anything about what happened to your friend?" Rogers asked. When he opened his eyes, she was studying his face as if it were a road map.

"Nothing that makes any sense," Corso replied. "I made some calls. The guy in the truck was a janitor for a local school district. Lived in a ratty little apartment down in the south end. The guy was so amorphous nobody even reported him missing."

"Really?"

"And that's not the good part."

"Oh?"

"Before somebody went to all the trouble of burying him and the truck, they shot him nine times." Corso looked over at Rogers and their eyes met. "With three different guns. Five of the shots postmortem."

Rogers whistled softly. "Curiouser and curiouser."

"Lotta anger there," Butler offered. "It's usually a family member who gets that pissed off."

"I've got a line on an ex-wife," Corso said. "I'm going to follow up on it this afternoon."

Klein was separating himself from the crowd. "I hope to God this thing is as cut and dried as Klein thinks it is," Corso said.

Rogers and Butler made faces at each other. "Next couple days will tell the tale," Butler said. "We've got our expert witnesses. Elkins has got his own expert witnesses." He shrugged. "A lot's going to depend on what shakes out in there. Balagula's done a great job of insulating himself from his business enterprises." He waggled a hand. "It's touch and go." He looked over at Renee Rogers as if seeking agreement.

She picked her briefcase up from the sidewalk. "Much as it pains me to say it, Raymond, if I had to bet I'd bet Warren is probably going to luck out."

Corso broke out in a grin.

"What's so funny?" Rogers demanded.

"I was thinking how somebody once said that we have to believe in luck, or else there's no way to explain the success of people we don't like," he said.

She laughed and followed Ray Butler up the short length of sidewalk toward Warren Klein and the thick pair of brass doors. Corso stood and watched them file inside. Above the buzz of the crowd, a voice called his name and then another. Absentmindedly, he turned toward the crowd and found himself staring into the lens of a TV camera. He only said one word. One was all it took to stay off the evening news.

Thursday, October 19 1:51 p.m.

"Dr. Goldman, would you please provide the court with a brief description of your present academic position?"

Dr. Hiram Goldman was perfect: just this side of sixty, aging but not elderly, with a big shock of white hair combed back from a billboard forehead. He coughed into his hand and said, "I currently hold the position of executive director of the National Information Service for Earthquake Engineering."

"And your offices are located where?" Klein asked.

"At the University of California at Berkeley."

"And how far is that from the site of the Fairmont Hospital?"

"Approximately thirty miles."

Elkins was on his feet, wearing his bored face. "Your Honor, the defense will stipulate as to the witness's expertise in the area of seismology and earthquake engineering."

Judge Howell gave a cursory bang of the gavel. "So stipulated," he said.

Warren Klein shuffled through his notes for a moment before continuing. "Dr. Goldman, for the sake of the jury could you give us a brief"—he looked over his shoulder at the jury box—"layman's description of the San Andreas Fault system."

"Certainly," he said. "What is commonly referred to

as the San Andreas Fault is quite simply an eight-hundred-mile crack in the earth's crust."

"Eight hundred miles?"

"It runs northwesterly from the Gulf of California all the way to Cape Mendocino, just north of San Francisco."

"Would it be safe to say, Dr. Goldman—"

Before he could finish the question, Bruce Elkins was on his feet again. "The defense will also stipulate as to the existence of—"

Klein raised his voice. "If Your Honor please, I would like to be permitted to present my case in the manner I see fit."

Now Elkins looked like his feelings were hurt. "I was merely trying to comply with the bench's repeated admonitions regarding undue delays," he said. "Mr. Klein is reinventing the wheel here."

"I don't require his forbearance, Your Honor," Klein complained.

Fulton Howell glared at the lawyers as if they were a pair of unruly schoolboys before waving them up toward the bench. "Approach," was all he said.

Renee Rogers leaned toward Ray Butler, her forehead pleated.

"Since when does Elkins stipulate anything?" she asked.

"Been bothering me all day," Butler said. "I've never seen him this agreeable before."

Renee Rogers turned the other way. On the far side of the courtroom, Nicholas Balagula sat, staring absently off into space, like a snake sunning itself on a rock.

Klein built a case the way a castaway builds a fire:

urgently, but with great care, adding one tiny twig at a time and letting it burn until ready for something bigger, then adding another.

Elkins had, on five separate occasions, offered to stipulate for the record the very avenue of inquiry upon which Klein was at that moment driving. On each occasion, the judge had admonished him for undue delay, reminded him to stop referring to Klein's case as "Earthquake 101," and invited him to sit down.

Klein had been pecking at Dr. Goldman for nearly three hours when he hurried over to the prosecution table and retrieved a document. Renee Rogers got to her feet and took him by the elbow. She leaned over and spoke directly into his ear. "You need to pick up the pace, Warren. They're going to sleep in there," she said, tilting her head toward the jury box. Klein looked over at Butler, who nodded his solemn agreement. Klein heaved a sigh, dropped the document on the desk, and he turned back toward his witness.

"Dr. Goldman . . . how many earthquakes occur in California every year?"

"Certainly thousands. An exact number would be extremely difficult to compute."

"How so?"

"A great many of the shocks are sufficiently small as to escape notice."

"What's the smallest earthquake noticed by humans?"

"Something like a two on the Richter scale."

"For the sake of our jury, Dr. Goldman, could you give us a layman's explanation of the Richter scale?"

"The Richter scale measures the magnitude of an earthquake. The jury needs to know"—he indicated the jury box—"that the Richter scale is logarithmic."

"Which means?"

"A recording of seven, for instance, signifies a disturbance ten times greater than a disturbance of six." Goldman began talking directly to the darkened black panel. "What you on the jury must also understand is the amount of energy released in a seven is *thirty* times greater than that released by a six." Klein opened his mouth to ask another question, but the doctor, unsure as to whether he'd made his point, kept talking. "If you push those figures up one more notch, you get a better idea of how the scale operates. A recording of eight, would be"—he drew in the air with his finger—"thirty times thirty, or *nine hundred times* more powerful than our original reading of six."

Klein gave the jury a minute to do the math, before asking, "So, if anything under a two on the Richter scale is at the lower end of the spectrum, what is the upper end of the spectrum like?"

Hiram Goldman thought it over. "The two largest earthquakes ever recorded happened in 1906 off the coast of Ecuador and Colombia and in 1933 off the east coast of Honshu, Japan. Both were recorded at eight point nine on the Richter scale."

"And in California?"

"The 1906 quake was listed at a magnitude of eight point three."

Klein spoke directly to the jury. "Ladies and gentlemen of the jury, in order to give you some sense of the magnitude of an eight-point-three disturbance, Dr. Goldman has been kind enough to bring along an exhibit from the Library of the University of California at Berkeley."

He turned on his heel and headed for the easel. He

put one hand on the white material that covered the exhibit and whipped it off like a magician producing a rabbit.

Black-and-white photograph. A crowd of people stood along the jagged edge of a road that had been torn in two. To the right of the spectators, risen up to head level, was the continuation of the road, as if the earth had been ripped asunder by some unruly child.

"Dr. Goldman, would you tell the court what it is looking at here?"

"That's a photo from the 1906 earthquake. You're looking at a road that ran across the head of Tomales Bay. The road was offset nearly twenty-one feet."

"Can you explain the forces that caused this to happen?"

"Certainly. In this case, the Pacific plate moved nearly twenty-one feet north of its original position along the North American plate. The scraping together of these two plates is what causes the seismic activity in this region."

"And this was caused by an earthquake of a magnitude of eight point three?"

"Yes."

"How large was the earthquake that destroyed the north wall of Fairmont Hospital?"

"Two point one," he said immediately.

Klein made himself look surprised. "I thought you said anything under two was not noticeable by human beings."

"I did," the doctor said. "It was a murmur, a belch." He waved a hand. "It was hardly noticed at all."

"Other than to the hospital, what was the extent of damage to surrounding property?"

"None."

Klein did his astonished routine. "How can you be sure of that?"

"Insurance companies run their claims by my department for documentation of the disturbance. As of this date, not a single insurance claim—other than those related to Fairmont Hospital, of course—not a single claim has been filed."

"No further questions," Klein said.

The judge checked his watch. "Cross, Mr. Elkins."

Elkins got to his feet. "I have no questions of this witness," he said.

Bang. "Court's adjourned until nine o'clock tomorrow morning." *Bang*.

16

Thursday, October 19 5:01 p.m.

"How'd you find me anyway?" Marie Hall demanded.

Corso reached into his jacket pocket and came out with the wedding invitation. He slipped the rubber band off, unrolled the picture, and turned it her way. "I went to the church. They sent me to your parents." He shrugged. "The rest is history."

She lived in the top half of a duplex at the south end of Phinney Ridge: a nicely furnished one-bedroom, overlooking an elementary school playground. Everything had color-coordinated ruffles and shams, right out of some decorating book.

She shook her head disgustedly. "I thought it was so romantic to have the invitation picture taken in the Japanese Garden," she said. "Never occurred to me for a minute that Donald picked it because it was free."

She poured herself a cup of coffee, and offered one to Corso, who turned it down.

"Like I told you on the phone, I don't see how I can

help you. I haven't seen or spoken to Donald since the day I walked out."

"When was that?"

"Fourteen months ago."

"Mind telling me why you walked out?"

"The question's not why I left Donald, it's how I managed to live with the guy for seven years. That's the mystery."

"Lotta people feel that way when it's over."

She stared off into space for a moment. "I just couldn't see myself without a man. The idea that I might be something above and beyond my role in a relationship was totally beyond me." She shrugged. "That's why I put up with it for so long. Why I lived like that."

She'd been pretty once: Kewpie-doll lips, nice even features, and a pair of big blue eyes. Somewhere in her mid-thirties and getting thick in the hips. Her shaggy blond hair had grown out brown at the roots and looked like she'd cut it herself.

"Was your former husband abusive?" Corso asked.

She sighed and stirred her coffee. "There's abusive, and there's abusive," she said. "If you mean did he physically assault me, the answer is no." For the first time, she made eye contact with Corso. "But if you're asking me whether or not I'm sorry he's gone, the answer is also no." She waved a hand. "I know how that sounds, and I don't much like it." She kept her gaze locked on Corso. "But there it is."

"If it's any consolation, seems like you have a lot of company who felt that way."

"Why do you say that?"

"Because Donald Barth dropped out of sight for the

better part of three months and nobody even reported him missing."

"Donald wasn't the type to inspire much of anything."

"Why's that?"

"Because he didn't have a life."

"Everybody has a life."

"He went to work; he ate; he slept; he'd screw me twice a week if I let him." She waved a hand. "That was it. If he really wanted to push the envelope, Donald would stop at a convenience store on the way home and buy himself a pint of buttermilk. Buttermilk was Donald's idea of a big time." She read Corso's face. "You think I'm making it up."

Corso held up a hand. "I'm keeping an open mind."

Her expression became almost wistful. "He could be very charming, when he wanted to be. He was better looking than that picture you got." She crossed the bookcase and eased an unframed photograph out from between a tall pair of art books.

He was thinner than in the wedding-invitation picture, with the craggy face of a mountain climber. A thick head of black hair was combed straight back from his forehead. He was smiling with his mouth, while his eyes said they wished they were somewhere else. "Quite the handsome guy," she said, in a practiced tone. "I was twenty-seven when I met Donald. I'd just run away from my first marriage. I was on my own for the first time in my life." She shook her head sadly. "I didn't realize it at the time, but I didn't really have an identity of my own. I was just part of whoever I was connected to."

"We all make mistakes."

"In the beginning, I thought he was saving money . . . so we could buy a house or something like that. So for the first four years or so, I shut up about only owning three dresses. I told myself you had to suffer a little to get what you wanted. Then, when he started giving it away—"

"Giving it to who?"

"Prep schools and then colleges."

She read Corso's confusion and continued. "He's got a son from his first marriage: Robert Downs. He uses his mother's name."

"How many . . . ?"

"I was his third."

"Uh-huh."

"He had this . . . this . . . thing . . . about how Robert had to have it better than he did. Robert had to go to the finest schools and get the best education so he could become a doctor."

"Lotta people feel that way about their kids."

"Yeah, but not like Donald. With him it was like a religion. It didn't matter that we lived in subsidized housing. It didn't matter that he never in seven years went out to lunch with the other guys or that the people where I worked were whispering behind my back about my ragged clothes. Nothing—none of that mattered as long as he could keep the damn tuition paid."

"You worked."

"Same job I've got now—except back then I came home and gave my check to Donald, who promptly sent it off to Harvard or someplace, while we didn't have a television. While we didn't turn on the lights until it was too dark to see." She jabbed at her palm with her index finger. "While we never once in seven years went out to a movie!" She heard the stridency in her voice and looked away. "I know I sound like a bitch, but it's true." She ran a hand through her hair. "I walked out of seven years of slavery with just over fifteen hundred bucks."

"What happened to community property?"

"What property?" she scoffed. "We didn't own anything but a pile of cheap furniture and that beat-up old truck he drove. I took the bus to work." She waved her hand around the room. "This might not be the Ritz, Mr. Corso, but it's way better than anything Donald Barth ever provided for me."

She was right. Her apartment and its carefully chosen contents were far newer and far grander than the rubble Donald Barth had left behind. She thrust her chin at Corso. "I'm halfway to my accounting degree. I've been going nights to Seattle Central. Unlike my ex-husband, I've got plans for the future," she said.

Corso leaned back in the chair and folded his arms across his chest. "So I guess you can't think of any reason why somebody would want to murder your ex-husband."

"The only person with a reason to murder Donald Barth was me."

Corso gave her a small smile. "What finally gave you the courage to leave?"

She turned away. "No one thing. It just sort of happened. I got so I couldn't stand being in the same room with him. About six months before we separated, I cut him off." She fixed Corso in her gaze, as if defying him to take issue with her. "That's the only time I ever thought he might get violent. He told me I was his wife and had an obligation to take care of his needs." She laughed a bitter laugh. "Can you imagine that? Like we had a contract or something." She sighed. "Next thing I know he's not coming home after work. I start getting these phone calls that hang up." She got to her feet and crossed the room. "I moved into a women's shelter." When she turned back toward Corso, her eyes were wet. "You know what?" she asked.

"What?"

"He never even came looking for me. Never tried to talk me into coming back. Not once. He just went on with his life."

"You think he had a girlfriend while you were still married?"

"I'm sure of it. Donald wasn't about to go without his Monday and Thursday screw."

"If he had a regular girlfriend, you'd think she'd have noticed his absence."

She laughed. "I said Donald liked sex; I didn't say he was any good at it."

A smile from Corso seemed to encourage her.

"What Donald liked best about sex was that it was free."

17

Thursday, October 19 6:36 p.m.

"He ain't got a clue," Gerardo said.

"Why's that?"

" 'Cause he's back here again. He had a clue, he wouldn't be comin' to the same place twice."

"Hmm," was all Ramón said.

They were parked a half mile north of the Briarwood Garden Apartments, backed out onto the dike that defined the north end of the marsh.

"He's spinnin' his wheels," Gerardo insisted.

"How'd he put the girl and the truck guy together?"

Gerardo shrugged. "What's it matter?"

"It matters because we're not clean on this thing until we figure it out. There's something . . . some connection he's following here we don't understand, and as long as he's following some trail we can't see, we got big problems."

"We never shoulda lied about the guy in the truck," Gerardo said.

Ramón could feel the anger burning in his cheeks. They'd been through it fifty times. He spoke through clenched teeth. "What fucking difference did it make? We shot him; some other asshole shot him. Makes no goddamn difference. Either way, him and the truck end up in the hill and then come sliding out on their own, and we gotta pop the Ball guy. Don't matter a rat's ass who done the work. All that other shit happens anyway."

"Nothin' been right since we done it," Gerardo said. "It's like the whole damn world's out of balance or something."

"Then we better spend our time figuring out what trail he's following, huh?" He looked over at Gerardo, who was slouched down behind the wheel with his lips pressed tight.

"Or maybe we just cut his trail and be done with it," Gerardo offered. "I'm startin' to think maybe that's the way to make things right again."

Ramón gave the smallest of nods. "Could be," he said. "Could be."

"I'm tellin' you."

"I'm listening."

"So?"

"So tonight we don't lose him. Tonight, we find out where he lives."

Thursday, October 19 7:16 p.m.

The Briarwood consisted of eight one-story four-plexes, built in the form of a square: two buildings to a side, facing outward, away from one another, with the parking lot in the middle. Only the bedroom and bathroom windows looked out over the lot.

Figuring Barth and the truck had to have been abducted from somewhere and that the Briarwood parking lot was as good a bet as any, Corso had decided to knock on doors, hoping maybe somebody had seen or heard something useful. No such luck.

Third or fourth door, the Somali family had invited him in and let him take a look around. That's when he knew he was screwed. The way the apartments were laid out, there was absolutely no reason to be looking out at the parking lot. Matter of fact, if you wanted to look out the bedroom window, you had to stand on the bed; if you wanted to look out the bathroom window, you had to stand on the toilet—which was where his hopes rested as he approached 2D, the apartment where Donald Barth had lived.

Probably a dozen residents hadn't answered their doors. Some of the apartments were dark and empty. In others, the sounds of shuffling feet or labored breathing had told him someone was there but was not opening the door. On several occasions he'd been told to go away. The only real speed bump was a guy on the ground floor of F building, who'd opened the door wearing a ripped T-shirt with spaghetti stains all over the front, a pair of plaid boxer shorts, and black socks. "What?" he growled from around the unlit cigar butt wedged in the corner of his mouth. "You got business with me, pretty boy?"

Corso started to answer, but the guy cut him off.

" 'Cause if you don't, and if you're trying to sell me some shit I don't want, I just might have to kick your ass."

He was about forty, almost as wide as he was tall, his cheeks sporting three days' worth of stubble. His arms and shoulders were covered with a carpet of curly black hair, thick enough to hide the skin below.

Behind him, the TV was blaring what had to be a porno movie. Bad jazz and a lot of oooing and aahing. "Oh, yeah, baby; don't stop; don't stop . . . that's it. . . ." Corso was at an angle to the screen. From where he stood the picture looked a lot like a bilge pump operating at high speed.

"I'm not selling anything," Corso said.

"What then?" the guy demanded.

Corso told him. The shrill TV voice was now demanding it harder and deeper.

"The guy over there?" The guy nodded toward D building.

"Yeah," Corso said.

"Before my time," he said. "He was gone by the time I got here. Once in a while, I talk to the old bat who lives in One-D, next door to him. I seen her yesterday. She told me all about how the cops was by and all. You talk to her yet?"

The frenzy on the TV had reached a peak. Either the room had spontaneously ignited or everybody involved was about to get their jollies at the same time.

"Talk to her. She's got nothing to do but mind everybody's business." He looked back over his shoulder. "Getting to the good part now," he said with a leer. For the first time he smiled, exhibiting a row of thick yellow teeth. "Unless maybe you want to come in for a while, pretty boy." He hefted and then dropped the package beneath his boxers.

Corso declined, turned quickly, and began striding away.

"Don't be shy," the guy rasped at his back. "Ya gotta

find your inner self." Gruff laughter followed Corso up the sidewalk and around the corner, like a pack of dogs.

A plywood ramp and a low metal hand rail had been built over the stairs to 1D, rendering the apartment wheelchair-accessible. He tried the bell but didn't hear anything, so he knocked. A little brass plate screwed to the door read KILBURN. Corso knocked again. From inside the apartment came the shuffle of feet and the clink of metal.

A bright white halogen light above the stairs tore a hole in the darkness and reduced Corso to squinting and shading his eyes with one hand. The door opened a crack.

"Whadda you want?" a voice said from the darkness. "We don't allow solicitors here."

"I'm not selling anything."

"Does Mr. Pov know you're here?"

"I know Mr. Pov," Corso hedged.

"What's his first name?"

"Nhim," Corso answered. "Mr. Nhim Pov."

The door closed and then, after a moment, opened all the way. She had to be ninety. Coke-bottle glasses. Thick silver hair in an old-fashioned pageboy cut. She held the doorknob in one hand and a golf club in the other.

"What do you want?"

"I'm looking into the death of Donald Barth. The man who lived in the apartment next door, up until a few months back."

She eyed him closely. "You another cop?"

"I'm a writer."

She peered up at Corso for a minute. "You're the one writes those crime books."

"Yes, ma'am. Frank Corso."

"Seen you on the tube a couple of times."

"That's me," Corso said.

She stepped aside. "Well, don't be standing out there like an idiot, come in."

She ushered Corso onto a threadbare green sofa. The floor was covered with twice as much furniture as the room called for, leaving nothing but plastic-covered trails winding among the furnishings. Wasn't the decor, however, that caught Corso's eye. It was the walls, nearly every inch of them was covered with framed photographs.

She used the golf club as a cane as she sat down in the brown recliner opposite the couch. "I lived too damn long," she said.

"Excuse me?"

"I said I lived too damn long. Had six children and outlived every damn one of them. Had sixteen grandchildren and outlived five of them too."

Corso considered saying he was sorry to hear it but rejected the idea.

"It's not right to outlive everybody who cares about you. It's unnatural." She waved the golf club in the air. "You ever see those commercials on the TV? About how one a these days everybody gonna be able to live to a hundred?"

"Yes, ma'am, I have."

"Well you tell 'em you met Delores Kilburn and she says the whole idea's not all it's cracked up to be."

"I will," he assured her.

"Cops was here the other day."

"So I hear."

"I'll tell you the same thing I told them. I lived next

to that pair for five years and never said more that ten words to either of them." The club waved again. "Some of the most unfriendliest people I ever met. So if you're looking for some kind of inside dirt, I'm here to tell you, you come to the wrong place."

She looked at her hand and realized she was still brandishing the golf club. She groaned slightly as she turned around in the chair and leaned it against the wall.

"Poor Mr. Pov's had enough trouble for three lifetimes."

"You mean like being in a refugee camp and all?"

"That and everything else." She leaned forward in the chair. "Lost almost his entire family over there in Cambodia, you know." She drew a finger across her throat. "Slaughtered by that Pol Pot guy and the Khmer Rouge. Just killed 'em all. His wife and kids, his parents, all of 'em. Just like that."

"A terrible tragedy," Corso offered.

"And then his sister's death." She waved a hand. "It's a wonder to me the man could find the strength to go on."

"Going on is what people do best. It's why there's so many of us running around the planet."

"After all those years. After all the struggle. And to have it end like that."

"What happened?"

"You haven't heard?"

"No, ma'am."

She checked the room, as if looking for eavesdroppers. "Took poor Mr. Pov nearly ten years to get his sister Lily over here from Cambodia. All kinda red tape about how they wouldn't let her go and then how

America wouldn't let her in . . . and all the money he had to spend and all."

"And?"

"And he had everything set up. Had her a husband and everything. Nice Cambodian man from Seward Park. Owns a grocery. Drives a nice new Lincoln."

"I take it the wedding didn't come off."

Her eyes narrowed. "She killed herself. Hanged herself in the laundry room."

"Any idea why?"

She thought it over. "Lily was much younger than Mr. Pov. More Americanized." She shrugged. "Who knows why those people do things? Live in a whole other world than the rest of us. Got their own idea of right and wrong that don't make a stick of sense to folks like you and me. They come over here to live, but they're not like us." A light flickered in her eyes. She stopped. "Don't mean to come off as prejudiced or anything. I was right down there with the rest of them at the Cambodian church or whatever they call it, right there on Rainier Avenue, for the funeral." She looked up at Corso. "Had a hell of a turnout. Mr. Pov's a bigwig in the local Cambodian community, you know. Musta been five hundred people there." She shook a finger at Corso. "And I'll tell you one thing, Mr. Writer. Those Asians treat an old woman like me a lot better that Americans do. Found me a seat right in the front row. Treated me like I was gold, they did."

Corso stifled a sigh. "About Mr. and Mrs. Barth."

"He had her buffaloed. You could see it in her face. Like a deer in the headlights. Afraid of every damn thing she saw. I'd say hello, and she'd just stammer something and turn away, like she was ashamed or something."

Corso got to his feet. "Thanks for your trouble," he said.

She held out a hand. Corso stepped over, took her hand, and pulled her up from the chair. "You tell 'em Delores Kilburn says old age is overrated."

"I will," Corso assured her.

Corso stood on the front steps and listened to the locks snap behind him. Overhead, the moon floated high in the sky, ducking in and out of a jigsaw of thick black clouds. Corso warmed his hands in his coat pockets as he walked the length of the sidewalk and turned left, back into the center of the complex.

He rang the bell. "Coming," the voice said from inside.

A moment later, the door opened and Nhim Pov stood in his doorway.

"Ah," he said. "Mr. Corso."

Corso fished Donald Barth's wedding invitation from his pants pocket.

"I wanted to return this," he said.

"Thank you," the little man said. "But perhaps you would like to return it yourself." His eyes crinkled at Corso's momentary confusion. "His son is here. He's down at the shed right now."

18

Thursday, October 19 7:07 p.m.

Corso leaned against the wall and watched as Robert Downs sorted through the remnants of his father's life. He was a tall thin young man, with a full head of lank brown hair that was going to be gone before he saw forty. The single overhead bulb sent his shadow lurching over the walls and ceiling as he pawed through the dozen cardboard boxes.

Ten minutes later, Downs sat on the patched plastic couch with his head bent forward and his hands hanging down between his knees. "It's not much, is it?"

"I guess he had all he needed," Corso offered.

"Not a scrap of paper—" he began.

"Cops probably took all the paperwork."

Downs tapped his temple. "Of course. I'm not thinking very clearly," he said.

"You've had quite a shock."

Downs looked around, as if seeing the place for the first time. "The manager, Mr. . . ."

"Pov," Corso said.

"Yes. Mr. Pov showed me the apartment he lived in.

There's an old woman living in there now, but she said it was okay."

"Nice of her."

"It was . . . it wasn't what I expected."

"Your father led a simple life."

"I had no idea. His letters always said he was in building maintenance."

"He was."

Robert Downs ran a well-manicured hand through his lank hair. "But I always assumed it was . . . somehow . . ." He searched for a phrase, didn't find anything suitable, and gave up.

"Something a bit more grandiose," Corso suggested.

Downs nodded. "Like he had his own firm or something."

"When was the last time you saw your father?"

"You mean like in person?" He read Corso's expression. "A couple of times he sent a videotape for Christmas, and I saw him that way."

"In the flesh."

"When I was eleven. He lived in southern California then. I went out to LA for two weeks. He took me to Disneyland. He had a nice apartment in Santa Monica, just a few blocks off the beach."

"What year was that?"

"Nineteen eighty-one."

"Long time."

Downs agreed. "My mother was bitter," he said. "She'd have preferred I never saw him again."

"What was she bitter about?"

"She always claimed he fooled around on her."

"I take it they didn't correspond?"

"Oh, no," he said. "I was six or seven before she

even admitted I had a father and that he was alive on the West Coast somewhere." He rolled his eyes. "It took me three years to get her to send me to California." He looked around again and jammed his hands into his pockets. "How could he live in a place like this?"

"His ex-wife says it's because he was sending all his money away to keep you in college and medical school."

His face was the color of ashes. "I had no idea he was living this way," he complained to the ceiling. "Those apartments . . . they're hovels." He stepped over to the storage unit and pawed at an open box of housewares. "I mean, look at the man's dishes." He gestured with the back of his hand. "This is it?" he demanded, of nobody in particular. "*This* is the total of a man's life, some broken-down furniture and a few cardboard boxes?"

Something in his tone annoyed Corso. "So then, if you'd known he was living in poverty, you'd have sent him his money back and enrolled in the state university?"

Downs's eyes narrowed. He opened his mouth to defend himself and then changed his mind. The muscles along his jawline rippled like snakes. He cupped his face in his long fingers and stayed that way for quite a while.

"You're right," he said finally. "I was being a first-class asshole, wasn't I? I mean, who the hell am I to be judging him? After everything he did for me . . . everything he gave up . . . and here I am, standing around judging the quality of the guy's life like I'm Martha Stewart or something."

Downs turned away from Corso and leaned his forehead against the chain link. He took several deep breaths and then began to cry. Corso watched until the shaking of his shoulders stopped; then he stepped into the storage area, found a roll of paper towels, and tore off a couple.

It took Robert Downs a few minutes to put himself back together. He honked three times into a towel and dropped it onto the floor.

"Why would anybody want to kill my father?" he asked.

"I was hoping you could tell me."

"The police called me yesterday morning."

"Where were you?"

"Boston. I live in Boston." He retrieved the other paper towel from his pants pocket and wiped his nose. "They asked me what I wanted done with the body." He looked to Corso, as if for forgiveness. "They had to say his name twice before I realized who it was they were talking about. That it was my father who was dead. And that I was . . . that nobody else had come forward for his remains."

"You know the details?" Corso asked.

"They said he was found in his truck. Buried in a hillside."

"Shot."

"That's what they said."

"My source says the medical examiner's office is going to report nine bullet wounds from three different weapons."

"That doesn't make any sense."

"No, it doesn't," Corso agreed. "None of this makes any sense."

They stood in silence. Somewhere out in the parking lot a car engine shuddered to a stop. A car door closed. They listened as the sound of footsteps faded to black.

"You going back to Boston?" Corso asked.

Downs wandered around in a circle, as if confused. "I'm . . . I mean, I was. . . ." He looked at his watch. "I'm getting married in three weeks," he said absently, then reached inside his sport jacket and came out with an airline ticket. "I've got a flight back in the morning, but I think . . . I think I'm going to stay for a while."

"Might not be a good idea for you to be mucking about in this," Corso said.

"Why's that?"

Corso told Downs about Dougherty.

"And you think what happened to your friend was a result of her looking into my father's death?"

"Yeah, I do."

"How could—"

"I have no idea," Corso interrupted. "But I'm going to keep turning over rocks until something crawls out."

"I can't just leave," Downs said. "I don't know why, but I can't. It's like I found something and lost it all at the same time." He looked to Corso for agreement. "You know what I mean?"

Corso said he did. He remembered his own father's army trunk with the big brass padlock, how his father kept it stored under a tarp in the garage rafters. In the years after he returned from the war, he'd opened it only once, when a friend from his army days had stopped by one hot August afternoon. They sat together all day, stripped down to their undershirts, sweating together in that stifling oven of a garage, talking quietly and looking at pictures. Together they drank a whole bottle of whiskey and then, late in the afternoon, they'd put their heads together and cried.

He could still hear the dry crack of the wood when, the day after his father's death, he'd torn the hasp off with a crowbar and rolled back the lid. He could still feel the stinging of his cheeks as he tried to ignore his guilt—the terrible guilt—about the sense of relief he'd felt when the VA doctor told them his father had passed away. About how his first thought hadn't been about the loss of a father or its effect on those he loved but had, instead, been about the trunk in the rafters and how now, in death, he might solve the riddle of his father in some fashion that had not been possible in life.

"It's a high-profile case. The cops are giving it the full treatment."

"That's what they said." Downs waved a hand. "There's nothing I can do, I know that. But . . . somehow . . . for some reason I don't understand, I can't go back to Boston until I try to sort things out here. Does that sound crazy?"

"Yeah, it does," Corso said. "But sometimes life's like that."

Robert Downs ran his hands through his hair. "I don't know where to begin."

"Maybe I can help you there."

"What do you mean?"

"You have a car?"

"Sure. A rental Chevy."

"Then start with the cops," Corso said. "Contrary to rumor, they're real good at what they do. Go see them first thing in the morning. See what they've come up with so far. While you're there, get a copy of your father's financial records."

Downs started to ask a question, but Corso cut him off. "If it's not about sex, it's probably about money."

"But my father didn't have a—"

"Let's eliminate the obvious, and then we can work from there."

"Okay." Downs sighed. "First the police."

"Get an official death certificate," Corso said. "Somewhere down the line you're going to need it."

"Then?"

Corso reached into his pants pocket and pulled out a business card.

"When you get that done, call me and we'll go down to the school district where he worked."

"Oh, listen, you don't have to. . . . I didn't mean to—"

Corso held up a moderating hand. "Mr. Downs," he said, "if you knew me at all, you'd know my offer's got nothing to do with charity. With you or without you, I'm going to find out what happened to my friend and why." He turned the hand palm up. "If, somewhere in the process, I can help you to come to grips with a father you never knew, all the better. What's true is that I think you can be of use to me."

"How so?"

"You've got the bona fides. You're his son and heir. The cops are going to give and tell you things they wouldn't tell anybody else. School districts are the most clamped-down, tight-mouthed organizations in the world. Other than admitting that somebody did indeed work for them, they generally won't divulge a thing."

"What makes you think they might know something worthwhile?"

"Your father spent a third of his life at work. As far as I'm concerned, that makes it a one-in-three chance that whatever your father got mixed up in was work-related."

"But what about . . . I mean, I saw it on TV. You're covering that gangster trial, aren't you?"

"Tomorrow's the day they try to tie Balagula to his businesses. Eight hours of charts and graphs, all of which I've seen before. If I'm going to miss a morning, tomorrow's the one."

"I don't know what to say."

"Good."

Thursday, October 19 8:21 p.m.

Lake Union lay flat and still, its surface gleaming like black oil beneath the full moon. Corso felt the unseen eyes the minute he got out of the car. He slowed down, allowing his vision to adjust to the darkness as he scoured the shadows for movement, looking for that slight vibration of line that separates blood from blackness. He whistled softly as he walked back up the line of cars toward the street. A Metro bus hissed by on Fairview Avenue, its bold advertising placards inviting folks to visit the Experience Music Project. Nobody between the cars. Nobody out on the sidewalk. He walked over and checked along the fenceline. Nothing.

He gave an exaggerated shrug, lengthened his stride, and began walking quickly back toward the dock. And then stopped dead, held his breath, listened. No doubt about it: He heard the click of heels. He was still working on what to do next when the sound of voices snapped his head around.

They were coming up from C dock. In the dim purple light, they seemed almost to emerge from the asphalt as they climbed the ramp to ground level. It was the couple from *Grisswold*, a Hans Christian forty-seven, about a quarter of the way down the dock. Marla and Steve Something-or-other from Gig Harbor. They used the boat maybe twice a year. When he'd left this morning, they'd been standing on the dock with Marty Kroll. Looked like Marty'd been giving them an estimate on refinishing the brightwork.

Marla tried to work up a smile and failed. "Hi, Frank," she said. She was pushing fifty. Tall and dark, she moved with a girlish grace that belied her years.

"Hey, how's it going?" Corso said.

"It's *going* to cost the better part of fifteen grand," Steve growled.

Steve was a big beefy specimen, red-faced and loud. Prone to sandals and Hawaiian shirts regardless of the weather. He sold something.

"Without new sails," Marla added.

"Which is *at least* another ten." Steve said.

Sympathizing about the cost of boat repairs with other owners was de rigueur. Especially on those fateful days when day-trippers find out why you can't let sailboats sit around for years.

"Those kinda boat units will kill you," Corso said.

"I'm gonna put her up for sale," Steve announced. Over Steve's shoulder, Corso thought he saw movement among the dark pillars that supported the marina office.

"We'll still have to do the work," Marla said. "And we won't have the boat."

Steve looked to Corso. "Whoever buys it's gonna want a survey," Corso said. "She's right. Nobody's going to give them a loan unless everything's in order."

"Shit," Steve spit out into the night air.

Marla tugged at his elbow. "Come on, honey. We'll get a bite and you'll feel better."

"Better be Burger King or something cheap," Steve grumbled as she moved him along. "I just wanted a place we could stay in the city," he groused. "Hell, we coulda flown over. Stayed at the Four Seasons. We coulda . . ."

Corso had seen it before, but it was always a little sad to see a grown man finally come to understand the folly of boat ownership. He wondered if Steve had ever uttered the much used line about how a boat is a hole into which you throw money. Now he knew what all real boaters know. Every minute of every day, your boat is rotting away beneath you, and all you can hope to accomplish, with all the sandpaper and Cetol, the brass polish and bottom paint, is an uneasy stalemate with the elements.

He watched as they got into a gray Cadillac Seville, backed out into the lot, and drove off. He stood still for another moment, waiting until the Cadillac's taillights were nothing but a red smear at the end of Fairview Avenue, before he turned and started down the ramp.

He used his key on the lock and then let the spring swing it shut with a dull *clank*. The line of boats sat silent and slack in the water as he hurried toward *Salt-*

heart, moored at the far end. He was halfway there when his hands, as if acting on their own, reached to raise his collar, and he realized that once again he could feel unknown eyes on his back.

19

Friday, October 20 10:34 a.m.

She'd become the body electric. A flesh-and-blood software application. An extension cord for millennial medicine. Her heart reduced to a series of green electronic waves, her brain functions to a skittering red line on a bright white screen, her lungs to the rise and fall of a small black bellows. Tubes going in, tubes coming out, everything stimulating, and simulating, and yet she lay as still as death, her fingers relaxed, her eyes motionless beneath the lids.

Corso found himself thinking funeral thoughts. About the nature of life and how precious little what we call *the body* has to do with the person we are. How the body is little more than a container for the spark that makes us alive, that makes us unique, that makes us divine, and is ultimately no more meaningful or permanent than the red velvet box that delivers the diamond ring.

The soft *whoosh* of the door diverted his attention: the day nurse, a tall no-name-tag no-nonsense African-American woman of maybe thirty-five.

"There's a young man upstairs," she began.

"The boyfriend?"

She nodded. "He seems to feel—"

"Yeah," Corso said. "I know. I'll be going."

"He objects to you being here."

"We got off to a bad start," Corso said. "He'll get over it." He fetched his coat from the foot of the bed and shouldered his way into it. "You've got my number?"

"Yes, sir. Both Ms. Taylor and Mr. Crispin were very explicit. Any change in Ms. Dougherty's condition, you're to be notified immediately."

The look in her eyes said she was vaguely annoyed by the extra instructions and wanted to know what the hoopla was about.

"Thanks," Corso said. "I appreciate it."

She headed for the bed, Corso for the door. In the hall, he turned right and made for the elevators at the far end of the corridor. At the moment he pushed the UP button his cellular phone rang softly in his pocket. He pulled it out, raised the antenna.

"Corso."

"Mr. Corso, it's Robert Downs."

"Where are you?"

Downs told him.

"You're finished with the cops?"

Downs said he was.

Corso gave him directions to the hospital. "I'll meet you out front," he said.

Friday, October 20 10:53 a.m.

Corso shuffled through the pile of papers in his lap. Pulled out a 1040 form.

"Last year, your father made thirty-seven thousand dollars." He pointed out over the dashboard. "Take the next exit. Stay left."

Downs put on his turn signal and moved to the right lane, running up the steep exit ramp onto Martin Luther King Way South. Doubling back over the freeway, running south alongside the northbound freeway.

"Thirty-seven thousand dollars netted him just over two thousand dollars a month." Corso shuffled some more papers. "From what I can see, he lived on eight hundred and spent the other twelve on your education."

Downs swallowed hard but kept his eyes on the road. Corso found a bank statement. "At the time of his death, he had a hundred thirty-nine dollars in his savings account." Corso scanned the bottom of the form. "His average savings account balance for the past two years is one hundred fifty-three dollars and twelve cents."

"I don't understand," Robert Downs said.

"Don't understand what?"

"How his average balance wasn't higher."

"Why's that?"

"Early last year, maybe a year and a half ago, my last year of med school, he missed a bunch of payments. I started getting letters from Harvard saying I better make other arrangements for payment or I was going to be dropped."

"And?"

"I called him. He was never there, so I kept leaving him messages."

"How long did this go on?"

"Three or four months. I'd already been to my bank. Signed the papers for a loan." Robert Downs looked over at Corso. "I was going to tell him it was all right. I had a loan. It was no problem."

"And?"

"He paid it off. Out of the blue. All of it. Not just what he was behind but the whole rest of the year."

"How much was that?

"Forty-something thousand."

Corso sat back in the seat. "Really?"

"Not only that, but the last time we spoke—"

"When was that?"

"A couple of months back."

"And?"

"I was telling him how I was probably going to have to go to work for an HMO. How private practice was so expensive I was going to have to spend a few years saving my pennies before I could even think about going out on my own."

"And?"

"And he told me to hang in there. Not to commit to anything. He said he might be able to help set me up on my own." He lifted one hand from the wheel and waved it around. "How could a guy with a hundred-fifty-dollar average balance be thinking about helping me get into private practice?"

"Beats me," Corso said. "Turn right at the bottom of the hill."

Downs did as he was told, making a sharp right, rolling the rented Malibu along an access road between a Fred Meyer store and an apartment complex.

"How much would it take to get yourself into private practice?"

"A hundred thousand, minimum." He threw a pleading glance at Corso. "That's why I always assumed he was . . . I assumed he had . . ."

"Means," Corso said.

"He made it sound like it was no problem. Like he just had to move some money around and it would be okay."

Corso ruffled the stack of papers. "If he had a portfolio he'd have been paying taxes on it." Corso turned the tax form over. "He claimed nothing but his salary and twelve dollars in interest income."

The haunted look on Robert Downs's face said he was as confused as Corso was.

"Take a right at the light. That's Renton Avenue. The school district building should be somewhere up the road on the right."

Half a mile up Renton Avenue, the Meridian School District was housed in a sleek modern building across from South Sound Ford. Robert Downs eased into a leaf-strewn parking space marked VISITOR and turned off the engine. He sighed and looked over at Corso. "What now?"

"Same deal," Corso said. "We're following the money. Did he cash in his retirement fund last year? Did he have an insurance policy he could borrow on? Was he into his credit union big-time? We're looking for any explanation of how a man with an average balance of less than two hundred bucks could come up with better than forty thousand dollars in a pinch."

Downs grabbed the door handle. "You coming?" he asked.

"They'll just make me wait outside," Corso said. "You better handle this one on your own." Downs heaved a sigh and got out of the car. As he stood for a moment with the door open, Corso could hear the rush of traffic and the car lot's colorful pennants snapping in the breeze.

Robert Downs was gone for thirty-three minutes. By the time he returned, carrying a thick manila folder, Corso had been through Donald Barth's financial records twice.

"Anything?" Corso asked as the younger man settled into the driver's seat.

Downs dropped the folder on the seat between them. "Nothing," he said. "He's got thirty-three thousand dollars in his retirement fund and a ten-thousand-dollar insurance policy, neither of which have been touched."

"You the beneficiary?"

"Yeah," Downs muttered, looking away.

"Nothing to be sad about, kid. It's how he would have wanted it. And you're damn near halfway to private practice."

Downs leaned his head against the window. "It doesn't seem right."

"What's that?"

"That I could occupy such a huge part in his life, when . . . you know."

Corso remained silent. Downs rubbed the side of his face.

"It's like he aimed his whole existence at me, and—you know—to me he was just an afterthought. This distant creep my mother talked about. And all the while he was toiling away so I could—"

He stopped talking and looked over at Corso.

"Listen to me," he said. "I sound like something off a soap opera."

"Fathers are tough," Corso said. "There's a lot of built-in baggage."

Downs silently agreed, turned the key, and started the engine. "The school district has a maintenance shop. He had a locker." He reached down, opened the manila folder, and came out with a small piece of yellow lined paper. "I got directions," he said.

Corso took the paper from his hand, studied it for a moment, and then pointed toward the opposite end of the parking lot. "Take the far exit. Turn right out of the lot."

"You find anything?" Downs asked.

"It's what I *didn't* find."

"Like what?"

"Like any records pertaining to medical school payments."

"Really?"

"He's got everything from your four years at Harvard. Every bill, every letter, every invoice." Corso spread his hands. "Then, for the past two years, nothing."

"You suppose the police . . . ?" Downs pointed the Chevy up a steep hill, into a seedy suburban neighborhood.

"Soon as we get back to town, you're going to check with them again. Make sure they didn't miss something."

"Maybe they're holding out on us."

"Maybe," Corso said, without believing it. "And then you need to call Harvard. Get a complete copy of your payment records. College, med school, the whole thing. Have them overnight it to you."

20

Friday, October 20 11:47 a.m.

"I'll tell you the same thing I told the cops. Donald Barth's been with us fifteen months. A model employee. Never missed a day."

Dennis—call me Denny—Ryder was foreman of the West Hill Maintenance Shop. Age was turning his thick blond hair the color of dirty brass, but it hadn't stopped him from plastering it back into a duck-tailed pompadour that would have made Elvis proud. A black Harley Davidson Road King Classic rested lovingly along the rear wall. Corso was betting it was Denny Ryder's.

Ryder wiped the corners of his mouth with his thumb and forefinger and then flicked a glance over at Robert Downs, who was holding his father's uniform shirt up in front of his face, studying the fabric as if it were the Turin Shroud.

"Nice quiet fella. Did his job. Kept his mouth shut."

"Where'd he work before?" Corso asked.

Ryder's eyes took on a furtive cast. "Before what?"

"Before fifteen months ago."

"Musta been somewhere else in the district."

"You don't know for sure?"

"He transferred in with his seniority intact, so he must have worked somewhere else in the district."

"Must have?"

"I don't do the hiring and firing," he said disgustedly. "The eggheads up in Human Resources do that. I just keep 'em busy when they get here."

Again, he flashed a quick look over at Robert Downs, who had folded the two uniform shirts over his arm and now stood, staring dejectedly off into space.

"Like I said. I really didn't know the guy very well."

Corso turned to Downs. "You ready?"

Downs looked startled by the question. "Oh . . . yes, sure." he seemed to shudder slightly as he started across the floor. He stuck out his hand. "Thanks for your help, Mr. Ryder," he said. Denny Ryder mumbled the obligatory condolences and then followed Corso over to the door, where he once again managed a furtive smile and a clumsy testimonial on the subject of Donald Barth. Hell-of-a-guy, good-bye.

Outside, the weather had gone to hell. A steady rain slanted in from the south. What an hour ago had been a bright blue sky was now a black blanket hanging twenty feet above the treetops like cannon smoke.

Robert Downs had raised his foot, as if to jog to the car, when Corso put a hand on his shoulder. "I'll meet you in the car," Corso shouted over the rush of the wind.

"I . . ." Downs began to stammer.

"I'll be right there," Corso assured him.

Downs nodded blankly and began jogging toward the car. Corso waited until the car door closed before turning and walking up the three stairs into the maintenance office.

Dennis Ryder's expression said he had half expected Corso to come back and wasn't happy about it. "Lose something?" he asked.

"Yeah," Corso said. "But I'm not quite sure what it is."

"What's that mean?" His tone held a challenge.

"It means I hear you talking, but I don't hear you saying anything. You sound like Jeffrey Dahmer's neighbors, talking about what a nice quiet boy he was."

Ryder swallowed a denial, scratched the back of his neck, and sighed. "I mean, what am I gonna say? With his kid here and all."

"I understand."

Ryder checked the room. "Barth was a first-class asshole," he said. "A complete loser loner. Thought he was better than everybody else." He waved a hand. "Cheapest sonofabitch I ever met." He threw a thumb back over his shoulder at the pop machine. "Never saw him so much as buy a pop. Never saw him buy a bag of chips or a candy bar. Two sandwiches and a bottle of tap water." He cut the air with the side of his hand. "That was it. Five days a week."

"So how come you don't know where Barth transferred in from?"

Ryder's eyes narrowed. "I didn't say that. I said Human Resources didn't provide me with that information."

"But you asked around."

"Wouldn't you? You come in one Monday morning." He waved a hand around. "I remember it was the fifteenth, because it was payday. And all of a sudden here's this guy who the district says is going to work full-time. They say he's got seven and a half years' seniority, which is more than anybody here but me." He shook his head, sending a single yellow lock down onto his forehead. "So naturally, I want to know where this guy came from. And you know what they say?" He waited for the question to sink in. "They say it's none of my damn business. Just put him to work. That's it."

"So?"

"I called the union."

"And the union said?"

"The union said, If they want to give us an extra position, we're sure as hell gonna take it."

"But you asked around anyway."

"Damn right I did."

"So?"

"So I find out he'd been working over in the North Hill shop. I call Sammy Harris—he's the lead over there—and I ask Sammy what the deal is, and he tells me pretty much the same thing I just told you. The guy's a loner. It's like he thinks he's better than everybody else or something. Eats lunch out in his truck by himself. Listens to classical music. Don't attend any of the social things. Just comes in, does his job, and goes home." Ryder stopped talking and squinted out the window. A white pickup with a Meridian School District logo on the door drove along the side of the building. Then another. And a third. "Crew's coming back for lunch," Ryder said.

"So how come they transfer Barth over here?" Corso asked.

"Well, that's the sixty-four-thousand-dollar question, now, isn't it?" Again he checked the room.

"Seems our friend Mr. Barth took a four-month leave of absence. By the time he got around to coming back, they didn't need him over on North Hill anymore, so they sent him here."

"Four months?"

"Yeah . . . from a job where if you're out more than three days in a row, you gotta bring a note from a doctor to keep from getting docked."

"Weird," Corso said. "When was this?"

"About this time last year is when he showed up. So he must have been out since early June sometime."

"Anybody tell you why he was gone?"

He shook his head. "Nope. District said I didn't need to know. Just put him back to work. Said it was confidential."

"What did Sammy have to say?" Corso asked.

Ryder chuckled. "Sammy said he don't have any idea either. Just gets a call from Human Resources one morning. They say Barth won't be in for a while. Period. That's it. Just won't be in for a while. But don't take him off the union rolls."

Corso pulled his notebook from his coat pocket. "Let me see if I've got this straight. Sometime last summer, Barth walks off his job and doesn't come back for over four months."

Ryder nodded. "Fourth of June to the eleventh of October. I looked it up for the cops yesterday."

Another pair of district pickup trucks rolled by the window.

"Then he shows up over here one morning, four months later, and you're supposed to just put him to work and not ask questions."

"That's it."

"Then what?"

"Then—what?—a couple of months ago, he stops coming in. I wait a few days—you know, HR already told me it was none of my business—so I wait a few days and call. They tell me to hang loose. Don't take him off the payroll. Don't do nothing. Just hang loose."

"And?"

Dennis Ryder's nostrils fluttered, as if the air were suddenly rank. "I'm still hanging when the cops come waltzing here Tuesday afternoon. Start showing me all these pictures of what's left of Barth and his truck." He eyed Corso closely. "I been straight with you, mister," he said. "How about a little comp time? You know what's going on here? Ain't often some guy we work with is found buried in the side of a hill like Jimmy Hoffa or something."

"Not a clue," Corso said. "I'm getting the same picture you laid out for me: a loner, kept away from everybody else, cheap." Corso shrugged. "If he had a vice it might have been that he liked the ladies a bit too much."

"Who told you that?"

"His ex."

Ryder took a deep breath, held it, looked around again. "You won't quote me." His eyes narrowed. "This kind of thing'd get me fired."

"No problem."

He pushed the breath out through his nose. "There *were* a couple of complaints."

"What kind?"

"Sexual harassment."

"Do tell."

"One over on North Hill and another one here."

"For doing what?"

Ryder made a rude noise with his lips and put on a disgusted face. "Who the hell knows, these days? You sneeze and somebody takes it wrong. You hang up a girlie calendar, and somebody feels like their constitutional rights are being shit on."

"You've got no idea what the beef was?"

Ryder shook his head. "District's real tight-assed about that kind of thing." He scratched a pair of quotation marks in the air. "Confidentiality," he said. "I'm not even allowed to ask."

Corso thought it over. "The person he was supposed to have harassed while he was here . . ."

Ryder was already shaking his head. "I can't tell you that. They'd have my ass in a New York minute."

"She—I'm assuming it was a she."

Ryder nodded vigorously. "Yeah."

"She still here?"

"Why?"

"I was thinking maybe you could ask her—you know, confidentially—if she might be willing to talk to me about it?"

Ryder chewed his lower lip.

"She says no, I'll take a hike," Corso added.

Ryder thought about it, made a what-the-hell gesture and turned and walked toward a door marked EMPLOYEES ONLY. "Stay here," he said, over his shoulder.

Corso watched the second hand sweep around four times before the door opened and a woman stepped into the room. She was younger than he'd expected: thirty or so, with a lot of city miles etched around her eyes and mouth, slim-hipped and flat-chested, with shoulder-length brown hair framing a pale oval face.

The patch on her uniform read KATE. She carried half a sandwich in one hand and a can of Diet Pepsi in the other.

"Cops were here yesterday," she said.

"I'm not a policeman," Corso said. "I'm a writer."

She recoiled slightly. "I don't want my name in the paper."

"No problem," he assured her. "I write books."

"Don't want my name in a book neither."

"Still not a problem," Corso assured her. "I'm just trying to figure out how a guy like Donald Barth ended up buried in the side of a hill."

She shook her head. "Weird, huh? Nothing like this ever happened anywhere around me before." She took a bite of her sandwich. While chewing, she took Corso in from head to toe. After washing the sandwich down with a big swig of Pepsi, she asked, "So what is it you want from me?" Her tone suggested she might be willing to entertain suggestions above and beyond mere information.

"You filed a complaint against Mr. Barth."

She rolled a piece of plastic wrap into a ball and threw it in the garbage can, then took another big pull on the Pepsi.

"He was a jerk," she said.

"Did he harass you?"

"What he did was piss me off," she said.

Corso kept his mouth shut, figuring she wouldn't have agreed to talk to him unless she wanted to tell her story.

"We had a thing going for a while," she said. "Nothing too serious, but you know . . . it was passable."

"Everybody says he was a loner. Did everything by

himself. How'd you manage to get involved with him?"

Her expression suggested she'd never considered the matter before. "I guess that was part of it," she said tentatively. "He had like this mystique about him. All secret and silent and withdrawn. He was different. He just sorta sat back and waited, like a spider." She skittered across the room as if she were on wheels. "Looking back on it, I guess that was his technique. He made it so's you had to chase after him."

"So what happened?"

She walked over to the window, spread the blinds with her fingers, and looked out. "It's like it was more exciting that way." She turned back toward the room and gestured toward the shop. "You know, what with the rest of the guys always coming on with the 'oooh babay baby' routine." She made a suggestive move with her hands and hips. "It's kinda refreshing to be on the other side of it once in a while."

"So?"

"So he's tellin' me how it's been years for him. How he hasn't been involved with a woman since his divorce and all that." She gave Corso a sideways smile. "You know; and that's got its appeal too. It's like you're in charge or something."

"Uh-huh."

She brought one hand up to her throat. "I know I'm clean. I get myself tested every time I—you know—strike up a new friendship, so to speak. And he's supposedly been living like a monk for years, so we can do it au natural, so to speak, which is a joy all to itself, if you know what I mean."

Corso's confirmation seemed to encourage her. "So

almost right away—soon as we get past the sweaty palms part in the beginning—I can tell something's wrong. Never back to his place. Always gotta be mine. We never go anywhere in public, 'cause—you know—we work together, and people might be thinkin' it's bad to mix business with pleasure." She made a rueful face. "At least that's what he said at the time."

She rested a hip on the desk and folded her arms. "So right away I'm thinking he's gotta be married or something." She held up a hand. "I got a rule. No married guys. Period. That's it."

"So?"

"So, I've got a friend in payroll, who tells me that, lo and behold, he's single. Got him a son who he doesn't have on the health plan, which means the son's either too old or has coverage someplace else."

"Either of which is okay with you."

"Sure," she says. "I'm not looking for anything permanent. I just want to make sure I'm not tearing up some other girl's world."

"Then?"

"Then it all goes to hell," she said. "We been together maybe two weeks, and all of a sudden he's not showing up at my place after work anymore. Doesn't say a word, just stops coming over." She bumped herself off the desk and put a hand on her hip. "So I see him at work and say, 'Hey, what's the deal? Haven't seen you lately.' And you know what he tells me?"

"What?"

"He tells me to get over it. Says he's moved on and I should move on too." Her free hand joined its mate at her waist. "Like I'm some snot-nosed kid or something."

"Ah," Corso said. "The woman scorned."

She laughed. "No, no," she said, "I was okay with it. I'm still thinking I woke this guy up after a long hibernation, and now he's running amok." She shrugged. "It figures. You know how guys are."

"Uh-huh."

"Until I tell my friend Susie about it—Susie's the one in payroll—anyway, a coupla days after I tell her about it, she calls me one night and tells me she went through his personnel file and guess what?"

"He's already had a sexual harassment complaint filed against him."

"Bingo." She began to smile. "Now I'm starting to get pissed. So I get the name and find an excuse to go over to the North Hill Shop, and, lo and behold, he ran the same number on her he ran on me." She raised her voice and added a singsong quality. "*I haven't been with a woman in years. I'm not sure I still know what to do*. Oh my, oh my." She shook her head disgustedly. "He gives her the same damn song and dance." She cut the air with her hand. "Unbelievable."

"And then he dumps her too."

"He doesn't even bother to tell *her*. She has to find out on her own." Corso waited. "Yeah. She comes back to the shop one night for something she forgot, and there he is sitting there in the parking lot in his truck mauling some little Asian honey."

"Not good."

"Damn right it's not good. Turns out this jerk is risking our lives. We're having unprotected sex with a guy who's screwing the known world."

"Ah."

"I hadn't even thought about a complaint until she—

the other girl—told me that's why she filed one." She nodded slightly, as if once again confirming her decision. "I decided she was right. This guy was putting our lives at risk. Any trouble I could make for that jerk was okay with me."

A buzzer sounded out in the shop.

"I gotta go," she said and headed for the door. She stopped and looked back over her shoulder. "As far as I'm concerned, Donald Barth got exactly what he deserved."

"Thanks for your time," Corso said.

She gave him a wicked smile. "Come back sometime."

"It's been years," Corso said with a grin.

She burst out laughing. "Yeah, sure."

21

Friday, October 20 5:05 p.m.

Warren Klein paced back and forth in front of the jury like a lion in a cage. Ray Butler stood ready at the easel, which held a picture of the collapsed back wall of Fairmont Hospital, taken from a slightly different angle, so as to exclude the tiny foot. Renee Rogers sorted through a mountain of paperwork on the prosecution table, handing Klein folders whenever he strutted her way.

"Mr. Rozan," Klein said, "can you tell the jury the magnitude of an earthquake that could be expected to cause damage of this nature?"

Sam Rozan looked like your local greengrocer: bald little guy with a big mustache and thick wrists. Turned out he was chief earthquake engineer for the State of California and an expert of world renown. A man whose consulting résumé included every major planetary shake in the past fifteen years.

"That would depend almost entirely upon soil conditions."

"Have you had occasion to inspect the soil around the Fairmont Hospital project?"

"I have."

"What were those conditions?"

"The ground is virtually undisturbed."

"Virtually?"

"None of the signs of ground failure are present at the scene."

"What signs would those be?"

He counted on his fingers. "Ground cracking, lateral transposition, landslides, differential settlement." He stopped with four fingers in the air. "And at the extreme end of the spectrum, the liquefaction of the soil beneath the structure."

"So you're saying that—"

"Objection." Elkins was on his feet. "Mr. Klein is leading his own witness, Your Honor. If Mr. Klein wishes to testify—"

"Sustained," Fulton Howell said.

"I'll rephrase the question," Klein said.

Turned out he didn't need to. Rozan spoke up. "None of the ground conditions consistent with damage of that nature were present."

"None?"

"Not in the slightest."

"Having satisfied yourself that ground failure was not to blame, did you and your colleagues make a subsequent examination of the site in order to ascertain other possible causes for the collapse?"

"Yes. My staff and I conducted a full-scale on-site investigation."

"Were you able to come to a conclusion as to the cause of the tragedy?"

"Absolutely."

Klein looked at the jury box like a kindly uncle. "For the sake of clarity, Mr. Rozan, are you saying that you were absolutely able to reach a conclusion, or that you believe the conclusion you reached to be absolutely true?"

"Both," Sam Rozan said, without hesitation. "The reasons for the structural failure were staring us in the face. It was a no-brainer."

The room caught its collective breath, waiting for Elkins to get to his feet and fight for his client, but Bruce Elkins remained seated and impassive.

"How so?"

"The building didn't meet any of the established specifications for seismic-resistant design."

"Which are?"

Rozan waved a hand. "There is, of course, no ideal configuration for any particular type of building." Klein opened his mouth to ask another question, but Rozan went on. "There are, however, a number of basic guidelines."

"Could you enumerate those guidelines for us, please?"

Rozan went back to his fingers. "One: the building should be light and avoid unnecessary masses. Two: the building and its superstructure should be simple, symmetric, and regular in plan." He looked over at the jury box. "You don't want the building to be too much taller than it is wide. Three: the structure needs to have considerably more lateral stiffness than structures in nonseismic regions."

"Why is that?"

"Because the stiffer and lighter the building, the less sensitive it will be to the effects of shaking."

"How is it possible to build a structure that is both stronger and lighter at the same time?"

"That's accomplished by the quality of the materials in conjunction with the quality of the workmanship."

"And you say that the Fairmont Hospital was built without any of these qualities?" Klein looked to the jury and aimed his palms at the ceiling. "How can it be, Mr. Rozan, that a publicly funded structure in the most seismically active area of the country would be allowed to be erected without these safeguards?"

"It was not constructed according to specifications."

Klein looked astonished. "Surely there must have been some system of checks and balances in place to assure that seismic guidelines were being adhered to?"

"On a project of that size, you'd normally have a pair of state building inspectors working full-time on the site."

"Was that the case?"

"Yes, it was."

"That would be Joshua Harmon and Brian Swanson."

"Yes, it would."

"Have you or any member of your staff spoken to either of these gentlemen?"

For the first time, Sam Rozan looked confused. "That wasn't possible," he said tentatively. "As you know, they . . . both of them were—"

Suddenly Elkins was on his feet. "Objection," he said in a weary voice. "It's obvious where Mr. Klein is heading with this, Your Honor."

"I'm merely asking an expert witness about the standard procedure for an investigation of this nature."

Elkins made a rude noise. "Mr. Klein seeks to inflame the jury with facts not entered in evidence. He seeks—"

Fulton Howell had heard enough. "Approach the bench," he said.

As Elkins and Klein shuffled toward the front of the courtroom, Renee Rogers rocked her chair back onto two legs and whispered to Corso, "Maybe Warren does have a trick or two up his sleeve. This is very slick."

Corso arched an eyebrow. Rogers checked the bench, where the muted discussion continued. "Ordinarily, we couldn't include anything about crimes other than those with which the defendant is charged." She flicked another glance at the front of the room. "Hell, we can't even bring up crimes the defendant's been convicted of. Except, in this case, where he's asking an expert witness about his method of investigation. . . ."

The sound of shoes snapped her head around. Klein wore victory on his face. "Mr. Rozan, allow me to rephrase my previous question," he began. "When assigned an investigation of the scope of Fairmont Hospital, where do you and your staff generally begin?"

"With the on-site inspectors."

"Always?"

"It's the professional protocol." He shrugged. "A courtesy."

"But in this case you were not able to do so."

"That's correct."

"Why was that?"

"Once again, Your Honor—"

The judge waved Elkins off. "Allow the witness to answer."

"I must take exception—"

"Exception noted, Mr. Elkins."

Klein stepped in close to the witness. "Once again, Mr. Rozan, could you please tell us why you were unable to question the on-site inspection staff?"

"They were dead."

"Move for a mistrial on the grounds that—"

"Motion denied," the judge snapped. He waved his gavel at Bruce Elkins. "As I explained to you during our sidebar, Mr. Elkins, so long as Mr. Klein's questions regarding Messrs. Harmon and Swanson are solely directed toward establishing Mr. Rozan's method of investigation, the information may be entered into evidence."

Klein's right shoe squeaked as he hustled toward the prosecution table. "The Alameda County file," he said in a stage whisper.

Rogers handed him a bright yellow folder. Klein strode past the jury, headed for the front of the room.

"The People would like to introduce into evidence two autopsy reports provided by Mr. Eugene Berry, who was, at the time, medical examiner for Alameda County."

"This is an outrage!" Elkins stormed.

"I am merely attempting to corroborate Mr. Rozan's testimony as to why he was unable to conduct his investigation according to his established pattern of inquiry."

"Continue."

He waved his fistful of reports at the judge. "We can

either have the reports read into the record in their entirety or we can stipulate that the circumstances of death surrounding Mr. Harmon and Mr. Swanson fall under the umbrella of common knowledge."

"So stipulated," Howell said. "But you will limit your stipulation to the barest facts of their disposition."

Klein turned to face the jury box. "Seven weeks after the collapse of Fairmont Hospital, Mr. Joshua Harmon and Mr. Brian Swanson were found floating in San Pablo Bay. Each man had been shot twice in the back of the head. The medical examiner lists these wounds as the cause of death."

Klein dropped the reports on the desk of the court clerk and walked back over to his witness. "You said earlier, Mr. Rozan, that you believed the causes for the collapse of Fairmont Hospital were"—he hesitated, putting a finger to his temple—"I believe your phrase was that it was a *no-brainer*. Is that correct?"

"Yes. It was."

"Could you give us an example of what you meant?"

Sam Rozan looked over at Ray Butler, standing by the easel. Ray pulled the collapse picture off and leaned it against the legs. The next photo was of a splintered square of concrete. A yellow ruler had been placed along the base, for scale, seventeen inches a side.

"Mr. Rozan, could you give us some idea of what it is we're looking at in this exhibit?"

"The picture is of one of the pillars that supported the rear wall of Fairmont Hospital." He started to get to his feet, stopped, looked at the judge. "May I?"

Judge Howell nodded his assent. Rozan walked to the oversized photo and pointed with a stubby finger.

"Here—where the outer layer of concrete has fallen off—you can see the honeycombing." His voice began to rise. "This is a main structural support. It's supposed to be solid." He brushed the back of his hand across the picture. "This is unconscionable."

"Was this defect present in other back wall columns?"

"It was consistent with virtually every other pillar and column in the entire structure."

"To what do you attribute this lack of solidarity?"

"Everything," Rozan said quickly. "The concrete mixing, the placement, the consolidation, the curing—all of it was cheap, quick, and dirty." He pointed at the picture again. "You could peel away the outer layer of concrete with the kick of a boot."

Klein walked him through four more photos without Elkins so much as clearing his throat. By the time Klein thanked his witness and returned to his chair next to Rogers, the jury could be heard twisting around in their seats.

"Cross," the judge intoned.

Elkins stayed seated. "Not at this time, Your Honor. I would, however, like to retain the right to question this witness at another time."

Klein got to his feet. "As would I, Your Honor."

"So noted." *Bang*. The judge sat back in his chair and sighed. "We've run considerably past the customary adjournment hour. And as Mr. Elkins does not wish to cross-examine the witness at this time, this seems to be a suitable place to quit for the weekend." He looked from lawyer to lawyer. "If neither of you gentlemen objects."

Friday, October 20 5:28 p.m.

Bruce Elkins sat down at the defense table and looked over at his client, Nicholas Balagula. "You pay me for my best legal advice," he said.

Balagula nodded in agreement. "Handsomely," he said.

Elkins's gaze was stony. "I've changed my mind about our strategy. I have an obligation to give you the opportunity to find new counsel, should you disagree with what I now consider to be your best legal option."

"What strategy would that be?" Balagula asked.

Elkins leaned in close to his client. "I don't think we should put on a defense," he said in a low voice.

Balagula and Ivanov exchanged glances. "Really?" Ivanov said.

"At this stage of the proceedings, that's my best legal advice."

"And if I disagree?"

"Then it is my advice that we seek a plea."

Balagula waved a hand, as if shooing a fly. "Not an option," he said.

Elkins ran a hand over his head. "I don't like it either," he said. "You heard the testimony. If the state can connect you in any way to the construction conspiracy, prison could turn out to be the least of your worries." He held Nicholas Balagula in an unwavering gaze. "You could very well find yourself looking at a lethal injection."

"Why no defense?" Balagula asked.

"Because that way—even if this Lebow person connects you to the conspiracy—that way you'll have grounds for appeal on the basis of having been provided an incompetent and insufficient defense."

"Mr. Lebow can connect me to nothing," Balagula said.

"That's not what my sources are telling me. I'm being told he's going to testify that he was in the room when you ordered the falsification of the core-sample test results." Balagula started to speak, but Elkins cut him off. "If that happens, the party's over. Not me or anybody else can get you out of this."

Nicholas Balagula got to his feet. "You do what you think is best," he said.

22

Friday, October 20 5:54 p.m.

She was right where he expected to find her. Leaning back in a booth at Vito's, a half-empty martini glass on the table in front of her. On the jukebox, Otis Redding was working his way through "I've Been Loving You Too Long."

Corso stood in the doorway until his eyes adjusted to the deep-space dark. Half a dozen regulars held down the bar stools. Renee Rogers had the booths to herself.

He got all the way to the table before she looked up and made eye contact.

"Well, well," she said. "I guess I'm going to have to work on being less predictable." She gestured with her hand for Corso to take a seat.

"Good thing Elkins didn't want to cross-examine," he said.

"Mercifully." She raised her glass in a toast, took a sip of the clear liquid.

"Klein's on a roll in there."

Her eyes were suddenly serious. "It's too damn easy," she said.

"How's that?"

She thought it over. "It's hard to describe," she said finally. "You do this for as long as I have and you get a feel for the pace of a trial. The ebb and flow. A trial falls into a rhythm, like a song."

"And?"

She waved a hand and looked at the ceiling. "Something's not right. Raymond can feel it too. It's hard to describe. The timing is off. It's like we're rolling downhill with no brakes." She looked over at Corso and made a face. "It's a lawyer thing."

"You shared this with Klein?"

She snorted. "Both Ray and I tried, but Warren doesn't want to hear about it. He's convinced his case is so airtight that Elkins's finally giving up the ghost and facing the inevitable."

"Last time I saw the evidence connecting Balagula to the construction companies, it seemed pretty thin to me."

"It still is. It's the weak link in the case. Balagula did a great job of insulating himself from their businesses. No matter how you look at it, the construction trail always leads back to Harmon and Swanson."

"The two guys they found floating in San Pablo Bay."

"And the only two people on earth who could tie Balagula directly to the contractors." She took another small sip from her drink. "You were at the second trial. Elkins objected to every chart, every graph, and every witness I put up there. He had citations for every instance and objection."

"I remember."

"Today, he's Mr. Rogers. He gets up just often

enough to look like he's doing something. Last time out, it took us two weeks to get through what we got through today in two hours. He's going through the motions. I don't get it."

"Maybe Klein's right. Maybe he has got Balagula by the balls."

She gave a grudging nod. "Maybe," she said. "If we can prove that Balagula and Ivanov arranged for the fake inspections and the fabricated core tests, then by extension we prove they must have had some interest in the companies involved; otherwise there'd be no reason for them to be going to all that trouble and taking all that risk."

"And this Lebow guy is gonna make the connection?"

"He says he was present when it was discussed. That both Ivanov and Balagula were in the room at the time and that Balagula gave the order."

"That ought to do it," Corso said.

Renee Rogers massaged the bridge of her nose several times and then waved her hand disgustedly. "Enough already," she said. "I don't know why I'm obsessing over it. Either way, I'm out of here when the trial's over."

The bartender wandered over. Corso asked for ice water. Rogers covered her glass with her hand and shook her head. "What about you?" she asked. "How's your friend doing?"

"The same."

"You making any progress?" She ran her finger around the rim of the martini glass, as he told her about what he'd learned. "Sex and money," she said, when he'd finished. "The deadly duo."

"None of it gets me any closer to finding out what came down."

"You sound like I feel," she said.

They sat in silence for a moment. The ice water appeared. Corso downed half of it.

"Where's that market where they throw the fish around?" she asked. "The one they always show on TV."

"First and Pike. Four blocks west and six blocks north. Why?"

"Since I'm off for the weekend, I thought I might do a little sightseeing. I spent four months here last summer and never saw anything except the hotel, the bar, and the courthouse."

She watched as Corso took another sip of water and then sat back in his chair. Her eyes sparkled.

"You're not very quick on the uptake, Mr. Corso."

His face was blank. "How's that?"

"This is the point in the conversation where you're supposed to go all gallant and offer to show me around town."

"I know," he said, with a chuckle.

"If you're not careful, you're going to have me worrying that I've lost my charm. I could get a complex or something."

He laughed again. "Your charms are intact."

"Well, then?"

"I'm not much on the tourist traps."

"Then show me something else. Something only the locals get to see. Something known only to one of the city's true chroniclers such as yourself."

Corso thought it over. "You bring a pair of jeans and some real shoes?"

She looked down at her feet and then back up at Corso. "Yes, why?"

Corso threw a five-dollar bill on the table and stood up . "Come on," he said.

"I'll need an hour," she said, as she gathered her things.

He looked as if she were standing on his foot.

"You don't spend a lot of time with women, do you?"

Friday, October 20 7:32 p.m.

Corso poked his head out the pilothouse window. "Okay, now the stern line!" he shouted. Renee Rogers freed the line from the cleat and looked up at Corso through a cloud of diesel fumes. "Just bring it with you," he said, not wanting to risk her throwing the line on deck. If she missed, it would end up in the water, uncomfortably close to the props.

She came down the dock and then up the stainless-steel stairs to the deck. Corso opened the starboard door and pulled her inside as he backed the boat out of the slip. A fender groaned as the big boat rolled it along the dock. Corso dropped the engines to idle, reversed the transmissions, gave the starboard engine a little diesel, and swung the bow out into the channel.

Renee Rogers climbed the three steps into the pilothouse. "This was not *quite* what I had in mind," she said.

"You said you wanted to see something only the locals get to see." Corso held the wheel straight and let the bow thruster push the nose out into Lake Union. "Hold the wheel," he said.

"But I've nev—"

He hooked her with an arm and moved her behind the wheel. Instinctively, she grabbed the big teak wheel with both hands.

"Just aim at the other side of the lake and don't hit anything," he said.

It took him less than five minutes to stow the stairs, clean up the lines, and get the fenders back aboard. He swung the hinged section of rail back into place and stepped into the galley. Renee Rogers looked down from the pilothouse. "This is really something," she said. "I had no idea this huge lake was right in the middle of the city."

Corso stowed his coat in the forward shower. He climbed into the pilothouse, slipped behind Renee Rogers, and settled into the mate's chair.

The lake was a choppy green field, foamy and frantic, falling all over itself from a dozen directions. *Saltheart* bobbed slightly in the chop. Without warning, a deepening roar began to fill the cabin. A Lake Union Air Service seaplane buzzed over, not more than forty feet above the deck. "Wow," Rogers said softly, as she watched the yellow-and-white De Havilland Beaver descend. Five hundred feet ahead, the pontoons cut silver slices in the dark water. They watched as the water pulled the plane to a halt and the pilot swung the plane on its axis, until the whirling propeller was pointed back their way.

Above the taxiing plane, the city stood tall and twinkling, the buildings shadowed by a black sky, glowing purple at the edges.

Corso closed his eyes and allowed the water to pull the weight from his shoulders, let the movement of the boat and the deep rumble of the diesels loosen the grime of the day. And then he seemed to swim downward in the thick green water, with the hum of the engines in his ears and the taste of the water on his lips.

"Hey," Rogers said. He opened his eyes. They were coming up to the south end of the lake. The Wooden Boat Museum loomed ahead.

"What now?" she wanted to know.

"Go around the red buoy," he said, pointing.

She gave the buoy a wide berth as she brought the boat about. Corso reached over and eased the throttle forward. Eight hundred rpms. About five knots across the surface.

"My father had a boat," she said, "when I was a kid."

"What kind?"

"A ChrisCraft." She waved a hand around. "Not a palace like this. Just a little boat he and my Uncle George used to go fishing in. Maybe twenty feet."

"What'd your father do?"

"He was a county sheriff."

"Where?"

"Anderson County, Virginia."

"Where's that?"

"Way down in the southern part of the state. Almost in North Carolina."

"Still alive?"

"Oh, no," she said. "He died back in 'ninety-one." She flicked a glance in his direction. "Yours?"

He offered a wan smile. "Mine was a regular guest of the county sheriff."

"Still alive?"

He shook his head. "His liver gave out at forty."

"A pity."

"We didn't think so," he said.

To starboard, the shoreline was awash with houseboats. Once cozy weekend retreats, they were now gussied up into million-dollar barges for the army of cellular-software-dot-com millionaires who swarmed the city like portfolioed roaches.

"Where are we going?" she asked.

"I told you: to see something only seen by the locals."

"You're not going to tell me, are you?"

"No."

"That's very childish."

"I know."

She feigned annoyance, frowning and looking out the windows into the bright moonlight, swiveling her head in an arc to take it all in, until the frown disappeared and she said, "Look at all these boats. Does everybody in this city own a boat?"

"Sometimes you'd think so," Corso said. "They say we've got more boats per capita than any other place in the country."

Corso played tour guide as they motored under the freeway bridge into the west end of Portage Bay, past the University of Washington and the Seattle Yacht Club and into the Montlake Cut, past the massive steel chevrons of Husky Stadium and out into Union Bay, where Corso reached over and pushed the throttles forward to fifteen hundred rpms and a stately twelve knots. "Moon's gonna be just right," he said.

For five minutes, they ran parallel to the 520 bridge, where the headlights of the traffic formed a solid line of amber that seemed to slide around the floating bridge's elegant curves like an android snake.

At the far end of the bridge, Corso finally took the helm, motoring *Saltheart* under the east high-rise and into the south end of Lake Washington. Ahead in the gloom, Mercer Island floated low on the shimmering water.

Corso cut back on the throttles and angled closer to shore. He checked his course and then set the autopilot. "Come on. Let's go down on deck. We can see it better from there."

The eastern shoreline was littered with million-dollar mansions: sterile steel and glass monoliths, neo-antebellum Greek Revival Taras, fifties Ramblers, and Tudor reproductions all huddled cheek-by-jowl along the narrow bank. Corso pulled open the port door and followed Renee Rogers out on deck. He pointed to a break in lights that lined the shore. "There," he said. "You can only see it from the lake, and only this time of year, when the leaves are off the trees."

Renee Rogers leaned on the rail and squinted out through the gloom. At first it looked like a park. Then maybe a trendy waterfront shopping center. Very Northwest. Lots of environmentally conscious exposed rock and wood, meandering its way up and down the cliff and along the bank for the better part of an eighth of a mile.

She traced the outline with her finger. "Is that all one—"

"Yeah, it's all one house," Corso answered.

"Who—"

"Bill Gates," Corso said. "Forty-five thousand square feet. Somewhere in the vicinity of a hundred and ten million dollars."

"No kidding."

"You get a little preprogrammed electronic badge. As you walk around the house, it adjusts everything to your liking. The temperature, the lights, even the electronic art on the walls."

"Wonder what it's like to live in something like that."

"When he married Melinda, she said it was like living in a convention center. She hired a team of decorators to make parts of it into something more livable."

"Funny how it's all relative," she said. "An hour ago, I thought your boat was decadent. Now"—she gestured toward the shore—"it seems like a rowboat."

"You think owning a house like that would change your life?"

She looked at him like he was crazy. "What do you mean?"

"Sometimes I cruise by here and wonder whether having all that would really make any long-term difference in my life."

"About a hundred-million-dollar difference," she scoffed.

"Over and above the money."

"There's no such thing as over and above the money."

"Would you be happier?"

She searched his eyes for a sign of irony. "You're serious, aren't you?"

"I wouldn't," he said. "If Bill gave me the place tomorrow, lock, stock, and barrel, paid for, tax-free."

"Yeah?"

"Once the buzz wore off, once I'd had everybody I know over for dinner and got used to the idea of owning the most expensive piece of residential property in

America . . . ?" He hesitated. "A week later I wouldn't be any happier than I was when I got up this morning."

As the house slid slowly to stern, she seemed to consider and discard a number of responses. The moon was directly overhead. The surface of the lake glowed like molten glass. "Me neither," she said finally.

"You hungry?" Corso asked.

"What I am is thirsty."

"What would you like?"

"What do you drink?"

"Bourbon."

"Then let there be bourbon." She toasted with an imaginary glass. "And come to think of it, I'm starved."

Corso pulled open the liquor cabinet and pulled out a half gallon of Jack Daniel's. In the cabinet above the stove, he found a pair of thick tumblers, filled each with ice, and added four fingers of bourbon. He handed Renee Rogers her drink and lifted his own. "Here's to putting Nicholas Balagula behind bars."

They clicked glasses. Corso took a sip. Rogers swallowed half the drink. Corso set the bourbon bottle on the drainboard next to the sink. "Bottle's here," he said. "From now on, it's self-service."

"Just the way I like it."

"We could probably rustle up a couple of steaks and a salad on the way back, if you want."

"I'm not very handy."

"Look in the bottom of the refrigerator. I think there's a new bag of salad greens in there."

She crossed the galley, pulled open the refrigerator door, and extracted a plastic bag full of greens. Corso put the transmissions into neutral, throttled all the way back, and switched off the engines. For a moment, the big boat floated in silence. Then Corso pushed the chrome button on the console and the generator sprang to life.

"You actually cook for yourself?" she asked.

"All the time."

"I eat out. Or do takeout or call room service or whatever."

"There was a time when I couldn't go out without attracting a crowd and having cameras shoved in my face. I kinda got in the habit of eating in."

She watched the memory wash across his dark face. "You actually hate it, don't you?"

"Hate what?"

"The celebrity."

"Doesn't everybody?"

"A lot of them say they do, but I don't think so. I think it's chic and humble to pretend you don't like being famous, but I think most people, once they've had their moment in the sun, would rather have it than not, no matter what they say in public."

"Celebrity as the opiate of the people."

She laughed. "Something like that."

She bounced the bag of salad greens in the palm of her hand. "What are we gonna put on this?"

"Look on the refrigerator door. There's a bunch of different things in there. Pick something you like."

She rummaged around in the door for a minute and came out with an unopened bottle of honey mustard dressing. "This okay?" she asked.

"Works for me," Corso said.

She downed the rest of her drink and poured herself another and then downed half of that. Corso sprinkled salt and pepper on a pair of T-bone steaks.

"I'm going to the stern and fire up the barbecue," he said. He reached over and flipped up the teak lid above the sink. Plates, glasses, silverware. "Why don't you set the table and then dump some of that stuff on the salad and mix it up. You think you can handle that?"

She took a pull from her glass. "Are you making fun of me?"

"Just a little," he said. "I'll be right back."

23

Friday, October 20 10:53 p.m.

Gerardo knew the drill. He'd been watching all day. The shift was about to change. For the next ten minutes, the hospital corridors would be virtually empty, as one shift of doctors, nurses, and orderlies left the floor and another came on duty.

He pushed his burnished aluminum cleaning cart to the side of the corridor and pretended to rearrange his cleaning supplies. Sixty feet down the hall, a pair of white-clad nurses came out of Room One-oh-nine and hurried up the hall toward the nurses' station.

He'd talked it over with Ramón, talked more than the whole fifteen years they'd been together. Nothing was going right lately. The way things had been going, it might be time to clean up their messes. Might be best if Gerardo was ready to run backup too, just to be sure. Lotta stuff going on in that part of the hospital. Might be best to have another gun, just in case somebody walked in or something. You never knew.

* * *

Ramón Javier looked like he belonged at a board meeting. He wore a somber gray suit, a blue tie, and a pair of tasseled loafers that gleamed from a recent shine. The .22-caliber automatic with the noise suppressor was tucked into the back of his pants, leaving the lines of the suit undisturbed as he stepped off the elevator and started down the hall.

He saw Gerardo standing behind a cart full of towels, wearing rubber gloves and a pair of baby-blue scrubs. Not his color at all. Made him look like a troll. Ramón pretended not to notice him, instead striding by, heading for One-oh-nine down at the corner. Probably could have just walked in and popped her on his own, but things were a little bit loosey-goosey lately, so they were playing it safe. The whole damn thing shouldn't take more than a minute. A minute, and they'd be halfway back to the kind of programmed normality upon which Ramón thrived.

At the corner, he stopped, checked the corridor to his left, and looked back at Gerardo, who offered a small nod that said the room was empty. Gerardo busied himself with a clear plastic spray bottle. Ramón took a deep breath, pulled open the door, and stepped into the room.

* * *

As the door closed behind Ramón, Gerardo began a silent count in his head. If he got to a hundred, it meant trouble and he was going in. His mother told him trouble came in threes. Sixteen, seventeen, eighteen. They'd already had three: the dead guy, the truck coming unburied, and the girl walking in on them. Twenty-three, twenty-four. Didn't need no more damn disasters. Just a nice clean kill and out the door. He checked the hallway. Nothing but a big-ass nurse, standing with her hands on her hips way down at the opposite end of the building. Thirty-seven, thirty-eight.

* * *

The room was lit only by the machines surrounding the bed. Ramón pulled the .22 from the back of his pants, thumbed off the safety, and placed the end of the suppressor against the side of the bandaged head. He listened for the sound of feet in the hall, heard nothing, and pulled the trigger. The pile of bandages rocked violently to the right and then snapped back into place. The electronic images went wild, dancing over their monitors like insects on fire. The small symmetrical hole began to leak blood, as Ramón placed the suppressor against the top of the head and fired again. Just to be sure.

* * *

He was at fifty-one when he heard the voice. "Hey, you," she called from the opposite end of the hall. Nigger bitch. Big enough to plow a field. Gerardo pretended not to hear. "You speak English? *¿Habla inglés?*"

Gerardo whistled softly and sorted through a pile of small towels until his hand came to rest upon the taped grip of the automatic. A warm feeling spread through his body, even as he listened to the sound of her shoes squeaking down the long corridor in his direction.

"You hear me down there?" she demanded. "We got a mess up in One-sixty-four."

She kept coming his way and then, suddenly, from

the direction of the nurses' station, a guy appeared, thirty-something, hair and brown beard in need of a trim. He carried a newspaper under his left arm. As he reached the corner, he hesitated for a moment and then grabbed the handle of One-oh-nine, pulled it open, and stepped inside.

"You got an earwax problem or what?" she demanded. No more than thirty feet away now. Beneath the pile of linen, Gerardo thumbed the safety off and turned her way, grinning maniacally. Pointing at his ear, as if to say he could not hear. When he peeked back over his shoulder, the hall was empty.

* * *

Ramón was halfway back to the door when it began to open. He stepped quickly into the shadow behind the door, which kept opening and opening until it had him pressed flat against the wall. The figure stepped into the room and stood for a second as the door hissed shut, letting his eyes adjust to the gloom. Ramón was already moving his way when the figure emitted a low moan and ran to the bedside. The bright white screen had gone black. The green hillocks of her heartbeat crawled over the screen like flatworms. The visitor reached out and touched her head, brought the hand up to his face, stared for a brief second at the stain, and turned, wide-eyed, toward the door. From a distance of two feet, Ramón shot him between the eyes.

* * *

A buzzer was going off. Her hand was on his elbow, pushing him up the hall. Gerardo's hand rested on the butt of his automatic. Eighty-three, eighty-four. He'd already decided: one hundred and the bitch dies. Then, a second later, Ramón was standing in the hall. He gave Gerardo a small nod that meant the job was done and then began following along in their wake.

"Come on." The bitch pulled harder on his arm. Gerardo snuck another peek, just as Ramón turned left at the exit sign and started for the stairs. At the far end of the hall, a trio of nurses hurried into Room One-oh-nine. He heard a scream and then another. The nurse loosened her grip and then let him go altogether. The door to One-oh-nine burst open. The front of the nurse's uniform was a glistening smear of blood. Her mouth was a frozen circle. Gerardo wrapped the automatic in a fresh towel and stuck it under his arm. For seventy feet, he shuffled along behind his captor as she hurried back toward the shouts and confusion. At the overhead exit sign, he straight-armed the door, stepped into the stairwell, and began jogging up the stairs. At the first landing, he threw his hip into the emergency exit door and stepped outside into the cool night air. "One down, one to go," he whispered to himself, as he started up the sidewalk.

24

Friday, October 20 10:57 p.m.

Along the north shore of Lake Union, the derelict ferry *Kalakala* lay beached like some moldering gray carcass washed ashore by the tide. Once the pride of the Seattle fleet, the Art Deco *Kalakala* had been rescued by a local businessman, whose sense of nostalgia had been offended by the notion that the ferry of his childhood seemed destined to live out its final days as an Alaskan fish-packing plant.

At considerable expense, he'd had her towed down from Alaska and berthed at her current location, only to find that his fellow Seattleites did not share his fondness for the old vessel. Not only were they unwilling to participate in her proposed multimillion-dollar renovation but most considered her little more than an eyesore and demanded that she be removed from sight forthwith. Under intense pressure from the city, her owner now sought a suitable buyer who might be willing to take her off his hands.

As the rusted hull slid to starboard, Renee Rogers

stepped over to the refrigerator and filled her glass with ice cubes, which she then drowned in bourbon.

"Warren would hate this," she said.

"Hate what?"

"Hate us bobbing around out here on the lake together. He gave me a little lecture the other day about what he called *commiserating* with you."

"Have we been doing that? And here I thought we were just trying to pick each other's brains over dinner."

She laughed and looked around. "We're almost back, aren't we?" she said.

"Up ahead on the left."

The purple had faded from the horizon, leaving a charcoal sky. The air had begun to thicken with mist, turning the full moon to a hazy nickel.

She took another pull from her drink. "So how come you never got married?" she asked, out of the blue.

Corso pulled his gaze from the lake and looked her way. Her eyes looked tired, and her words carried just the hint of a slur.

"How do you know I've never been married?"

She laughed. "I've read your file, of course. You don't think we let you in the courtroom without doing our homework, do you?"

"What about you?" Corso asked. "You've never managed it either."

She made a *tsk-tsk* sound. "You've got a file on me too, don't you?"

"Of course."

She laughed again. "You ever notice how small talk suffers when you're talking to somebody you've got a dossier on?"

Corso's shoulders shook with laughter. It took him a moment before he was able to speak. "Especially when they don't know."

Renee Rogers threw her head back and laughed. Corso kept on.

"You already know everything you'd normally ask them at a time like that, so you're five minutes into a conversation with a stranger, and if you're not careful you're asking them about that mole they had removed last year, a story that they can't, for the life of them, remember having shared with you."

"And they spend the rest of the night looking at you out of the corner of their eyes."

They shared another laugh, before Corso asked. "So? How come you never managed it either?"

"I asked you first."

He thought it over. "I was engaged once, but things didn't work out," he said, after a moment. "It's not like I planned it that way or anything. Always seemed to me like I might be ready to settle down after the next assignment or after the next big story." He shrugged. "It just kept getting pushed somewhere down the road until I was so used to being like I was"—he took one hand off the wheel—"that it stopped being an issue."

She folded her arms and turned her eyes inward.

"You like living alone?" she said, after a short silence.

"I'm used to it. The longer I do it, the more it suits me."

"You don't get lonely?"

"You can be married with five kids and still be lonely."

She gestured with her glass. "Your Honor. The witness is being unresponsive. Please direct him to answer the question."

He chuckled. "Yeah . . . Sometimes, I guess—you know—sometimes it would be nice to have somebody to do things with."

"I hate eating out alone," Renee Rogers offered.

"Me too. That's another reason why I cook."

She finished her drink. "When I get home, I'm going to dust off all the cookbooks I've gotten as presents over the years and give it a try." She held up two fingers, Boy Scout–style. "I hereby resolve to be more domestic." The slur was stronger now. She seemed to notice and turned her face toward the windows.

Corso pulled back on the throttles, allowing the wind and the water to slow the boat's momentum and ease *Saltheart* to a stop alongside the floating dock.

Renee Rogers pushed herself from the seat. "I'll help," she announced.

"No need," Corso said. "I've got it. Docking's easier," he lied.

He moved quickly down the stairs and out onto the deck. First he went forward and threw the bowline down onto the dock, then grabbed a trio of fenders and spaced them along the rail as he made his way to the stern. By the time he'd finished getting the stairs in place, the wind had moved the boat six feet from the dock and he had to step inside and readjust the bow thruster. Renee Rogers was leaning back against the sink, rolling her icy glass across her forehead. Corso stepped back outside, climbed to the bottom step, and hopped down onto the dock.

Took him five minutes to moor the boat to his satisfaction and reconnect the electrical power and the phone line. When he stepped back into the galley, Renee Rogers was leaning over the counter, taking deep breaths through her open mouth.

"You okay?" he asked.

She gave a silent shake of the head and continued staring down into the sink as Corso stepped around her and turned off the engines.

"Anything I can do?" he asked.

She stood up straight and brought a hand to her throat. "I don't know, I think maybe it's the rocking of the boat. I feel dizzy."

"Come on," he said, offering a hand. She took it, and he led her down into the salon and sat her on the couch. "Relax."

She leaned back on the couch, brought a hand up to her forehead, closed her eyes, and took several deep breaths.

"This is so embarrassing," she said.

"The water affects people differently."

She massaged the back of her neck and nodded slightly.

"Relax," Corso said. "I'm going to do a few chores. I'll be right back."

It took him the better part of ten minutes to round up all the plates and glasses, rinse everything, and get it into the dishwasher. When he returned to the salon, Renee Rogers hadn't moved. He sat down next to her on the sofa and jostled her arm. He tried three times before her eyes blinked open. "How ya doin'?" he asked.

"Not very well, I'm afraid. One minute I was feeling fine. . . ."

"Listen," Corso said. "I've got an idea. I've got a

real nice forward berth with its own head. Why don't you lie down there until you're feeling better."

She started to protest, but Corso kept talking.

"You wake up and feel better, we'll call you a cab. You sleep till morning, and I'll make you breakfast. Whatta you say?"

She tried to get to her feet. "I couldn't, really." Her hand slipped on the arm of the sofa, and she fell back onto the couch.

Corso held out his hand. "Come on," he said.

He left his hand extended until finally she reached out and took it. Slowly, he pulled her to her feet and led her back through the galley to the four stairs leading down to the forward berth and the chain locker. She slipped slightly on the second step, but Corso was there to take her by the shoulders and ease her to the lower deck.

He slid open the door to the berth. "Here it is," he said. "Take it easy for a while. See how you feel."

"This is terrible," she said. "I'm so embarrassed."

"Nothing to be embarrassed about," he said as he steered her into the room until the backs of her legs were against the bed. "Just make yourself comfortable."

She pulled the coverlet back, sat, and swung her feet up onto the bed, then noticed her shoes. She used her right foot to pry off the opposite sneaker, then reversed the process. Corso grabbed the Nikes and set them on the floor next to the bed.

"Just till I'm feeling better," she said.

"I'll button things up for the night and then come back and see how you're doing. We'll figure out where to go from there."

"Okay," she said, closing her eyes.

She was snoring before he got the door closed. He reached over, drew the coverlet over her shoulder, and made his way up and forward. Turned off the dock lights and the heat and finally, almost as an afterthought, flipped on the carpet alarm. He started outside to pull up the stairs but stopped himself. Figured he better wait and see what was going on with Rogers. On his way through the salon, he cracked a couple of windows.

25

Saturday, October 21 1:34 a.m.

The cornstalks stood dry and broken among the furrows, their shattered shafts pale against the frozen brown earth. Here and there, snow had gathered along the windward edges of the rows, like lace along the neck of a dress.

The preacher had to ask the operator to shut down the backhoe so he could be heard above the wind. Then he started on about other lives in other times, as the mourners stood hand in hand, waiting for him to speak his piece, so they could put the box in the ground and finally be free of everything but the memory. Or so they hoped.

As he read from the book, the sky darkened and the air was filled with the rush of wings. A flock of blackbirds filled the sky, soaring together, veering off at angles, and then, as if by signal, landing in the cornfield, where they began to pick among the stubble like refugees. And above the droning voice, above the whine of the wind and the rustle of the birds, the hollow metal sound began, metric and mechanical: bong . . . bong . . . bong . . .

Corso sat up in bed. The muted gong of the alarm system beat a rhythm in his ears. He checked the digital clock by his bedside. One thirty-five. Probably a dog, he thought. That big ugly shepherd they take out on the Catalina thirty-six.

He lay back and waited for the dog to wander off and the alarm to go silent. The wind had died. *Saltheart* floated lightly in the slip. The moment he felt the boat move, his heart began to pound in his chest. Somebody was coming up the stairs he had left in place. Nobody in the marina would come on board without permission. It just wasn't done. You hailed from the dock. You hammered on the hull. You did whatever you had to, but you didn't come aboard without permission. He sat back up and flipped the switch, turning off the alarm. Then the boat rocked again as a second person climbed the ladder to the deck, and he felt his mouth go dry.

He bumped himself down off the berth. Wearing only a pair of Kelly-green basketball trunks, he climbed the three stairs and poked his head up into the galley. Maybe Rogers was up and wandering around. It took a single glance to stop the breath in his chest and make his blood feel cold.

Shadows, two of them: one tall, one short. Short had come on board first. He was halfway to the stern when he stuck his fingers into the window crack and slid the window all the way open. Then the curtains were eased back. The cops maybe?

Tall came in head first. With the grace of a gymnast, he used his hands to cushion his roll down onto the couch, came up lightly on his feet, then reached back out the window. When the hand reappeared, it held a silenced automatic. Corso felt his insides contract. So much for the cops. Tall set the automatic off to the side on the settee and put both hands out the window. The sight of a pump shotgun in his hands got Corso moving.

He swallowed a mouthful of air and backed down the stairs. Once at the bottom, he quietly closed and locked the companionway door. He knew the puny barrel bolt wouldn't stop a determined child; he just hoped to slow them down. A movement beneath his feet announced the second man's arrival in the salon. Corso crawled down under the stairs.

His fingers trembled as he unlatched the brass dogs holding the engine-room hatch, but his brain was starting to work again. He knew what he had to do. They were only expecting one person on board. If they went forward, they'd find Rogers in the bunk, kill her, and then come looking for him. He had to draw them toward himself and then make his way through the engine room to Rogers in the bow, hoping like hell they didn't know anything about boats, didn't immediately realize that all they had to do was go up to the main deck and they could stroll wherever they wanted.

He pulled open the three storage drawers that were built into the bulkhead. Open, they prevented the door from swinging inward. He banged his hand hard on the door and ducked down under the stairs. They came his way. He heard the door handle rattle and the wood groan. Somebody walked back to the salon and then returned.

An instant later a deep muffled boom shattered the air, and the companionway door was reduced to splinters. The air was filled with floating pieces of fabric and fiber. They'd used a couch cushion to muffle the shotgun's roar. A second smothered blast, and the opened drawers were history. The splintered remains were still in the air, as Corso crawled into the engine room and snapped the four inside dogs closed.

He reached to his right, switched on the light, and moved as quickly and quietly as possible toward the bow. He duckwalked his way between the twin Lehman diesels, picked his way carefully over the exhaust manifolds and electrical lines. Through the forward storage area to the forward watertight door, where he sat on his haunches and took a deep breath. If they'd figured it out and were waiting, he was dead.

The first dog took him three tries. After that, he was cool. He pulled the door toward himself. He winced as he stuck his head out and peered up at the bottom of the stairs. Nothing, so he crawled out into the hall and stood up. Ran the same door-locking strategy with the barrel bolt and the open doors and then slid open the berth door.

Renee Rogers was sitting up in bed. She wore an expensive-looking gray bra-and-panty set and a serious frown. He clamped a hand over her mouth. She grabbed his wrist and tried to pull the hand away. "Shhhhh," Corso hissed. She began to struggle, digging her nails into his wrist. Corso reached for her free hand but missed. Her fingers were hooked into a claw, on their way to remove his eyes, when the shotgun roared out in the hall and the air was suddenly full of gunsmoke and debris. Her nails stopped an inch from his face. When he removed his hand, her mouth hung open.

Corso got to his knees and opened the overhead

hatch. He fought his fingers as he twisted the knob on the restraining arm, until it finally came off in his hand, allowing the hatch to flop all the way open. The shotgun roared again. Corso could hear them kicking out the remaining splinters of the door. He pointed up at the hatch.

Didn't have to tell her twice; she scrambled up and out in an instant. Corso wiggled his shoulders through the narrow opening and then used his arms to lever himself on deck. He took her by the hand. To port was the dock, to starboard, Lake Union. He pulled her toward the lake.

"Over the side," he whispered. "It's our only chance."

She nodded and put one leg over the rail.

"Stay close to me," he said.

"I can't swim," she said. Her lower lip quivered.

"I'll take care of you," he said.

They stepped off together. Her eyes were wide. Her instincts pulled her knees to her chest, as they hovered for a moment before plummeting down into the black water.

The icy water raked his skin like nails, froze the air in his lungs, and gave him an instant headache. He surfaced, shaking the water from his eyes. To his left, Rogers was making gasping sounds and thrashing the water to foam, in a frenzied attempt to stay afloat. He reached over, grabbed her wrist, and pulled her to him. Her face was white with terror. She locked her arms and legs around him in a death grip, sending them both below the surface. Corso held his breath and pried her loose, spun her in the water, and threw his arm around her chest in the classic lifeguard manner.

She came up gasping, whimpering. Her body shuddered uncontrollably as Corso began to stroke his way toward the stern. His "Shhhh" failed to stop her gasps. The effort made his legs ache. A cramp tore at his right calf.

From inside the boat, two more muffled shotgun blasts. They'd be on deck in a minute. At the stern, Corso grabbed the swim step with one hand. With the other, he spun Renee Rogers in the water. He slipped his knee between her legs and used it to keep her afloat. "Listen to me." Her lips were turning blue, but she nodded slightly. "You and I are going down under the swim step. There's room under there to breathe. Ready?"

He didn't wait for an answer, just put his arm around her waist and pulled her underwater. He managed a pair of scissor kicks before she struggled loose from his grasp and shot to the surface, banging her head on the underside of the swim step.

Corso came up facing her. The space between the underside of the swim step and the surface water was just big enough to keep their heads out of the water. Corso brought his finger to his lips. She was shaking so violently, he couldn't tell if she'd understood. Her face was the color of oatmeal. She was gasping for air.

The swim step was a lattice of teak, designed to keep water from collecting on its surface. She had her hands thrust up through a couple of the spaces, holding on for dear life. Unfortunately, anyone looking down from the stern would surely see her fingers and then they'd both be dead.

Corso pointed to her hands and shook his head. "Let go."

"No," she breathed.

Corso swam to the rear of the step, put his back against the hull, and grabbed hold of the support bracket. He gestured for her to come. She refused to move. "Theeey're gonnnnna seeee your fiiiiingers," he stuttered out. She looked up at her hands, over at Corso, and began to cry. He extended a hand. His legs were going numb from the cold. He could barely keep them moving. "Come on," he said.

She came his way hand over hand, exchanging one grip for another until she was locked against his side. "Hang on to me," he whispered. She tried to speak but couldn't get her jaw muscles to cooperate. She was shivering and clinging to him like a barnacle when he began to feel movement in the hull. They were coming toward the stern. He brought a finger to his lips, but she was too far gone to notice.

He heard the hinged section of rail swing up and the gate swing open. Ten seconds passed before the visitor stepped down onto the swim step. All Corso could see were parts of the bottoms of his shoes as he moved tentatively around the platform. Someone whispered in Spanish and the feet disappeared. Half a minute later, a slight roll of the hull told him at least one of them was on the dock.

He couldn't be sure, but above the gentle lapping of the waves and the chattering of his own teeth he thought maybe he heard the sounds of shoes on the dock.

He waited. What if it was a decoy? What if one of them was still on board? She was sobbing silently now. He held her tight and waited. Seemed like he waited for an hour. Until finally he knew that if he waited any longer, he'd die there in the water. Drown six feet from safety because his muscles wouldn't carry him the distance.

He pushed off the hull with his aching legs, propelling them out from under the step. His left arm was wrapped around Rogers. He threw his right arm up onto the wood and pressed her back against the edge. "You gotta help out here," he whispered in her ear. "We're almost there." She shivered harder but opened her eyes. "Just roll up onto the step." In slow motion, she loosened her left arm and grabbed a piece of the step. Her teeth chattered like castanets. He felt her grip loosen, lowered his body in the water, and grabbed her around the hips. "Ready? One . . . two . . . three!" He managed to force one leg and one hip up onto the surface. Then he got his shoulder under her and kept pushing until the rest of her torso and the other leg followed suit. She flopped over onto her stomach and began to vomit. Corso gathered his strength and forced a knee over the edge but couldn't muster the power to pull himself aboard. Then he felt her hands, pulling at him, and he tried again, finally flopping up next to her on his belly, breathing like a locomotive.

He lay there for a moment and then rose to his knees. He crawled to the port side of the step, hooked a frozen hand into one of the indented footholds, and pulled himself upright, where he could grab the handrails. He stood leaning against the transom. He couldn't feel his legs or his feet. And then the boat rocked . . . twice. His heart threatened to tear his chest. They must have been nearby . . . watching . . . waiting.

Rogers felt it too. She looked up, read the expression of helplessness on Corso's face, and began to sob.

They were on the stern now, just above his head. When he looked up, he was staring down the barrel of a gun. He closed his eyes and waited to die.

"Frank Corso," a voice boomed, "you're under arrest for the murders of David Rosewall and Margaret Dougherty. Anything you say can and will be used against you. You have a right to an attorney. If you cannot afford an attorney . . ."

Another voice was muttering in the background. "This is Sorenstam. Get me an Aid Car," it was saying. "Forty-seven-ninety Fairview. Send two if you've got 'em."

26

Saturday, October 21 2:04 a.m.

Wasn't till one of the uniforms came up with Rogers's wallet that Detectives First Class Troy Hamer and Roger Sorenstam begin to take what Corso was telling them seriously. They didn't give a damn about the damage to the boat. They were stuck on crimes of passion. All they knew was they had a witness to Corso's fight with the boyfriend, a nurse who said he'd objected to Corso's presence in Dougherty's room, and an LPN who saw a tall man with a black ponytail exiting the ground-floor side door of the hospital at the time of the murders. Dead to rights. Hold the sirens.

Corso sat on the couch wrapped in a wool blanket. The last of the EMTs were up front with Rogers when the uniform handed the wallet to Hamer. "She's telling the same story he is," he whispered, and shot a glance at Corso.

Hamer made a sour face. "We better get a crime-scene team down here," he said to Sorenstam.

Corso got to his feet. "I'm leaving," he said.

"We're still conducting an investigation here," Hamer snapped.

"I'm going to the hospital," Corso announced. "You need anything from me, I'll be there." He felt like the Tin Man as he shuffled across the carpet.

His exit stalled at the top of the stairs. The stairway and the hall were littered with exploded wood. Fresh splinters poked up like teeth. Corso used a foot to roll a pair of boat shoes out from under his writing table and then slipped them on.

The refuse snapped and popped beneath his feet as he made his way to his berth. His body ached as if he'd been beaten all over, and his fingers felt thick and clumsy as he struggled into a shirt and a pair of jeans.

The EMTs had immediately thrown them in the showers, Rogers up in the guest head and Corso in his own. Left them sitting under warm water until the water heater couldn't handle it anymore.

"There's nothing you can do up there," Sorenstam said.

"I'm going anyway."

"Don't be such an asshole," Hamer said. "The more I look around, the more I'm feeling like you don't want to burn any bridges here." He swept an arm around the boat. "Whoever wanted your ass, wanted it real bad." He left a little silence for Corso. "Looks to me like the kind of people who just might try, try again, if you know what I'm sayin'."

"Maybe you guys better get to protecting and serving."

"Maybe it's time you got straight with us," Sorenstam said.

"How's that?"

Hamer made an elaborate move to scratch the back of his head. "Let me see here. We got your girlfriend"—Corso opened his mouth to argue the point, but the cop waved him off—"taking her little pictures, until a pair of skels in a black Mercedes chase her down and damn near kill her. Somehow or other they find out she's still among the living and hustle their bustles down to Harborview Medical Center, where they off both her and her boyfriend and then"—he paused again—"they come down here and make a very determined effort to pop your scrawny ass."

"You want to give us a hint here?" Sorenstam asked. "Sounds like you may have rattled somebody's cage."

Corso looked from one to the other. Despite his best efforts, a sneer crept onto his lips. "You don't have shit, do you?"

"We've got you," Hamer said.

"You've been on this for four days, and you haven't got a goddamn thing." He tried to keep the disgust out of his voice. Tried to say something neutral. What came out was, "What the fuck have you been doing with your time, anyway?"

"We've been looking at you and the boyfriend," Sorenstam snapped.

Sure. That was the protocol. Eliminate those closest to the victim before widening the investigation. For the first time since he'd been given the news, he could feel the loss burning like a cold flame. Inside his head, a familiar voice said that another pair of cops was already looking into Donald Barth. Said there was no reason to put it together for these two bozos—except. And then the voice changed. Except that Dougherty was dead, and the way things were shaking out he might have inadvertently been a player. The new voice asked him what might have happened if he'd shared what he knew with the cops.

"It's got something to do with the guy they found buried in his truck," he said.

Sorenstam pulled out a notebook and a pencil.

"His name's Donald Barth." It took Corso a full five minutes to lay it out for them. "Now you know everything I do," he said as he finished. "I suggest you talk to whoever caught the truck squeal and whoever they've got looking for this Joe Ball character. Maybe one of them has come up with something useful."

Sorenstam checked his notes. "So you're saying the missing person, this Joe Ball guy, the dead guy in the truck, the assault here, and the murders at the hospital are all tied together somehow."

"That's what it looks like to me."

"Any idea about the connection?"

"None."

"So how does any of that help us?" Hamer asked.

"It doesn't," Corso said.

"Where'd he get the forty thousand?"

"No idea."

"You think any of these women was pissed off enough—"

Corso was already shaking his head. "No."

Corso stepped around the cops and pulled a black leather jacket from the closet. He stuck one arm into the coat. "Find these guys," Corso said. "Find 'em before I do."

"What you're going to do"—Hamer jabbed a finger at him—"is keep the hell out of an ongoing investigation." Corso settled the jacket on his shoulders and started toward the bow. "Do you hear me?" Hamer bellowed after him.

Hamer was angry. Corso didn't blame him. They'd wasted a lot of manpower going around in circles. Last thing they wanted was to hear from some jive-ass writer about how they'd fucked up.

The forward passage was still clogged with cops and EMTs. Corso shouldered his way to the front. Renee Rogers sat on the bed, wearing the outfit she'd come aboard in. She looked small inside the clothes, as if the outfit belonged to an older sister.

"How you feeling?" Corso asked.

She had to think it over. "Like I'll never really be warm again."

"I'm going up to the hospital."

She reached out and touched his cheek. "Oh—your friend. I'm so sorry."

Corso nodded. "You walking okay?" he asked, after a moment.

"My legs feel like rubber bands, but they work."

"Let's get out of here. They've got a forensics team on the way. The place is about to be crawling with cops."

She put her hand on his. "You saved my life."

"We got lucky," he said.

Her eyes said she didn't believe a word of it but was too tired to argue.

"I'll drop you at the hotel."

She searched his eyes. "You sure you want to go up there?"

"It'll never be real to me if I don't," he said.

She said she understood and got to her feet. "Let's go," she said.

The walk started off shaky; she nearly fell off the stairs. Leaning on each other, they got steadier as they made their way up the dock to the gate. Corso's legs would barely push him up the steep ramp. When he looked back, Renee Rogers was having the same problem. She stood at the bottom shaking her head. He took her hand and pulled her to his side. Then walked to the top and repeated the process.

They were still holding hands when the flashbulbs began to pop and the reporters stepped from behind the cars, firing questions from the darkness. They'd had word of a shooting. Could he elaborate? Was he involved? If there was a shooting, did the police have a suspect? "That's the Rogers woman," he heard somebody say. "You know, the U.S. Attorney from the Balagula case." Her name joined his in the air as they pushed their way through the crowd toward the car.

Ten yards from sanctuary, Rogers was jostled by the crowd and dropped her purse, which burst open on impact, spilling some of the contents out on the ground.

Corso straight-armed the nearest photographer, setting off a stumbling chain reaction as she bent to retrieve her bag. Flashbulbs rendered him nearly blind as he led her to the car, let her in, and threw himself into the driver's seat.

Saturday, October 21 2:40 a.m.

"I'm sorry, sir, but you can't. . . ."

Corso ducked under the yellow police tape and started down the stairs. They'd fixed the elevators so they wouldn't go to the basement and strung enough plastic police tape across the stairwells to circle the globe.

She couldn't have been more than twenty. "Please, sir," she whined at his back as he held on to the handrail and walked deliberately down the stairs. At the first landing, he looked up and saw her still standing at the top. "The police—" she began.

At the bottom, he pulled the door open, poked his head out into the hall, looked one way and then the other. In both directions, the corridor was full of people. To the left, it was mostly hospital employees, people the police would want to interview before allowing them to go home. To the right was One-oh-nine, where a pair of medical examiners, in bright yellow jackets, sipped coffee from plastic cups while they stood talking with a couple of county mounties.

His eyes stopped on a pair of metal gurneys, end to end along the wall. Resting, larvaelike, on top of each cart was a black rubber body bag, red straps around the chests and ankles. He felt like he always felt in the face of death, light and disconnected. Like he was coming unglued from the earth.

His legs ached as he started down the hall. A voice behind him called, "Hey!" He kept going. The door to One-oh-nine popped open. Rachel Taylor stepped out into the hall. As the door eased shut, Corso could hear the sound of angry voices coming from inside. She caught sight of Corso and stopped. "Oh," she said. "Miss Dougherty—"

The door opened again. Crispin, Edward J.: red-faced, disheveled, looking like he'd been rousted from his bed. Followed by what had to be a couple of cops.

He went slack-jawed at the sight of Corso coming his way.

"She's not here," he said. Corso stopped. "Your friend," Crispin tried. "She's not here anymore."

Corso's eyes moved to the body bags.

"No," Crispin said. "That's . . ." He looked to Nurse Taylor for help.

"Mrs. Guillen," Taylor said. "Ruth Guillen."

"I found her a room," Crispin blurted.

Rachel Taylor walked to Corso's side and took hold of his arm. She cast a baleful stare at Crispin. "Mr. Crispin circumvented the normal room-scheduling procedures." Another stare. "Second shift saw the room was empty and put Mrs. Guillen in it."

"She'd been in a head on-collision," Crispin added, as if her condition somehow mitigated whatever the problem was.

"Mr. Rosewall didn't know either," Taylor said. "He just walked in at the wrong time."

"I don't understand," Corso said, feeling himself beginning to sway.

"Miss Dougherty is upstairs in surgery," Rachel Taylor said.

27

Saturday, October 21 6:10 a.m.

They cut a hole in her head. "Not very big," the post-op nurse said with a smile. She held her fingers about an inch apart. "About the size of a stamp."

She busied herself changing an IV bag and straightening the covers. "Her vital signs are better this morning," she announced. "I think doctor is going to be pleased." Not *the* doctor or Dr. Something-or-other. Just *doctor*. Corso grunted.

He was holed up in a brown leatherette chair under the window, sipping lukewarm coffee through an articulated straw, trying not to wonder if things could get worse.

The door opened and another nurse marched in and dropped both morning papers in his lap. She stood with hands on half-acre hips, waiting for him to have a peek. Without looking down, Corso thanked her, folded the papers in two, and stuffed them between the cushion and the armrest. She huffed once, looked at the post-op nurse as if to say *Some people*, and left. Post-op was still chuckling when she completed her tasks and squeaked out of the room.

Corso waited a minute and then crossed to the bedside. Her rest was more troubled now. Her extremities twitched and, just after the last doctor had left, she groaned once, as if to say enough was enough, and tossed her head back and forth. He had the urge to pull the covers up over the spiraled words and images that encircled her bare arms, but she seemed so fragile, and her hold on life so tenuous, he couldn't bring himself to touch a thing.

He returned to the chair and looked down at the papers. He used two fingers to pry the top paper off and turn it face up on the seat. The *Seattle Times*. Lunar-landing-sized picture. He and Rogers, hand in hand at the top of the dock ramp, looking like they'd been rode hard and put up wet. Banner headline: EASTLAKE GUN BATTLE. He winced. Turned it over and grabbed the other paper. After the *Times*, how bad could it be?

Bad. MARINA SHOOT-OUT. The *Post Intelligencer* photographer had caught them by the car: Corso snarling at a cameraman, Renee Rogers, down on one knee, gathering her things back into her purse. You could see it plain as day, the strap and one cup of her brassiere hanging out on the asphalt. And the little wet bundle still nestled inside the bag that you knew just hadda be the panties. Warren's really gonna hate this, he thought.

Corso deposited both papers in the bathroom wastebasket and was on his way back to the chair when Detective Sorenstam poked his hat in the door and gestured for Corso to come out in the hall.

Hamer leaned against the wall, picking his teeth with a blue twist tie. Sorenstam had his notebook out. "We talked with Jonesy and his partner," he said.

"They caught the Barth squeal." Corso waited for him to get to the point. "The number crunchers read it like you do. Guy's living like a mouse for years. Sending all his cash back east so's his kid can get an education."

"Then, last year, he gets behind," Hamer offered.

"Med school's a bitch."

Hamer chewed the piece of plastic like a cigar. "He tries to borrow thirty grand from his credit union, but they turn him down. Back in Boston, the kid's trying to finagle a loan for himself."

"And then, *bingo!*" Sorenstam snapped his fingers. "All of a sudden he pays off the whole damn thing. All the way to the end of the year."

Hamer dropped the twist tie to the floor. "And while that's going on, this Barth guy is leaving the house every day, kissing the little woman good-bye and going where?" He didn't wait for a reply. " 'Cause he sure as hell wasn't going to his job at the school district. He's on leave June through September of 'ninety-nine."

"Neighbors say everything was status quo. His truck came and went as usual." Sorenstam shrugged. "Wife swears it was same-old same-old."

"So where did he go?" Corso asked.

"Someplace you could get forty grand," Hamer said.

"What about this Joe Ball guy?" Corso asked.

"Still missing," Hamer said.

"Missing Persons has a guy says your friend Miss Dougherty was the last person to see Mr. Ball before he turned up lost."

Corso held up a hand. "So let's assume our friend Mr. Ball was responsible for burying Donald Barth and his truck."

"Why would he want to do that?" Hamer asked.

"Probably because somebody paid him to."

"Okay."

"And whoever paid him is unhappy when the truck turns up."

Hamer bumped himself off the wall and wandered over. "And you're thinking your girlfriend here walked in on them expressing their displeasure."

"Could be," Corso said.

"There's a chase," Sorenstam prompted.

"She crashes."

"One of them gets out to finish the deal, but civilians show up."

"How'd they know she was still alive?" Corso asked. "How'd they know which hospital to find her in?"

"Maybe they followed the ambulance," Hamer said.

"Maybe," Corso muttered, without believing it for a minute.

"Doesn't explain their beef with you, though," Hamer said.

"Assuming they're the same people, of course," his partner added.

They stood in silence for a moment, before Corso asked, "You gonna put somebody on the door?"

Hamer looked puzzled. "What door?"

"This one."

"What for?"

"In case you haven't noticed, somebody's trying to kill her."

"She's safe up here. Nobody knows where she is," Hamer said.

"She's unlisted," Sorenstam assured him.

"*You* found her," Corso said.

"What's that supposed to mean?" Hamer demanded.

Corso leaned down and put his face in Hamer's. "You'll excuse me, won't you, if I'm not exactly dazzled by your investigative footwork?"

Hamer dropped his hands to his sides and leaned on Corso with his chest. "I was you, I'd worry about my own ass."

"You was me, you'd probably have detected something by now."

Sorenstam was using his forearms to push them apart. "Hey, now . . . hey, now . . . take it easy. We're all on the same side here." He looked from one to the other but came away empty.

"She needs protection," Corso insisted.

Hamer used his finger to pry something out from between his teeth and then spit it to the floor. "You think she needs protection, you do it," he said with a grin. "According to the papers, you seem to be on a roll when it comes to saving damsels in distress."

28

Saturday, October 21 12:09 p.m.

Joe Bocco just *happened* to be Italian. When you've got a name like that, a scar on your cheek, and you break legs for a living, a number of stereotypes come immediately to mind, not the least of which would be the assumption that, with his ancestry and occupation, he must be part of some wider, more well-known criminal conspiracy, involving others whose names likewise end in vowels.

Not so, though. Joe was an equal opportunity thug. Billed himself as private security. For the right piece of change, he'd dance the tarantella on somebody's spinal column for you or, if he was sure you were a pro, maybe even follow you through the front door of a rock house.

They'd met five years ago, when Corso had been working a story about the longshoremen's union. Lotta pension money turned out to be missing. Lotta people thought union president Tony Trujillo was responsible. Some of those same folks wanted him dead. Corso had interviewed Trujillo on a sweltering hot August day, down on Pier 18, while Joe Bocco sat in the corner wearing a turtleneck and a full-length raincoat. Never broke a sweat. Never even blinked. Two days later, a pair of cowboys tried to force Trujillo's limo off the Fourth Avenue Bridge. Bocco killed the driver and left the passenger paralyzed from the waist down. Front-page news.

Bocco checked the room, then looked over at Dougherty. "This the one from the paper?"

"Yeah."

He stroked his chin. "Which ain't the same one you was on the front page with?"

"No."

He marinated the thought for a moment and then turned his gaze back toward Meg. "So somebody tried to cap her and offed a couple of civilians instead."

Corso frowned. "Where'd you get that from? That wasn't in the papers."

"It's all over the radio."

"Shit," Corso said.

"Be better off the hitters didn't know, wouldn't it? They any kind of pros, they're gonna be pissed as hell." He pulled open the bathroom door and peered inside. "Obviously, you think they're coming back."

"Could be."

"And you want me to make sure she doesn't get any unwanted visitors."

"That's what I had in mind."

"I quoted you a rate on the phone. That gonna work for you?"

"Yeah."

"Sooner or later I gotta sleep."

"You got any brave friends?"

He shook his head. "Know a couple of fools, maybe."

"Have one of them relieve you."

"Be another seven-fifty."

"And Greenspan said there was no inflation."

Joe Bocco sneered. Did the insurance company commercial. "How can you put a price on peace of mind?" he asked.

Saturday, October 21 1:13 p.m.

Not a word in six hours. Not since this morning, when they seen the TV news about the bitch still being alive. Just sitting there on the bed, cleaning his piece over and over again, staring out the window at the water. When Ramón finally spoke, Gerardo nearly choked on his room-service burrito.

"Comes a time you gotta listen," Ramón said suddenly. "Somethin' in the world is talkin' to you, tryin' to take care of you, and all you gotta do is open up your ears and listen to what it's got to say."

"That what you been doing?" Gerardo asked around a mouthful of bun. "You been listening to the world?"

Ramón felt his anger rise. "I meant like, you know, metaphorically."

Gerardo dredged a pair of french fries in ketchup and stuffed them into his mouth. "What's that mean?" he asked. "Meta . . ."—he waved a pair of red fingers—"whatever you said. What's that mean?"

"It means I'm thinkin' we ought to maybe lay low for a while," he said, as much to himself as to Gerardo. "Maybe take a little time off." He looked at Gerardo. "You could visit your sister in Florida."

Gerardo washed the burrito down with Coke. "Kids must be getting big by now," he mused. He flicked a glance at Ramón. "You could maybe see your mom."

Ramón sighed. "We got nothing to say to each other."

"She's your mother, man."

"I'm telling you. It's not me, it's her. She don't want nothing to do with me. Got this new husband. Plays fucking golf. Don't want none of the old-time shit coming back at her. She don't talk to my sister neither."

Gerardo stopped chewing. Frowned. "We gonna tell the Russians?"

"Fuck, no. They'll cap us for sure."

Gerardo started to argue, but Ramón cut him off. "We'll get replaced just like we replaced those Colombian dudes." He held up two fingers. Two in the head. "They ain't gonna want us walkin' around. We know where the bodies are buried."

Gerardo waved the burrito around. "That's another one of those meta things, huh?"

Ramón wanted to explain that it was and it wasn't, but instead he kept things simple. "Yeah," he said.

"When we gonna go?"

"Soon as we take care of business."

Saturday, October 21 1:13 p.m.

"I told you he was in her pants," Nicholas Balagula said in Russian. It came out with a bit of reverberation because of the way the hotel's Swedish masseuse was pummeling his vertebrae as he spoke. She was a large red-faced woman with thinning blond hair and a pair of big red hands strong enough to strangle a heifer.

She grabbed a double handful of his smooth rubbery flesh and began to knead it like bread. Balagula put on his glasses and read the text beneath the picture of Renee Rogers stuffing her underwear into her purse. He looked up at Mikhail Ivanov, who was holding the paper in front of his face. "You didn't—"

Ivanov raised an eyebrow. "Of course not."

"Not the Cubans?" Balagula asked.

"I did what you told me," Ivanov said. "They followed him home to the boat and then reported in. That was it."

Balagula nodded. "When this is over," he began.

"I'll see to it personally," Ivanov said. They'd agreed. When the trial was over, they disappeared into retirement. No need for the likes of Ramón and Gerardo.

She was using the sides of her hands like cleavers, working her way up and down his spine. The thick skin of his torso vibrated from the blows.

"The timing is interesting."

"I thought so too."

"Or perhaps Mr. Corso merely has a knack for making enemies."

"I wouldn't be surprised," Ivanov said.

Balagula reached back and grabbed the woman's wrist. "Enough," he said in English. The woman stepped back, offered a curt bow, and crossed the suite to a black athletic bag she'd left on the side bar. She pulled a white hand towel from the bag and wiped her hands. "Charge to the room?" she asked.

"Please," Ivanov said, and she was out the door and gone.

Nicholas Balagula pulled the towel from his buttocks and sat up. "Some company for tonight." Ivanov looked away. "Something fresh. Something not so long on the vine this time."

"You think this is easy?" Ivanov snapped. "In a strange city?"

Nicholas Balagula shuffled across the floor. As he walked, his privates swung to and fro beneath his belly. He put a hand on Ivanov's shoulder. "Soon, Mikhail," he said, "this farce will be over, and you can run to that house of yours in France. Find yourself a cow to service you." Ivanov stepped out from under the hand. "In the meantime . . ."

"I'll do the best I can," said Ivanov.

29

Saturday, October 21 4:54 p.m.

His mother, his brothers, and his sister were inside with the relatives, huddled around casseroles and coffee, the air filled with hushed talk about moving on to a better place and how maybe it was all for the best or was part of some grand plan not apparent to humble folk such as themselves.

He stood on the dirt floor of the garage, looking up at the trunk in the rafters, half expecting some specter to appear and demand to know why he wasn't inside with his mother and what in hell he thought he was doing. He shivered.

He pushed the rusted wheelbarrow over to the center of the room, stepped up into the bucket and grabbed the trunk with both hands. Somehow, he'd always imagined the trunk to be of great weight and so was momentarily taken aback when it turned out to be a mere fraction of what he'd expected.

The metal strapping was cold to the touch as he slid the trunk into his arms and then stepped down onto the floor and started across toward the ancient GMC pickup truck backed halfway into the garage.

He wasted no time. Just set the trunk on the tailgate, hurried over to the workbench, and grabbed a claw hammer. The brass key that opened the lock was probably around somewhere, but he wasn't inclined to look.

With a single snap, the hammer pulled the hasp free of the trunk. He took a deep breath and pushed open the lid. The top layer was a shallow tray, divided into compartments. Closest, a pair of rusty dog tags and three dull brass shell casings. To the right, an American flag folded into a tight triangle. A stack of letters, written in his mother's childish hand. Got as far as Dear Wayne *before his eyes refused. Bunches of army insignia, campaign ribbons. A small porcelain figure of a smiling hula dancer with* HAWAII *painted across the base.*

He grabbed the brass rings and lifted the tray from the trunk. On top was a neatly folded dress uniform and hat. He carefully pulled the hat and uniform out and set them on the tray. Beneath the folded pants was a brown paper sack from Baxter's Market.

He peeked inside. His breath caught in his throat. A leaner, younger version of his father stared back at him. He stood knee-deep in snow, leaning on an M1 rifle, looking like he'd rather be any other damn place on earth. When he pulled the picture out, the headline hit him in the face: LOCAL POW COMES HOME TUESDAY. *His hands shook as he picked the yellowed newspaper article from the bag and carefully unfolded it. The* Buford County News, *November 10, 1954: Longtime Tiree resident Wayne D. Corso returned to his wife and family after nearly three years in a North Korean pris-*

oner-of-war camp. Captured early in the Korean conflict, Mr. Corso . . .

As he stood peering down into that broken vault, he'd felt his childish sense of certainty float off and disappear into the winter sky, until he was left with only the disquieting suspicion that, from that moment forward, the world would always be something other than what it first seemed to be, a thought that left him shivering in that dank garage, feeling more alone than he'd ever felt in his life.

And then an iron hand gripped his shoulder, and he knew it was him, come back to . . .

Corso opened his eyes. Joe Bocco stood next to his chair.

"I think she's waking up," he said.

Corso blinked twice, ran his hands over his face, and got to his feet.

Something certainly had changed. She was restless, trying to move her hands, which were secured to the metal bed rails by elastic bandages, designed to keep her from disrupting the IV tubes sprouting from her body like vines.

Corso walked to the side of the bed and put his hand on her arm. Her body jumped as if she were startled by the intrusion.

"Should I get somebody?" Bocco asked.

Corso said yes. Joe Bocco buttoned his coat and left the room at the exact moment when her eyes popped open. Her eyes squeezed down in pain when she tried to move her head and survey the room. She groaned and then tried to speak. Nothing.

Corso poured a glass of ice water from the chrome

pitcher by the bedside, stuck one of the hinged hospital straws in, and held it to her mouth. Took her lips three tries to master the sucking thing. She closed her eyes and made noises like a puppy having a bad dream as she slowly but surely emptied the glass. When her lips released the straw, he refilled the glass and repeated the process.

She was halfway through the second glass when Joe Bocco returned with a nurse. She was maybe thirty, a big woman but nicely shaped. Apple cheeks and sparkling blue eyes, hair a little too red to be real. Had a name tag with rhinestones around the edge that read TURNER. "Easy now," she said to Dougherty as she took the cup from Corso's hand. "There's no rush."

Dougherty's eyes opened and found the new voice.

"Nice to have you back," the nurse said, as she began to unwind the elastic. "You don't have to answer me; just listen," she said. "I'm going to free your hands now. I'm going to need you to keep your hands away from the top of your head."

Dougherty tried to nod and immediately regretted the action, as even a slight movement squeezed her eyes closed in pain. As the nurse made her way to the other side of the bed, Dougherty took her freed hand and rested it on her stomach. She looked over at Corso. "Hey," she croaked.

"Hey yourself," he said.

She swallowed twice and asked, "How long?"

"Since the crash?"

She blinked what Corso took to be a yes. He counted backward in his head.

"Four days," he said.

"What day?"

"It's Saturday the twenty-first."

"David?"

Corso looked over at the nurse, who gave him a somber shake of the head.

"He's been in a lot," Corso assured her, and then abruptly changed the subject. "Just blink if I'm right, okay?" *Blink*. "You walked in on something going on at Evergreen Construction." *Blink*. "A killing?" *Blink*. "You saw the killers?" *No blink*. "You didn't see the killers." *Blink*. "They chased you." *Blink*. "You crashed your car into a moving van." *Blink*. "That's all you know." *Blink*.

She looked over Corso's shoulder and noticed Joe Bocco for the first time. She frowned and mouthed the word *who*.

"His name is Joe," Corso said. "He'll be over there in the chair in case you need anything." On cue, Bocco crossed the room and settled himself into one of the chairs, facing the door.

Nurse Turner came back around the bed. "The young lady's had about all she can handle at a time like this," she said. "Why don't you come back tomorrow? She may be feeling better then." Corso started to protest, but when he looked over at Dougherty her eyes were closed and her mouth hung open in a manner she wouldn't have permitted if she had been awake.

He looked over at Joe Bocco. "You got everything you need?"

"Marvin gonna do ten to six," he said. "I'll be back after that."

Corso let the nurse lead him by the elbow toward the door. She looked back over her shoulder at Bocco. "You too. Come on."

Corso shook his elbow free. "Mr. Bocco will be staying," he said.

She wanted to argue, but something in Corso's flat gaze brought her brain around. "Oh, you mean from like before . . . downstairs."

Corso pulled open the door and followed her out into the hall.

30

Sunday, October 22 9:41 a.m.

Corso held his breath as the straps began to tighten. Somewhere beneath his feet a timber groaned and then the sound of falling water began, as the engine whined and the Travel Lift started to raise *Saltheart* from the water, pulling the big boat higher and deeper into its belly until the keel came clear of the dock and swung gently between the massive tires of the machine.

Paul's son Eric fed diesel to the engine, and the Travel Lift began to ease *Saltheart* forward, down the ramp, into the boatyard.

"You said you called Dave Williams."

Paul Hansen was third generation. His family had owned the Seaview Boatyard for over seventy years. "Yeah," Corso said, as he watched *Saltheart* roll off across the asphalt. "He said he'd start on the woodwork first thing Tuesday morning."

"So what that means is Thursday or Friday." Hansen waggled the clipboard. "You know how he is. He'll be shacked up with some Betty and I'll have to send one of the boys to roust him."

"He does good work."

"The best," Hansen agreed. "Long as you're not in a hurry."

"So how long you figure?" Corso asked.

Hansen checked his list. "Ten days minimum. You got any unauthorized through holes, maybe two weeks."

"All I'm sure of is that I've got a forward bilge pump that won't quit running, so either something clipped a waterline somewhere in the boat or I've got a bullet hole somewhere in the hull."

"Heard you had a little excitement the other night."

Across the yard, an old man with a white beard was sanding the window casings on an ancient tug, whose chipped and peeling transom announced her to be the *Cheryl Anne IV*. He was humming as he worked. Not a whole song, just some little part that he kept recycling over and over.

"Let's do the bottom the same color it is now," Corso said.

Hansen chuckled and scribbled on his clipboard. "She was due for bottom work in the spring, anyway," he said.

"Tell the crew I'm grateful for them coming down on a Sunday."

He shrugged. "Christmas is coming. They can use the extra cash."

A burst of static hit his radio. He pulled it from his back pocket, pushed it against his lips, and spoke. Another longer burst of gibberish crackled from the speaker.

"Bernie says your cab is at the gate."

"Have him let it in, will you? I've got more crap than I want to carry that far." He gestured toward the dock, where a suitcase, a garment bag, a backpack, and an Igloo cooler lay in a heap.

Hansen relayed the message and returned the radio to his pocket. "Got a number where you're staying?"

"I'll call *you*," Corso said.

Hansen permitted himself a small smile. "Can't be too careful, I guess," he mused. "Be sure you keep in touch. You know how it is. There's always something we didn't count on in the estimate."

"That's what insurance is for."

"You call them yet?"

"Said they'll have somebody out tomorrow."

"What's your deductible?"

"Fifteen hundred."

Paul Hansen snorted. "So you're out what? Maybe five percent of the tag?"

Corso shrugged. "I'd rather have the boat."

The sound of tires pulled Corso's head around. Yellow cab. He crossed to the pile on the dock, threw the backpack over one shoulder, handed the garment bag and the cooler to Paul Hansen, and grabbed the suitcase.

Satisfied that any hard work was past tense, the cabdriver got out and opened the trunk. Hanson and Corso threw his stuff inside and closed the lid. Corso sighed and gazed blankly out over the forest of grounded boats.

Paul Hansen smiled and bopped him on the arm. "You getting that hard-core boaty look, Frank."

"What look is that?" Corso asked.

Hansen inclined his head toward the old man on the *Cheryl Anne*. "You're gonna end up like Ole there. I can see it coming."

"How's that?"

"Got him a nice snug little apartment over in Fremont. His kids pay for everything, utilities and all."

"Nice kids."

"He only goes there to shower and do his laundry."

"Why's that?"

"Because he can't sleep anywhere but onboard anymore. Don't matter whether she's afloat or on the hard. Either way, it's the only place he can get a wink."

"I'll call you," Corso said, as he got into the cab. "The Marriott on Fairview," he said to the driver.

Corso kept his eyes straight ahead. Something about the sight of *Saltheart* up on jacks always bothered him. Like somehow being on land took her one step closer to joining the legion of derelict vessels who were pulled from the water for repairs and then, for one reason or another, never made it back afloat and now languish in backyards, along waterways, or in forgotten corners of boatyards, hoping for a last-minute pardon, as the brass turns green and the paint curls to the ground.

The driver bounced out into the street and turned right down Leary Way, running along the ship canal, where the last of Seattle's commercial boatyards, dry docks, and parts suppliers still held out against the yuppie condo tribe, whose insatiable appetite for waterfront has reduced what was once the very soul of the city to something like an outnumbered cavalry troop, holed up in the fort, brave and defiant but knowing it's just a matter of time before it gets dark and the Apaches come and kill them all.

An electronic beep pulled Corso's attention to his

jacket pocket. He extracted his cell phone and looked at the caller ID number. Nothing he recognized, so he figured it must be Robert Downs. "Corso," he said into the receiver.

A woman's voice. "I hope you're having a better morning than I am," Renee Rogers said. "I just got off the phone with the AG herself."

"Trading recipes?"

"Getting canned."

"Really?"

He heard her sigh. "They're never quite that direct. If you read between the lines, I'm being offered the opportunity to resign. Nice letter of recommendation and out the door."

"I take it Warren was much displeased."

"Actually—to tell you the truth—the little jerk was happy about it."

"That figures."

"Tomorrow's my last day in court. They're sending a replacement to take over on Tuesday morning."

"I'm sorry to hear it . . . assuming you are."

"Tell you the truth, Corso, I'm feeling ambivalent as hell. Part of me says, Good, let's get on with whatever comes next in life and be done with it."

"Yeah."

"And another part of me feels like I've failed at something. Like I'm being sent home in disgrace with a brand on my cheek."

"Know the feeling well," Corso said.

She sighed again. "Yeah. I'll bet you do."

After a moment of silence, she asked, "How's your friend doing?"

Corso told her. The news seemed to buoy her slightly. "Well, at least there's *some* good news," she said.

"Except she doesn't know her boyfriend's dead."

"Jesus."

Corso cleared his throat. "I didn't mean for my life to slop over on yours," he said.

"Oh, hell, Corso. I was already on the skids." He heard her laugh. "It was as much my doing as yours. I'm the one wangled the invite from you."

His first instinct was to argue about who was more to blame, but he stifled it.

"You coming to court tomorrow?" she asked.

"Wouldn't miss it for the world."

"Should get Lebow on the stand sometime tomorrow afternoon."

"I'll be there."

"See you tomorrow," she said.

"Yeah."

Corso pointed at the Fremont Bridge and the western shore of Lake Union. "Go that way," he said to the cabdriver. "Let's take a slow drive around the lake." He scooted over to the water side of the seat, rolled down the window, and stuck his nose into the salty breeze.

He closed his eyes and let the wind take him out onto the water, out past the channel buoys and then dead north, to where the tall-tale monsters lurked beneath the hull, until, suddenly, he was among the islands. In his mind's eye, he saw Dougherty leaning over the bow, directing him this way and that, as they rode the flood tide through Thatcher Pass, *Saltheart* so close to the rocks they could smell the barnacles as they eased through the crack into the nearly landlocked body of water, smooth and black as oil in the lifting morning mists. And how, just as they'd put the rocks to stern, she'd pointed to the north shore of Blakey Island, at a family of deer as they emerged onto the shore like a smudged pencil drawing.

31

Sunday, October 22 10:59 a.m.

Joe Bocco leaned back against the wall. He had his feet crossed in front of him and wore an expression of extreme boredom. Sergeant Sorenstam popped the clip from a serious-looking Glock .40-caliber and worked the slide, sending a single round down onto the floor, where he accidentally kicked it once before picking it up and dropping it into his pocket. Sergeant Hamer had a pair of black-framed half-glasses resting on the end of his nose as he read the document in his hands.

"What's this?" Corso demanded.

"National asshole week," Bocco offered.

Hamer stepped over and waved a finger under Bocco's nose. "I'm not telling you again. You watch your mouth, you hear me?"

Sorenstam pocketed the piece. "This"—he looked over at Bocco in disgust—"Mr. Bocco here says he's in your employ."

"Yeah. He is."

"In what capacity?"

"As a private security consultant."

"Doing what?"

"Doing what you guys ought to be doing. Guarding Miss Dougherty."

The cops exchanged looks. Bocco looked over at Corso, then nodded at Hamer.

"Asshole here told her about the boyfriend," he said.

Hamer started for him. Sorenstam stepped between them, using his palms to keep his partner at bay. "Take it easy, take it easy," he said.

Hamer stepped back, adjusted his coat, and shrugged. "How the hell was I supposed to know?"

"Musta been sick for the sensitivity workshop," Bocco said.

This time it was Corso who stepped between the men. "Something wrong with his carry permit?" he asked Hamer.

"I'll let you know when I'm finished with it," Hamer snapped.

Corso turned his attention now to Sorenstam. "His license in order?"

"Seems to be."

"Then what's the problem?"

"The problem," Hamer said, "is we don't like cop wannabes."

Bocco burst out laughing. "Cop? Wannabe? Are you shitting me? I'd rather be Judge Judy's toilet slave," he said.

Hamer was red-faced and pointing again. "Watch your damn mouth."

Sorenstam sighed and took his time as he pulled the clip from his pocket and thumbed the loose round in on top of the others. From his other pocket he produced the Glock. He kept the business end pointed at the floor while he inserted the clip and snapped on the safety, then turned it handle first and handed it back to Bocco.

"Try not to hurt yourself," he said.

Bocco rocked himself off the wall, slid the gun into the holster on his hip, and then stepped around Sorenstam and held out his hand.

"Whadda you want?" Hamer demanded.

"My paperwork."

"I'm gonna call it in," Hamer said.

"Let's go," Sorenstam said.

They stood for a moment like statues. Bocco with his arm extended. Hamer with the paperwork held back, out of reach.

Sorenstam started up the hall. "Let's go, Troy. He's not worth the trouble."

Hamer opened his fingers, allowing the papers to float to the floor, turned, and followed his partner up the hall.

Bocco waited until they were out of sight before retrieving his PI license and gun permit from the floor. "Is it just me," he wanted to know, "or didn't cops used to be more competent?"

"Don't get me started," Corso said.

Joe Bocco stuffed the paperwork back into his wallet. "I didn't get a chance to see how she took the news. Minute I started ragging on them, they rousted me out into the hall. That's where you came in."

"Why don't you go downstairs and get yourself a cup of coffee or something," Corso said. "I'll see how she's doing."

Corso stood in the hall for a moment, composing

himself, and then pulled open the door and stepped inside. She was up on her right side facing the wall. As he crossed the room to her bedside, a slight movement of her shoulders told him she was aware of his presence.

He stood there with his hands on the top rail. She slid deeper into the covers and sniffed up a runny nose. He waited for what seemed like an hour before she carefully rolled over onto her back and looked his way. He could see the long-ago little girl in her tear-streaked face. Lost her kitten Buster and wasn't believing a word about this kitty heaven stuff. "Sorry you found out that way," Corso said.

She started to cry. "He was so sweet to me . . ." she began, before sliding into a series of racking sobs. Something about crying women brought out the worst in Corso. He felt compelled to *do* something. To right whatever wrong had brought forth the sorrow. To turn back time, if necessary. To do whatever it took to make it stop, not so much for the sufferer as for himself, because, for reasons he'd never understood, it was the suffering of others that connected him most readily to the well of sorrow he carried around in his own heart and forced him to wonder, once again, why his own pain was so much easier to ignore than that of others.

He clamped his jaw, as if to lock the homilies in his mouth, the preacher talk of better days in better places. Of lives cut short as part of the grand plan. Of divine justice, the power of acceptance, and how time heals all wounds. Instead, he reached down and put a hand on her shoulder.

Sunday, October 22 9:00 p.m.

"I'm going back to Boston on Tuesday," Robert Downs said. "I'm not accomplishing a damn thing here." He ran his hand through his hair and looked around the hotel suite.

It had been nearly seven o'clock when, after devouring a room-service cheeseburger and downing a pair of Heinekens, Corso had finally gotten around to checking his messages: six, all from Robert Downs.

"All I'm doing here is beating myself up for not knowing my father, and I can do that from home." He pulled a handful of papers from his back pocket and dropped them on the coffee table. "My Harvard financial records," he said. "Undergrad, grad, and med school. The whole thing."

"You're getting married pretty soon, aren't you?"

"Seventeen days," Downs said.

"Probably a lot of details to be attended to back in Boston."

He blew air out through his lips. "Pamela—my fiancée—she's obsessing. She calls every fifteen minutes. It's like I'm supposed to—" He stopped himself. "Listen to me." He wandered over and sat down in the chair on Corso's right. "I want to thank you for the help," Downs said.

Corso waved him off. "I told you before, Robert. I'm pursuing my own ends here. The school district would have stonewalled me. I'd never have gotten a peek at those," Corso said, gesturing at the folded pile of papers on the table. "We're even."

"I've been reading *Backwater*," Downs said, naming Corso's first book, "and I'm amazed at the way you take these people you didn't even know and imbue them with life." He waved a hand in the air. "It's like what I've been trying to do with my father: take all this disparate information and somehow shape it into the picture of a man who makes sense to me. I just can't do it."

"It's easier when you don't know them at all," Corso said. "That way you can start from scratch without any preconceptions."

"But how can you be sure you get it right?"

"You can't. All you can do is look at what a person leaves behind. Look at his art. Look at his children. Look at the feelings he's left behind in others. Then look at the little things in his life. Ask people about how he kept his car. Find out if he returned things on time. Did he remember birthdays? Send Christmas cards? Show up at graduations? You do enough of that, and you start to get a picture of the character who does things for reasons that make sense to other people."

"That's exactly it," Downs said. "I can't, for the life of me, understand this fixation the man had on me and my education. We hardly knew each other. I hadn't seen him in nearly twenty years, and then I find out that his every waking effort went toward me, while—I mean, I've gone years at a time without even *thinking* about him."

"Reasons is where you have to be most careful," Corso said. "That's where the self-serving bullshit and the psychobabble rear their ugly heads."

"Why is that?"

"Because, first off, when you start ascribing reasons for people's behavior, you're kind of assuming *they* were aware of why they were doing whatever it was, aren't you?" Corso didn't give him a chance to answer. "And that doesn't square with my experience at all. Seems to me a great deal of human behavior is every bit as mysterious to the person doing it as it is to those watching." Corso shrugged. "Let's say we knew your father had an impoverished childhood. We knew he always wanted to get an education but had been thwarted by circumstance. The natural leap would be to assume that his desire to see you become a doctor was just him living out his own desires vicariously through you."

"I don't know anything about his childhood," Downs said sadly.

"Doesn't matter," Corso said. "Because whatever we say after the fact, even if it seems to fit, is just conjecture. All we can be sure of is that your father did the things he did because, in his mind at least, that was what worked out best for him. Somehow or other, he got more pleasure sending his money off to schools than he would have gotten spending it himself."

Downs got to his feet. Jammed his hands deep into his pockets. "That doesn't leave much room for things like altruism or heroism."

"No, it doesn't," Corso said. "Mother Teresa did what she did because that's what felt best to her. Maybe she had a longer worldview than the rest of us. Maybe compassion made her all gooey inside. All I know for sure is that there was something in it for her."

"That's pretty cynical."

"Ask war heroes and they'll all tell you the same thing. It was over and done with before they ever thought about it. They were so scared or so mad or so outraged they acted on impulse. And you know why?"

"Why?"

"Because, for them, being heroes was the line of least resistance."

"How can that be?"

"It *can* be, because something inside was telling them they wouldn't be able to live with themselves if they didn't take action."

A silence settled over the room. Corso got to his feet, walked into the kitchen, and poured himself a glass of water. It was one of those businessman's suites: living room, kitchen, and a little office area downstairs; bedroom and bathroom upstairs. Extended Stay, they called it. "What are you doing tomorrow?" Corso asked.

Downs was pacing the living room. "I've got to sign the insurance paperwork and the pension fund paperwork. Stuff like that."

"What are you doing with his stuff?"

"Mr. Pov. He's going to take care of it for me."

"He'll probably find a home for a lot of it."

"Hard to believe."

Downs stopped pacing, took a deep breath. "You'll let me know if anything develops? If you ever figure out what this is all about?"

"Hell, I ever figure this one out I'll write a book about it."

Downs walked into the kitchen and offered a hand. "Thanks," he said. The men shook hands, and then Downs turned and walked to the door. He didn't sneak a last look, just pulled open the door and left.

And it was as if the whisper of the door and the clicking of the lock were the sounds of Corso himself hissing to a halt and coming to rest. Suddenly he felt bruised and tired and old. His throat was dry and seemed to be getting sore. His eyes felt scratchy, as if they were packed with fine sand.

He sipped at his water as he wandered into the living room and sat back down on the couch. He set the water on the glass top of the coffee table and picked up the packet of financial records. He unfolded papers and used his hands to iron out the wrinkles.

Later, when he recalled the moment, he knew he'd have to spice it up a bit in the book. Add a little drama. Like how he'd studied the records for hours and was just about to give up when suddenly, in a flash of insight, it came to him. Readers didn't want to hear he'd been using the heels of his hands to straighten Robert Downs's financial records when the back page became separated from the others and he glanced down and read the last item, the list of those who had previously requested these records. Mr. Donald Barth, thirteen times. Mr. Robert Downs, four times. South Puget Sound Public Employees Credit Union, once. Fresno Guarantee Trust, once. Boston Hanover Bank, one time.

32

Monday, October 23 11:23 a.m.

Sam Rozan, chief earthquake engineer for the State of California, twirled an end of his mustache as he thought it over. "That's hard to say," he said finally. "At least thirty million dollars."

Warren Klein leaned on the witness box. "So the perpetrators of this fraud, in your opinion, profited to the sum of what you estimate to be thirty million dollars."

"At a conservative estimate," Sam Rozan said.

"Thank you, Mr. Rozan. That will be all."

The judge pointed to Bruce Elkins. "Cross."

Elkins got slowly to his feet. "Not at this time, Your Honor."

Fulton Howell was scowling now. He opened his mouth to rebuke Elkins but instead turned his attention to Klein. "Mr. Klein, am I to understand that the government's next witness will be its last?"

"Yes, Your Honor." Klein had his Boy Scout face on.

The judge shuffled though a stack of papers on the bench. Unable to find what he was looking for, he leaned over and whispered to the court clerk, who picked her way through several files before handing one to the judge.

"Mr. Elkins," the judge began. "In your pretrial brief you indicated the defense's intention to call nine witnesses. Could you please indicate to the court how long, in terms of days, you believe the defense will require to complete its case?"

"It is the defense's intention to rest, Your Honor."

"Without calling witnesses?"

"Yes, Your Honor."

He crooked a finger at both lawyers. "Approach the bench." Neither Elkins nor Klein had gotten a full step closer to the judge, when suddenly Fulton Howell bellowed, "No! Stay where you are. I want this on the record."

For the first time, Howell was visibly upset. Wagging a finger like a parent to a child, he directed his ire toward Bruce Elkins.

"Mr. Elkins, if you think for one minute that you are going to subvert the justice system by laying the grounds for an incompetent-representation defense, you've got another think coming. Do you hear me?"

"Your Honor—"

"Shut up, sir. Because, Mr. Elkins, if that is indeed your intention, I will personally take you before the ethics board and see to it that, in addition to never practicing law again, you are punished to the fullest extent possible under the law. Am I making myself clear?"

"Yes, Your Honor."

A moment passed. "Well?" the judge demanded.

"It is my considered legal opinion that it is in my client's best interest not to offer a defense."

Fulton Howell's hands were shaking. A deep, ruddy glow had consumed his throat. "Perhaps you would be so kind as to explain to the court how it is you have reached that conclusion."

"Certainly, Your Honor," Elkins said. "It's quite simple. We do not believe the state has proved its case within a reasonable doubt. We don't believe they have provided this jury with a single strand of connective tissue that attaches my client, Nicholas Balagula, to any of the sundry enterprises responsible for the tragedy at Fairmont Hospital. Not one witness. Not a single piece of paper with my client's name scribbled on it." His voice was rising now. "The state's case is nothing but inference and innuendo." He pounded the table. "I believe resting the defense best expresses our utter contempt for the pile of unsubstantiated rumors the prosecution calls a case. And I believe that tactic will best enable this jury to experience our complete faith that they can be trusted to see through the lies."

Fulton Howell was unimpressed. "That's quite a risk, Mr. Elkins."

"I have discussed the matter with my client and offered him the opportunity to obtain different counsel, should he so desire."

Howell looked over at Nicholas Balagula. "Is that so, Mr. Balagula?"

"Yes, it is."

"And you understand that Mr. Elkins is risking your life on the single throw of a dice, so to speak."

"I understand. I am innocent," he said. "I have nothing to fear."

Howell searched Balagula's face for irony, and finding none, sat back in his chair.

"I am informed by the U.S. Marshal's Service that for security reasons they will require fifteen minutes and an empty courtroom in order to safely deliver the prosecution's final witness to these proceedings." He checked his watch. "Normally, with the approach of the noon hour, we would adjourn until after lunch. However, owing to the unusually stringent security required in this case, we will adjourn for twenty minutes only." *Bang*. "Court will reconvene at eleven-fifty sharp," *Bang*. "Bailiffs, clear the courtroom."

Warren Klein was having a discussion with the court clerk. Ray Butler and Renee Rogers gathered the piles of papers and folders together in the center of the table. At the far end of the room, Balagula, Ivanov, and Elkins formed a tight muttering knot as they moved leisurely up the long aisle together behind a phalanx of bailiffs.

"Hey."

The sound pulled Corso's head around. Renee Rogers. Black leather purse slung over one shoulder, big pile of files in her arms. "You were late this morning."

"I slept in," Corso said. He'd had twelve hours of dreamless sleep. If the maid hadn't come to the door, he'd probably still be in bed.

"I slept all day Sunday," she said. "I just couldn't seem to get enough."

Corso pulled open the gate. Renee Rogers stepped through, and they started up the aisle together. "I'd offer to help with the files," Corso said, "but I'm afraid it'd look like I was carrying your books."

She laughed. "The whole world already thinks we're sleeping together. We were on CNN last night. Did you see it?"

"I don't watch much television."

"Neither do I, but Warren called and insisted I turn it on."

"Thoughtful."

"In living color. Looking like we just got out of the shower."

Corso pulled open the arched door and allowed Renee Rogers to precede him into the lobby. Two of the street doors were open. The breeze rushed in with the noise of the crowd on its back, swirling around the marble canyon like a squall.

"My mother called this morning," Rogers said. "She allowed as how you were a good-looking specimen and, according to the news, quite well off, but she wanted to know if maybe we couldn't keep it a bit lower-key. She said the postman had looked at her oddly today."

Corso laughed as they angled over toward the nearest corner. "So what do you think of the no-defense defense?" Corso asked.

Rogers shrugged. "Risky," she said. "It's going to come down to whether or not the jury believes what Victor Lebow has to say."

"Any reason they shouldn't?"

"Juries tend not to like witnesses who've been granted immunity."

"Must be what Elkins is counting on."

"He's done his homework. He's hoping he can discredit Lebow in front of the jury. If he manages that, we've got us a horse race."

"What kind of witness is Lebow?"

She waggled her free hand. "I've seen better. He didn't immediately come forward—which Elkins is going to be all over—and he's got a criminal record."

"I came upon something last night," Corso said.

"What kind of something?"

"Something that could tell us how Balagula compromised your jury."

"Really?"

"Rogers," a voice called.

Her gaze remained riveted to Corso. "You're sure?"

"Not quite."

"We've got work to do, Rogers," Warren Klein bawled. "Courtroom C. Two minutes." He wiggled a pair of fingers and then clicked off across the floor, with Ray Butler trotting along behind like a pack mule.

For a moment, Corso thought she was going to launch the files, shot-put style, at his back. Sanity prevailed, however. She hitched her purse strap higher on her shoulder, took a better purchase on her folders, and turned to Corso.

"I shall be professional to the end," she said, with exaggerated solemnity.

"To the end," Corso said.

"Or until I kill him," she said, and marched off.

Corso wandered over to the open door. For security reasons, the entire media swarm had been moved to the area adjacent to the back door of the courthouse. Bruce Elkins was outside, addressing the assembled multitude.

". . . whose entire case is about to hang on the word of a convicted felon: a man who has been convicted of federal perjury charges. A man who was granted immunity on a variety of federal charges in return for testifying against my client, and whose only function will be to obliquely connect my client to a conspiracy in which they have otherwise found it impossible to demonstrate my client's involvement."

At eleven forty-five, the courtroom doors were re-opened. When Corso strolled back inside a minute later, Elkins, Balagula, and Ivanov were already ensconced at the defense table. At the front of the room, a dozen U.S. marshals stood shoulder to shoulder, gazing impassively out at the empty seats.

A minute later, the prosecution team arrived. Renee Rogers cast a wish-us-luck gaze Corso's way as she walked by. Corso got to his feet and slipped out of his coat. By the time he folded it over the seat and sat back down, Judge Howell had resumed his place behind the bench and located the gavel. *Bang*.

33

Monday, October 23 11:53 a.m.

"Would you tell us your name, please."

"Victor Lebow."

Unlike those of the previous witnesses, Victor Lebow's physical presence did little to inspire confidence. He was a thin man in his late fifties, with greasy hair and a twitchy left eye that flickered like a candle every time Klein asked him a question. He sat in the witness box, sweating into a gray wool suit that looked like it belonged to somebody else.

Predictably, Warren Klein wasn't taking any chances. He seemed determined to take his witness from childhood up until the minute he entered into a criminal conspiracy with Nicholas Balagula. Equally predictably, Bruce Elkins objected to every word Victor Lebow uttered.

Two minutes into Lebow's testimony, however, Judge Howell lost patience with Elkins's repeated objections and threatened to have him removed from the room if he didn't sit down and keep quiet, an attitude Elkins now adopted with an air of stoic martyrdom.

"Could you please, Mr. Lebow, explain to us in what capacity you were employed on the Fairmont Hospital construction project?"

Lebow coughed into his hand. "Inspection liaison officer."

"And could you explain to the jury, Mr. Lebow, precisely what an"—Klein made quotation marks in the air with his fingers—"inspection liaison officer does?"

Lebow thought it over. "I worked in between the testing lab and the state inspectors."

"What exactly were your responsibilities, Mr. Lebow?"

"Mostly I took the concrete core samples from the job site and delivered them to the lab for testing."

"Testing for what?"

"Strength and rigidity."

"Could you tell us something about how such tests are conducted?"

Lebow crossed and uncrossed a leg. "Sure," he said. "They put them in a hydraulic press and stress them to the breaking point."

"What laboratory conducted the tests?"

"Phillips Engineering Technology of Oakland."

"How often were these tests conducted?"

"Once a week."

"So once a week you took concrete core samples from the Fairmont Hospital job site to the laboratory for testing."

"Objection, Your Honor. Asked and answered."

"Sustained."

Klein walked quickly over to the defense table, where Ray Butler handed him a piece of paper. "Mr.

Lebow, can you tell us what amount of stress the core samples were expected to endure before failing?"

"The specifications called for a minimum of fifty thousand pounds per square inch," Lebow said. He craned his neck around the courtroom as if searching for someone who might disagree. "Theoretically," he added.

Klein walked to the side of the witness box, handed the piece of paper to Victor Lebow, and looked up at the judge. "Your Honor, I have handed Mr. Lebow a copy of People's Exhibit Thirty-eight, already offered in evidence."

"So noted," the judge said.

Klein now stepped in closer to Lebow. "Can you tell me, Mr. Lebow, whether or not you recognize the document you are presently holding?"

Lebow's eye was flickering like a signal flare. "Yes, I do."

"Would you tell us what it is, please?"

Again Victor Lebow nervously checked the room. "It's the week-to-week test results of the core samples."

"Is that your signature at the bottom of each week, attesting to the validity of the results?" Lebow nodded silently. "Please answer out loud for the record, Mr. Lebow?"

"Yes," he stammered. "That's my signature."

"Your signature attests to exactly what, Mr. Lebow?"

He looked confused. "I don't understand," he said.

"Well, Mr. Lebow, as you didn't conduct the stress tests yourself"—Klein reached into the jury box and turned the page over—"you can see here that the tests themselves were attested to by several employees of Phillips Engineering. I'm assuming that those signatures attest to the testing validity, and I was asking you specifically what *your* signature attested to."

Lebow thought it over. "I guess it says that the samples I gave them for testing were the same ones I got from the inspectors on the job site."

"Were they?"

"Excuse me?"

"Were the samples you delivered to Phillips Engineering for testing the same samples you took from the job site?"

Lebow looked up at the judge, as if asking for relief. Fulton Howell glowered down at the little man like the Old Testament Jehovah. "Answer the question."

"No," Lebow said in a low voice.

Klein cupped a hand around his ear. "Could you speak up, please?"

"No," Lebow said again, angry now. "They weren't the same samples I got from the job site."

Klein took his time now, milking the moment for all it was worth, casting his eyes from the judge to the jury and finally to Bruce Elkins, as if daring him to object.

"Mr. Lebow, if the samples you delivered for testing, and whose validity you attested to with your signature, did not come from the job site, where *did* they come from?"

"They were made up special."

"So the samples you delivered to Phillips Engineering—"

Elkins was on his feet. "Your Honor!"

Judge Howell waved him back down. "Move along, Mr. Klein, once again, the question has already been asked and answered."

"Who made up the samples you took to Phillips?"

"I don't know." He threw his hands up. "I mean, I didn't see 'em get made or anything."

For the first time in days, Warren Klein frowned. "Who did *you* get them from, Mr. Lebow?"

"I got them from the on-site inspectors."

"You're referring to Joshua Harmon and Brian Swanson."

"Yeah."

Klein paced in front of the jury box. "If you don't mind my asking, Mr. Lebow, what induced you to take part in a fraud such as this?"

Victor Lebow hesitated and then looked down into his lap. "I needed the money."

"Excuse me?" Klein taunted.

"I said I needed the money," Lebow answered angrily. "I had a consulting business, went tits up. . . ." He looked up at the judge. "Sorry. I went bankrupt. I was under a lot of pressure."

"And how much were you paid to perpetrate this fraud?"

"Two thousand dollars a week."

"For how long?"

"The whole project."

"Sixty-some weeks."

"Yes."

Lebow was squirming around in the seat like he was on a griddle.

"Would you tell us please, Mr. Lebow, how it came to pass that you were drawn into this conspiracy?"

"They knew about my money problems." He looked up at the judge again, pulled at his collar, and continued. "Said I could get myself out of debt if I played along."

"Played along how?"

"You know, if I dumped the real samples and delivered the ones they made up special."

"Dumped?"

"Yeah," Lebow said. "In the bay. I've got me a little boat. For striper fishing, you know." He looked around for other anglers but found the cupboard bare.

"I'd take 'em out on Saturday mornings with me and dump 'em while I was fishing."

"Tell me, Mr. Lebow, was anyone in this courtroom today present when you were offered the two thousand dollars a week to switch samples?"

Victor Lebow pulled a pair of black-framed glasses from the inside pocket of his suit jacket. He put them on and slowly surveyed the room. Satisfied, he returned the glasses to his pocket.

"Well?" Warren Klein prodded.

Lebow looked up at the judge.

"Answer the question, Mr. Lebow."

Lebow looked around the room again. "No," he said, in a low voice.

"Excuse me?" Klein managed.

"I said no."

Nicholas Balagula never blinked. Neither did Ivanov. They sat there like they were at the movies. Bruce Elkins flicked a confused glance at his client and then tentatively began to rise.

"Perhaps you didn't understand my question, Mr. Lebow," Klein began.

"Your Honor," Elkins said.

"Yes, Mr. Elkins," the judge replied.

Elkins brought a hand to his brow, then shook his head. "Never mind, Your Honor. Please excuse the interruption," he said, as he sat back down.

Warren Klein wore his most conspiratorial smile as he wandered over to the witness box and leaned on the rail. "I think you may have misunderstood me, Mr. Lebow, so let's start from the beginning, okay?"

"Whatever you say," Lebow said.

"I asked you whether or not the parties responsible for drawing you into this conspiracy were present in this courtroom today."

"And I said *no*," Lebow said.

Before Klein could collect his wits, Fulton Howell leaned out over the bench and shook his gavel at the witness. His voice shook as he spoke. "Mr. Lebow," he began. "Unless I'm mistaken, you have signed a deposition stating that the defendant Nicholas Balagula and his associate Mr. Ivanov were present in the room when the falsification scheme was hatched. That's true, is it not, Mr. Lebow?"

Victor Lebow sat staring down into his lap.

"Mr. Lebow," the judge prompted. "I direct you to answer my question. Did you or did you not sign a deposition in which you swore that the defendant Nicholas Balagula was present at the time of the conspiracy?"

"I did, yeah," Lebow answered, without looking up.

"Are you now contradicting that sworn statement?"

"Yeah. I guess I am."

"There'll be no guessing here, Mr. Lebow. Was Mr.

Balagula or Mr. Ivanov or both present when the conspiracy was proposed?"

Lebow pulled the glasses from his pocket, put them on, and peered over at the defense table. "I never seen either of those guys before in my life," he said.

34

Monday, October 23 2:09 p.m.

The air seemed to have been sucked from the room. In disbelief, Bruce Elkins looked back over his shoulder at his client, only to find Nicholas Balagula sitting quietly in his chair, whispering to Mikhail Ivanov from behind his hand. Elkins felt cold and unable to draw breath, almost the way he'd always imagined the onset of a heart attack would feel. Then, without willing it so, he found himself on his feet.

"Call for an immediate dismissal of charges," he said.

Fulton Howell's face had already moved through the deep-red stage and was now something more akin to blue.

"Your motion is noted, Mr. Elkins. Now sit back down." He squeezed the words out from between his teeth like putty.

"Your Honor—" Klein began.

The judge waved him off. "Sit," was all he said. He leaned out over the bench again. "Would you tell this court, Mr. Lebow, why it was you saw fit to give false witness in a matter of such seriousness?"

Victor Lebow had an answer ready. "They threatened me."

"Who threatened you, Mr. Lebow?"

He pointed at the prosecution table. "Over there," he said. "Them."

"Are you referring to Mr. Klein, Mr. Butler, and Ms. Rogers?"

"Not her. The other two."

"How did they threaten you, Mr. Lebow?"

"With jail. I mean, they kept saying I was going to prison for a long time." His face was a knot. "And, you know, all the bad things that were going to happen to me in jail. How I was gonna get fucked up the ass and all. They kept telling me I was gonna be the only one who took the rap. And that the real bad guys would go free, and it was just gonna be me in the jailhouse."

"And so you decided to implicate Mr. Balagula."

Lebow shook his head. "I never heard of the guy before"—he pointed at the prosecution table—"until that Klein guy kept saying his name."

"What else did he say?"

"He said Harmon and Swanson were on the pad and that it was this Balagula guy who was paying the freight."

"And you merely took their word for the fact that Mr. Balagula was the guilty party?"

Lebow shrugged. "Tell you the truth, I didn't much care," he said. "By the time they started talking about how I could maybe not go to jail if this guy Balagula was convicted, I woulda signed just about anything."

"Your Honor," Klein protested, "we have both transcripts and tape recordings of our conversations with Mr. Lebow, and I assure you—"

Fulton Howell ignored Klein. "You are aware, Mr. Lebow, that your testimony here today forfeits any immunity agreement you may have been granted in return for your testimony against Mr. Balagula."

Lebow's lower lip was beginning to quiver. "I know."

"And that you are, in all probability, facing a sizable term in a federal prison."

"Yeah, I know."

"And with that in mind, you still insist that Mr. Balagula was not present when you entered into this conspiracy and that your original statements were false?"

"I do."

The judge sat back for a moment, taking the witness in. "Could you perhaps tell the court why it is that you have chosen to change your story at this late stage in the proceedings?"

"I hadda to do the right thing," Lebow stuttered. "If I kept on with this Balagula story, they were gonna send the wrong guy to jail and the real bums responsible for all those dead babies was going to be walking around the streets."

"So you've changed your story in the interest of justice."

"Yeah, that's it."

"Why did you wait until now?" The judge's voice was rising. "For pity sake, why did you allow the expenditure of so much time and money before you told the truth? You could have come forward months ago."

"I was scared," Lebow said. "People said they were gonna kill me. I didn't know what to do. I . . . wanted . . . to . . ." He hiccuped once and began to sob. The judge watched for a disbelieving moment, then dropped his hands to the bench with a slap and shook his head in disgust.

"I want to see Mr. Klein and Mr. Elkins in my chambers. Mr. Lebow is to be remanded to custody." He pointed at the defense table. "I want to see the transcripts of your conversations with Mr. Lebow and the recordings thereof, ASAP."

"I'll need a little time, Your Honor," Warren Klein protested.

Howell ignored him, turning his attention to Elkins instead. "I want you to consider your position as an officer of the court, Mr. Elkins, as well as the ramifications of suborning perjury."

Elkins puffed his chest. "I take exception to that remark, Your Honor."

"Exception noted. Court is adjourned until nine o'clock Wednesday morning, when I will rule on Mr. Elkins's call for a dismissal of charges."

Fulton Howell jerked a thumb back over his shoulder. "Chambers," he growled.

Klein walked over to Ray Butler. They stood together whispering before Klein disengaged and made his way to the front of the room.

* * *

Bruce Elkins lingered at the defense table. The jury could be heard rustling out the side door, and the spectators disappeared through the door at the front of the room. Elkins leaned in close and swept his eyes from Balagula to Ivanov and back. "You set this up, didn't you?"

Neither man answered.

"You arranged the whole thing," Elkins persisted.

"I think they're waiting for you," Nicholas Balagula said.

"I won't be party to it," Elkins hissed. "I will not sit idly by and allow you to subvert the criminal justice system." He pounded the desk, caught himself, and looked around. "I'll resign before I'll be part of this"—he searched for a word—"this abomination."

Balagula looked at him like he was a schoolchild. "We have been miraculously spared the wrath of an *unjust* and *spiteful* prosecution," he said, using Elkins's own words. "Just do your job, Mr. Elkins. As I keep telling you, I'm innocent, so the rest will take care of itself."

"Mr. Elkins." It was one of the bailiffs. "The judge is waiting."

Elkins reluctantly got to his feet. Balagula smiled up at him. "Have you no faith that truth and justice will prevail, Mr. Elkins?"

The lawyer was talking to himself as he made his way out of the courtroom.

* * *

Renee Rogers scratched her chair back along the floor and stood up. She stretched and then wandered over to Corso's side.

"Can you believe this?"

Corso shook his head in disgust. "It was a setup, all the way. Balagula took one look at Klein and knew all he had to do was give him a shiny new witness and Warren would be just the asshole to run with it."

"But Victor Lebow is going to prison. How in hell do you induce a guy into going to prison for you?"

"For how long?"

"Eight to fifteen."

"So he serves what?"

"Fifty months minimum."

"A million bucks."

"Huh?"

"You're broke. You're facing felony charges from the hospital disaster. You're getting death threats from the victim's families. You've just declared bankruptcy. Balagula comes to you with an offer you can't refuse. Go to the cops. Claim it was Balagula who gave you the phony core samples. Claim you were there. That you can put the smoking gun in his hand. After what happened to Harmon and Swanson, they're gonna lock you up like Fort Knox. Then, when the time comes to testify, you change your tune. Take the rap. You let the heat die down, let everybody forget about you, and walk away four years later with a million bucks. A quarter million a year. Twenty thousand a month. Tax-free."

She thought it over. "Assuming you're right, you think Elkins knew?"

"Unless he's the greatest actor I've ever seen," Corso said, "he was just as blown away as the rest of us." She nodded solemnly. Corso continued. "There'd be no reason to tell Elkins. He's too fond of appearing on talk shows to agree to suborn perjury. All Balagula had to do was put things in place, let Elkins do his job, and wait."

"I don't believe this," Rogers said. "That sonofabitch has screwed us again. He's gonna walk."

"The judge said he wanted to see the transcripts."

She laughed. "Which are going to show that Lebow is telling the truth. That's exactly how it's done. You scare the crap out of them and then offer them a way out. It's standard operating procedure."

"You never know with juries."

"No way," she scoffed. "Howell's not going to send it to any jury. He's going to come down with a directed not-guilty verdict, and Balagula's going to waltz out of here a free man."

A door opened at the top of the aisle. A green-jacketed U.S. marshal started down the aisle. As the door stood open, the noise of the media horde outside rushed into the courtroom, more of a snarl than a roar—and then, as the door snapped shut, silence again.

"Sounds like the grapevine has delivered the news," Corso said.

"Amazing how that works," she said disgustedly.

They went silent as the cop walked past them, lifted the rail, and made his way over to the nearest bailiff. They leaned together in animated conversation.

"Question," Corso said.

"What?"

"Last trial. Here in Seattle."

"Yeah?"

"You had the jury in a hotel for the duration of the trial."

"Uh-huh."

"Which hotel?"

"The Carlisle Tower."

"And you fed them three meals a day, right?"

"At least."

"Who paid the bill?"

"Initially or ultimately?"

"Both."

"Initially, it was King County, who then bled the General Accounting Office for reimbursement."

"How detailed do you figure the bill was?"

She pursed her lips. "Knowing the GAO, I'd say they probably wanted it itemized down to the last Q-Tip. Why?"

"Which department do you figure would handle that for King County?"

"I'd start with the county auditor."

The door to the judge's chambers burst open and banged against the wall. Warren Klein came storming out into the courtroom. He strode quickly across the floor, threw his coat over one arm, and grabbed his briefcase before turning his attention to Renee Rogers. Three words into his speech, and you knew two things: one, he'd rehearsed it; two, it needed more work. "If your busy social schedule will permit, Ms. Rogers, we'll be working at the hotel this afternoon. Two o'clock." Showed two fingers. "Despite your unfortunate lame-duck status, we're hoping you'll contribute some final advice about how to avoid this impending disaster you and the other incompetents have foisted upon us."

"I'll see if I can't pencil you in," she said.

They stood for a moment, their gazes locked, before Warren Klein barged through the gate and up the aisle. "Professional to the end," Corso whispered.

Halfway between the bench and the defense table, Ray Butler stood with his cell phone pressed to the side of his head. Occasionally his lips moved, but mostly he listened.

The movement of his hand caught Renee Rogers's attention. He was pointing at the phone and rolling his eyes. He began to move her way, talking now. "Yes . . . yes, I understand. I'll see to it. . . . Yes." He rested one cheek on the table and listened for a full minute before heaving a sigh and pocketing the phone. His expression made it clear he hadn't been chortling with his wife about the new house.

He looked up at Renee Rogers. "You want to guess?" he asked.

"We'll be having breakfast with the AG tomorrow morning."

"She's coming here?"

"As we speak."

Her lips were nearly invisible. "She's going to make sure the shit rolls downhill."

"We're gonna need wheelbarrows," Butler said.

"Dump trucks," she amended.

35

Monday, October 23 4:21 p.m.

"Try the county auditor," she suggested.

"Already been there," Corso said. "And the accounting office. And county records." Before she could respond, he said, "And I have been assured that hard copies of the material I'm looking for are to be found somewhere in your files."

Wearily, she checked the clock. "It's closing time. You come back tomorrow and maybe we can—"

"I really need it tonight," he interrupted. He gave her his best smile.

The woman shrugged. "Then you're out of luck, buddy," she said. "If Marcy were here, it might be a different story."

"Marcy?"

"On vacation with her sister. Maui. Two weeks." She checked the clock again. "I'm from accounts payable. I'm just holding down the fort until she gets back."

Corso waited. The woman leaned over the counter and, in a stage whisper, said, "Not to speak ill of the suntanned, but King County better hope she comes home in one piece."

"Why's that?"

"Because otherwise she might take her filing system to the grave with her, in which case nobody is ever going to find anything in here again."

She turned her back on Corso and began to straighten up. Pushing things around on the desk, sliding the chair in. When she walked to the long line of gray file cabinets and began to push the lock buttons, Corso piped up. "I've got an idea," he said.

She stopped and looked dubiously over in his direction. "Such as?"

"Such as, the bill I'm looking for went out sometime in the last half of last year. Can you find the paperwork from that time frame?"

"Yeah, " she said. "But she doesn't file the material by date or category. Or by any other method I've ever heard of." She waved a disgusted hand. "We'd literally have to start at the front and work our way back to find what you're looking for."

"Maybe not," Corso said.

She raised an eyebrow and went back to pushing buttons.

"Which one has the accounts payable for the last half of last year?"

She stopped and walked eight feet down the row of identical cabinets. She patted the next-to-last one. "Someplace in here."

"Open it up," Corso suggested.

This time, she gave him the other eyebrow.

"Please," he said.

With a sigh, she thumbed open the latch and jerked the drawer out.

"Just open the drawers in that cabinet and pull out whatever appears to be the biggest file. If that's not the one I'm looking for, I'll go away and leave you alone."

"The biggest?"

"Thickest. The one with the most pages."

She looked at Corso and then the clock. She bent at the waist and pulled open the bottom drawer. Then the next and the next and finally the top one again. She slid the top two closed and reached into the third drawer down. "No contest," she announced. "This one's way bigger than anything else in there."

She used her foot to close the remaining drawers as she perused the file. "Hmmmm," she said. She looked Corso over again.

"What is it?" Corso asked.

"Jury expenses."

"That's the one."

She hefted the file in her hand. "Biggest one I've ever seen."

"Could you make me a copy?"

"You're kidding, right?"

"Do I look like a guy who's kidding?" he asked.

Corso pointed to the sign on the wall. COPIES, $1.00 PER PAGE.

"I hear it's gone up to two bucks a page," he said.

"Three," she deadpanned.

"Damn Republicans."

Monday, October 23 7:45 p.m.

Forced onto a jury, torn from their friends and families, sequestered in a downtown hotel for months, the jurors tended to take it out on the menu. Surf and turf. The thirty-six-ounce porterhouse. Don't forget the cheese sauce for the asparagus. Once the revenge factor burned off, most seemed to settle into a routine. Some ended up eating hardly anything at all. By the time it was over, juror number 3 was living on cereal and dry toast. Juror number 5, on the other hand, never met a cheesecake he didn't like. Corso figured he'd either spent his out-of-court hours on a treadmill or he'd gained fifty pounds.

That's how they had them listed: Jurors 1 through 12 and then 13A and 14A, alternates. The expenses incurred by each were itemized on separate documents. He'd started at juror number 1 and was working his way toward the back. He'd been at it for nearly two hours, and was only halfway through, when the waitress came out from behind the counter again with the coffeepot. Without looking up, Corso said, "No, thanks."

"We close at eight," she said.

"Okay," he said, without looking up.

"Maybe a little earlier so's I can make the ten bus."

Corso began to laugh. "No shit," he said.

"Hey, now, mister—" she began.

He pointed to the page with his finger. "Big as life." He turned the page and then the next. "Every night. Same damn thing."

"You okay?" she asked.

He looked up and smiled. "Depends on who you ask," he said. He sorted through the pile of pages and selected half a dozen, which he folded into fourths and stuck in his inside jacket pocket. He threw a twenty on the table and slid out of the booth.

"You got anything smaller?" she asked.

Corso threw his arm around her. She drew the steaming pot back as if to defend herself. Corso kissed her on the cheek. "Tell you what. You throw away the rest of those papers for me and keep the change. How's that?"

"Works for me," she said, without hesitation.

Corso patted her shoulder once and headed for the door.

The sky was black on black. A flash of lightning skittered above Elliott Bay. A cold winter rain angled in from the south. Corso cursed silently, wishing he hadn't left the Subaru up at the hospital this morning before court. Especially since Dougherty had never stirred, and he'd been forced to spend an hour and a half talking with Joe Bocco's leg-breaker buddy, Marvin, whose entire stock of misinformation seemed to be garnered from ESPN.

Corso turned his collar up and began to lope uphill. Despite the effort, he couldn't keep from smiling. Wait until he told Dougherty. Give her something else to think about, other than David.

By the time he reached Ninth Avenue he was beginning to pant, so he slowed to a walk. Rain or no rain, he didn't want to be winded when he told her the story. Ahead in the distance, Harborview Hospital peeked out from a curtain of rain, its edges wavering and uncertain against the sky. He stopped under the canvas awning of a print shop and shook the rain from his clothes and hair.

Standing there, brushing at himself, facing away from the street, with the rain snapping and popping against the awning, Corso never heard it coming. He was still muttering to himself, practicing his delivery to Dougherty, when the steel wire slipped around his neck and dragged him to his knees.

His first instinct was to get his fingers between the wire and his neck. He clawed at his throat until the warm wetness whispered it was too late. His head felt as if it might burst. He tried to throw himself onto his back, but his assailant could not be moved. His eyes burned, his vision was beginning to blur. The next-to-last thing he saw was another set of legs in front of him on the sidewalk. And then the shoe starting at his face. He jerked his head to the left and, in that instant before the shoe connected, he saw the black Mercedes sitting at the curb with the doors open.

36

Monday, October 23 7:51 p.m.

As the four men slipped the ropes through their gloved hands, lowering the casket into the frozen earth, the birds went silent, the sky went white. . . .

Suddenly Corso was awake, his ears pricking at the sound of the voices.

"We'll put him where we put that Ball motherfucker. He like goin' down there so bad, we let his ass stay there till kingdom come."

Another voice, farther away. "He come around yet?"

"Startin' to."

"We want him awake. I don't want to be carrying that shit."

"We gonna do that again? Make 'im carry his own weight?"

"You want to do it?"

Close voice chuckled. "You know what I been thinkin', man?"

"What's that?"

"I been thinkin' this whole fuckin' mess started with

that asshole in the truck that we was supposed to pop but what was dead when we got there."

"Yeah."

"And how that was like a hit we got paid for but didn't do."

"You got a point here?"

"And now we end up doin' a hit we *ain't* gettin' paid for. All kinda evens out in the end. It's like one of those 'meta' things of yours."

Corso was wedged along the floor in the backseat of a moving car. His hands were tied behind his back. A foot suddenly pressed hard against his neck, driving his face down into the rubber floor mat. "You stay real still, hombre," a voice said. "We just about there."

Seemed like an hour, but it couldn't have been more than three minutes until the car began to slow, and then it turned and they weren't on paved road anymore. He could hear the whisk of grass and brush on the undercarriage as the car eased along.

"We'll put him down with the other one," the voice from the front seat said.

The car glided smoothly over a series of bumps and then swung in a slow circle and eased to a stop. The shoe on the back of his neck was replaced by the feel of cold metal. "Easy now," the voice behind him whispered. Above the sound of rain beating on the car, he heard the click of the door and the shift of weight as the driver got out and opened the rear door. "Ready?" the driver asked.

The guy in the backseat grabbed Corso by the belt. Another pair of hands gripped his shoulders, and in a single heave he was dragged from the car. He landed on his chest in the wet grass. He heard a pair of doors close. "Look," he heard Backseat say. "Fuckhead's feet are starting to float. We need to add some more weight."

"Better put two on nosy man here," Front Seat said.

And then they had him by the elbows and were jerking him to his feet.

"Gotta get up and walk now, nosy man. Not like we gonna carry your ass or nothin'."

When they began pulling on his arms, Corso realized he couldn't feel his hands. His knees nearly buckled from his own weight. He staggered slightly, regained his balance, looked around. Two of them: one nearly as tall as he was, long black hair worn in a ponytail. The other was a troll, a short dark specimen with a pockmarked face and one ear noticeably higher than the other.

"Get movin'," the troll said. "That way, down the end."

Corso looked around. Something was familiar, but he couldn't quite fathom what it was. "We figure you like it here so much," Ponytail said, "we'll let you stay."

And then Corso saw the bright light reflected in the water on his left. He looked to the south and saw the marsh and, beyond, the Briarwood Garden Apartments. They were parked on the levee that defined the northern extreme of the Black River marsh. Beneath the low sky, the water was stippled by the falling rain, its wavering surface broken here and there by grassy hillocks and broken-tooth stumps protruding above the surface. Along the edges, reeds and clumps of bulrushes waved in the wind like signal flags.

The only light came from the Speedy Auto Parts sign up the road. As he followed the reflection back across the marsh, he saw a pair of feet sticking up from the water. The shoelaces had burst, the bloated ankles were three times their normal size, pumped floating full by the expanding gases of death, forcing the feet up and out of the water as if the owner had dived into the muck and stuck.

They'd driven as far as they could. Three concrete pylons blocked the grassed-over road that ran along the top of the levee. Ponytail walked around and stood directly in front of Corso. In his right hand he carried a silver automatic with a gray silencer screwed onto the front. "Open your mouth," he said. When Corso failed to comply, he dug the barrel hard into Corso's solar plexus. Corso grunted and leaned forward. Next thing he knew his mouth was filled with metal and the pressure of the suppressor clicked on his teeth, forcing him up straight. "You just stand real still, nosy man," Ponytail said, pushing Corso's head back as his partner began to untie Corso's hands.

The steady rain beat down onto his face, wetting his cheeks, forcing his eyelids to flutter from the aerial assault. With the final strand removed, his arms flapped around to his sides. His wrists burned, and he could feel the cold blood struggling to move in his fingers. Slowly, the silencer slid from his mouth.

Ponytail motioned with the automatic. "That way," he said.

Corso hesitated, only to be propelled forward by a blow to the kidneys.

"Move your ass," the troll growled.

Corso rubbed at his wrists as he lurched forward; his hands were beginning to tingle as he stepped between the pylons into knee-deep grass.

Ahead in the darkness, the road was blocked by a pile of rubble. The troll passed by on Corso's left, hurrying up to the pile. He pointed at a spot about halfway up the pile. "This one," he said. "This one first."

As Corso approached, he could see that what had appeared to be a pile of light-colored rock was, in reality, a pile of broken concrete. Somebody's driveway, jackhammered to pieces, loaded into a truck, and surreptitiously dumped along the top of the levee. "Here," the troll said again.

The shards varied between six and eight inches in thickness, smooth on the top, wavy and rough with aggregate on the bottom. The troll slapped the pile with his hand.

"Come on, asshole. Hurry up."

The chunk of concrete was shaped like a triangle. Three feet in length. Nearly that long at the base, tapering to a point at the apex. "Let's go," Ponytail said, prodding Corso forward with the silenced automatic.

Corso bent his knees, got his left forearm beneath the jagged piece of stone, and straightened his legs. Must have weighed a hundred and fifty pounds. Corso lurched under the weight, adjusted his grip for balance, and turned back the way they'd come.

Ponytail held his gun by his side as he backed up, beckoning Corso forward with his free hand. "Come on," he said.

Corso moved carefully. His head roared and throbbed from the strain. Mindful of his footing, he shuffled along beneath the burden, until he was parallel with the submerged body, where Ponytail held up his hand.

"Dump it over the side," he said.

Corso staggered to the edge of the levee. The marsh was six feet below. It wasn't until he noticed the wavering, stippled surface of the black water that Corso remembered it was raining. He bent at the waist and let the chunk of concrete fall from his arms. It thumped onto the steep slope, rolled end over end, and stuck, point down, in the shallows.

"Go get it," the troll said.

Corso did as he was told, sliding down the muddy bank into the cold ankle-deep water. Unable to get under the piece, he was forced to lift it with his arms. He staggered and went to one knee, then righted himself and straightened up.

The troll was in the water with him now. Water up to Corso's shin was over the troll's knees. He waved Corso toward the half-submerged corpse, a dozen feet from shore. "Put it over the legs," he ordered. "Right behind the knees."

By the time Corso was in place, the frigid marsh water covered his knees. Three feet beneath the surface, the remains of Joe Ball lay festering and bloated, his torso held beneath the shimmering surface by another piece of concrete.

For some odd reason, Corso was overcome with the urge to be gentle. As if to spare the dead further indignity, he carefully placed the stone across the backs of the knees and let it go. When he straightened up, the protruding feet were gone. In another month, the gases would dissipate and the weight would push the corpse into the bottom of the marsh, where the body would begin to come apart. Small pieces of flesh would float to the surface, where, one by one, they'd be discovered by the birds and eaten, until finally nothing remained of Joe Ball save metal and bone.

"Let's go," the troll said.

Corso had to pull his feet from the gurgling muck one at a time as he labored back to the levee. His throat was constricted, but his mind was racing, trying to find a way out. Stifling an overpowering urge to run, he clawed his way back to the top of the levee and got to his feet. He knew he wouldn't get thirty feet before they shot him down and dragged him back to join Joe Ball, facedown in the muck.

"Let's go. Do it again," the troll said.

Corso steadied himself and retraced his footsteps back to the pile of broken concrete. They walked on either side of him, out of each other's line of fire, guns at the ready. The second chunk of concrete was nearly square and harder to carry. Corso had to keep adjusting his grip as he shuffled along the berm and finally let it fall from his arms and roll, end over end, down into the water.

"One more," Ponytail said.

Corso was beginning to shake. From fear, from the cold rain— he couldn't tell. Music was playing in his head now, voices and organs, getting louder and louder, something he'd never heard before. As if, all his life, he'd carried the sound track of his death inside himself, waiting, all this time, for the credits to roll and the end to be at hand. His legs wobbled as he started back. The troll prodded him in the side with his gun. "You get this one, nosy man," he leered. "You make us carry it, I'm gonna put a couple in your balls. Let you lay around a bit before I cap you."

He moved forward as if he were sleepwalking. The

music was blaring now. Morose and multivoiced, it filled his ears. "This one." Ponytail pointed to a jagged piece of concrete slightly smaller than the others. As Corso grabbed it and began to lift, the side of the pile collapsed, sending a dozen pieces of concrete bouncing down into the grass at the troll's feet. "Goddammit," the little man screamed, rubbing at his ankle with his free hand. He growled and grabbed the offending piece of stone from the grass and hurled it out into the marsh, where it landed with a splash. "Son of a—"

He didn't get all the words out before a movement in the marsh jerked his eyes from Corso. The snap of six-foot wings cut the air as a great blue heron took flight. Corso shifted his burden, getting his hand and elbow beneath it, and then, with every bit of strength left in his body, shot-putted the concrete at the troll.

It landed on his ankles. The troll howled like an animal and fell over onto his back, screaming at the sky. He had one foot jerked free when Corso landed on him, driving the breath from the small body. Corso had both hands on the gun when the flat report of Ponytail's silenced automatic split the air. Corso saw the back of his left hand explode in a mist of blood and bone but hung on with his right, allowing his momentum to pull the gun from the little man's grasp, as he slid down the side of the levee on his stomach. He fought for traction with his knees and then brought the gun to bear. He felt the tug of a bullet at the collar of his coat, before he heard the sound of the gun.

Ponytail had covered half the ground when Corso squeezed off his first round. It took Ponytail high in the right shoulder, spinning him nearly around in a circle, sending his gun off into space. He fell to one knee, then quickly jumped up, looking desperately around his feet for his weapon.

Corso crawled to the top of the bank. "Don't" was all he said.

Ponytail clutched his damaged shoulder and stood still. A scraping sound pulled Corso's vision toward the pile. The troll had extricated his other foot and was now kneeling in the grass. "Over here," Corso said, but the little man merely curled his lips and spat down onto the ground. Corso pointed the gun in his direction and let fly. The slug hit a chunk of concrete about two feet from the side of his head, sending a geyser of stone and dust into the air. The troll ducked behind his hands.

"Over here," Corso said again. This time the little man struggled to his feet and hobbled across the levee to his partner's side.

"Keys are in the car," Ponytail said.

Corso started for the car.

"You better drive far away," said the troll. " 'Cause this ain't over, motherfucker." He jabbed a finger at Corso. "We gonna find you. Maybe not today. Maybe not tomorrow. But you can make the rent on it."

"Find that fat cunt in the hospital too," said Ponytail with a smile. "Take care of her big ass, once and for all."

And then his lips moved again, but Corso couldn't hear the words because the music was deafening now, rolling out of every pore of his body. As he raised the gun, the music reached a crescendo and stayed there, pounding in his head like hell's hammers.

From a distance of eight feet, Corso shot the troll between eyes. The man's face was a mask of astonishment as he sank to his knees and then fell backward onto the ground, twitching.

Ponytail's mouth was agape as he knelt by his partner's side. "Gerardo," he said quietly, shaking the little man's shoulder as if to rouse him from sleep. "Oh, Gerardo!" The muscles along his jaw moved like knotted rope, but by the time he turned his fury toward Corso it was too late. The silencer was no more than a foot from his temple when Corso pulled the trigger, sending the man's brains spewing out over his partner's body. He toppled onto his back and lay motionless. A small trickle of blood ran from the corner of his mouth. And suddenly the night was silent.

Corso stood for a moment, breathing deeply and listening to the hiss of the rain. Only then did the burning red pain in his left hand float to the level of consciousness. Clutching the hand to his chest and moaning, Corso walked over to the men. He stood there rocking on unsteady legs for a moment, and then he pointed the gun and again shot each man in the head. Then again and again, until nothing was happening because the gun was empty.

He dropped to one knee. Set the gun in the grass and used his good hand to pat each man down. Extracted a wallet from each man's pocket and used his foot to roll one and then the other down the levee, into the water. He then retrieved the gun and, with all his might, heaved the automatic out into the marsh, before he started stumbling toward the car.

37

Monday, October 23 9:09 p.m.

The desk clerk didn't like what he saw, not a bit. Guy standing there with one hand jammed in his coat pocket, like he had a gun or something, looking like he'd spent the last week holed up under a bridge. As the man approached the registration desk, the clerk's index finger hovered over the button marked SECURITY. He pushed it.

"Robert Downs, please," the guy croaked.

Wasn't till he got close that the clerk noticed he was leaving wet tracks on the carpet. That he wasn't wearing socks. That his pants were soaked from the knees down and that, despite having his coat buttoned all the way up, his throat appeared to be circled by an angry purple welt. He fingered the button again. Twice.

"Room number?" the clerk said.

"I don't know the room number," the guy said in his rough voice.

"I can't connect you, sir, unless you know the room number."

"You call him," the guy rasped. "Tell him Frank

Corso is downstairs and needs to have a word with him."

Over the guy's left shoulder, a pair of hotel security guards emerged from the luggage room. The desk clerk breathed a sigh of relief as they advanced toward the desk.

The guy picked up something in his eyes and looked back over his shoulder. The movement brought a grunt from somewhere deep inside. "Please," the guy said. "I know I look like hell. Just call Mr. Downs for me."

The clerk held up a hand. Security stopped about six feet away. He dialed the phone and waited for a moment. "Mr. Downs," he said. "This is Dennis at the desk. Yes, sir. Sorry to bother you, sir, but there's a gentleman down here in the lobby asking for you." He listened and then looked up at Corso.

"Frank Corso," the guy said.

"Frank Corso," the clerk repeated. He pressed the phone tighter to his ear.

"Ah, yes. . . . Mr. Downs, I was wondering if instead of sending the gentleman up—I was wondering if it might be possible for you to come down to the lobby instead." He nodded. "Yes, sir. Thank you, sir." He hung up. "Mr. Downs will be down in a moment."

It was more like five minutes before Robert Downs appeared, wearing a black turtleneck over a pair of rumpled gray slacks. His hair was tousled and his face puffy. He crossed the lobby to Corso's side. "I was—I have an early . . ." He stammered as he took Corso in. He stepped in closer and studied Corso's throat. "What—?" he began.

Corso touched him on the shoulder and pulled him closer. "We need to go upstairs," he whispered.

Robert Downs hesitated for a moment and then nodded his head. He took Corso by the elbow and, under the baleful gaze of the security guards, led him back across the lobby to the elevator, where they waited no more than thirty seconds before a muted *ding* announced the arrival of the car. Downs put his arm around Corso's waist and drew him into the elevator.

They didn't speak on the ride up to the third floor or on the walk down the long hall. Corso leaned against the wall as Downs took three tries at swiping his card before he got the door open. He stepped to one side and ushered Corso into the room. Downs gestured toward the desk. "Sit down," he said. Corso shook his head and walked slowly into the bathroom. Downs followed. Corso's face twisted into a knot as he slowly, incrementally, pulled his left hand from his coat pocket and set it gently in the sink.

The black sock covering his hand was completely soaked with blood. He'd used the other sock for his right hand as he drove the Mercedes, so as not to leave fingerprints.

"Jesus," Downs muttered, his hands beginning to peel the sock from Corso's hand. The sink's drain was closed. Blood was beginning to collect. Corso groaned as Downs lifted his hand and inched off the last of the sock. "Steady now," Downs said, as he turned on the water and then tested it with his finger.

Satisfied, he gently moved Corso's palm beneath the warm trickle. Again Corso groaned. Downs scowled as he turned the hand over and washed off the back.

"This is a—" he began. "You've been shot."

"Nice to see a Harvard education paying dividends," Corso said through gritted teeth.

Despite himself, Downs managed a weak smile.

"Fix it," Corso said.

"We've got to get you to a hospital," Downs declared.

Corso shook his head. "I can't go to a hospital. They'll report it as a gunshot wound. You're going to have to fix it for me."

"The hand is a maze of nerves," Downs said. "There's no way I can possibly—" He looked around. "In a setting like this—"

Corso got nose to nose with him. "You're going to have to do the best you can."

"Your hand will never function properly again."

"That's a chance I'll have to take."

Downs broke the stare-down, stepped out into the hall, and ran a hand through his hair. "Did this . . . is this about my father's death?"

"Yes," Corso said.

"Do you know who—"

"I've got an idea," Corso said.

Downs thought it over for a moment. Corso imagined him weighing his obligations against his medical license. Then, without a word, he took Corso's hand again and ran it beneath the warm stream of water until it was free of blood, took a washcloth, doubled it over the exit wound in the palm, and then did the same for the back.

"Stay still," he said to Corso. "This is going to hurt for a minute." He took a hand towel and twirled it into a tightrope, then slipped the middle beneath Corso's hand. "Hang on," he whispered, as he tied the towel around the hand as tightly as he was able. Corso's vision went white for a moment. When his knees buckled, he braced himself against the sink.

Downs put an arm around Corso's waist and led him over to the small sofa by the window. "Take off your coat," he said, and helped Corso remove the jacket. He gently pushed Corso's head back and inspected the oozing line of purple flesh encircling his neck. "Nasty," he muttered to himself.

Corso didn't seem to hear.

"Is there an all-night drugstore in the city?"

"Bartell's on Broadway," Corso croaked.

"How do I get there?"

Corso gave him directions. "I'll be back," Downs said.

Corso waited until he was sure Robert Downs was gone and then retrieved his jacket from the floor. He put the two wallets on the bed and went through them. Pair of Florida driver's licenses: Gerardo Limón and Ramón Javier. Cubans, Corso guessed: Limón with a Miami address, Javier from Boca Raton. He dropped the licenses onto the couch and sat for a moment with his head thrown back, trying to muster his strength.

He felt nauseated and unsteady on his feet as he made his way to the closet and pulled open the door. On the shelf above the ironing board, he found what he was looking for, the extra pillow. He carried it back to the couch, where, using his good hand and his feet, he managed to remove the cover.

He rested again and then fished the keys to the Mercedes from his pants pocket and dropped them into the pillowcase, followed by the wallets and the licenses. He crossed to the desk, hefted a large glass ashtray, and returned to the couch, where he added the prize to the pile in the sack.

He tied a knot in the pillowcase and carried it over

to the curtain covering the west wall. He found the cord and pulled until the sliding glass door was exposed. It was one of those fake balconies; little more than a railing to keep guests from falling into Puget Sound. As he leaned against the wall, gathering himself, he remembered the famous picture of the Beatles, fishing out of a window in this very hotel, back in the sixties. During the last remodel, they'd added the faux balconies and banned angling.

When his stomach settled down, he popped the lock and slid the door open. He could hear the lap of waves under the hotel and the shrill cries of gulls. His nostrils caught the smells of creosote and salt water. His mouth hung open as he leaned against the rail, twirled the bundle in the air, and let fly. The pillowcase hit the water, floated for a moment, and then quickly disappeared beneath the waves.

The strain sent his senses ajar again. He reeled across the room and threw himself on the couch. Next thing he knew, he was dreaming of flying. Just holding his arms out and being borne above the branches by a spring wind. Of soaring and gamboling in the sky, beneath a bright yellow sun.

When he opened his eyes again, Robert Downs was kneeling by his side, opening a blue-and-white box of gauze. "You passed out," Downs said.

"Yeah," was all Corso could manage.

"Probably for the best. It let me stitch you up without you twitching on me."

Corso looked down at his hand. The jagged hole in

his palm had been drawn together by half a dozen black stitches. Same thing on the back.

"In about a week, take a pair of nail scissors to the knots and then pull out all the pieces," Downs said. He looked into Corso's eyes, trying to get a read on him. "Okay?" he said.

"Yeah."

Downs took Corso's hand in his and began to wrap it with gauze. By the time the gauze ran out, the hand looked like that of a boxer, ready for the ring. Downs secured the end with a piece of tape and looked up at Corso.

"I'm going to call the airlines and change my flight," he said.

Corso swallowed several times. "Go back to Boston," he said finally.

"There must be something I can do. . . ."

Corso reached out and grabbed the young man by the shoulder, squeezing hard.

"Go home. Go back to your girlfriend. Get married. There's nothing you can do here except get in the way."

"Are you—?"

"I'm sure."

Robert Downs searched Corso's face and then reached into the white plastic bag that lay on the floor by his side. He pulled out a plastic prescription bottle and placed it on the table next to Corso; then he got to his feet and walked into the bathroom.

Corso heard the water running. In a minute Downs reappeared, carrying a glass of water, which he set down next to the prescription. "You take two of these, three times a day," he said, shaking a trio of orange capsules out into his palm. "For infection. Make sure you take them until they're gone."

The plastic pills stuck in Corso's mouth like stones; it took the whole glass of water to wash them down. Corso lifted his bandaged hand toward his throat, winced, and returned it to his lap.

"I cleaned the throat laceration," Downs said. "There might be a little permanent scarring, I can't tell. It'll be all right, but there's nothing I can do about the short-term cosmetics."

Corso whispered his thanks and got to his feet, at which moment he realized he wasn't wearing trousers. He looked around the room and found them hanging over the heater, crossed the room gingerly, making no sudden moves. Took him about twice as long as usual to get his pants on, and he probably would never have gotten the belt hitched if Downs hadn't taken pity on him and lent a hand. Corso sat on the edge of the bed. "Could you spare a pair of socks?" he said.

Downs furrowed his brow and said, "Sure." After maybe thirty seconds of messing with his suitcase, he came up with a rolled pair of athletic socks. "Clean," he announced, pulling the socks apart and dropping them in Corso's lap.

The socks were easier than the pants, his shoes easier still. Corso looked down over the front of himself. The once forest-green polo shirt was streaked with blood and littered with bits of wood and straw. Corso eased it over his head and dropped it on the floor. He smirked at Robert Downs. "Sooner or later, it was bound to happen," he said.

Downs looked confused. "What's that, Mr. Corso?"

"Somebody was gonna want the shirt off your back."

The younger man looked down at himself. "You mean this?" He fingered the turtleneck. "My shirt?"

"The very same," Corso said.

"It's not clean. I've worn it a couple of—"

"Doesn't matter."

Downs shrugged and pulled the shirt over his head. He started to hand it to Corso, changed his mind, and took it back. Pulling the sleeves right side out, he rolled the neck down and put it over Corso's head. Getting his left hand the length of the sleeve left Corso panting. The sleeves were a couple of inches short, but otherwise the shirt fit fine.

Robert Downs adjusted the turtleneck and then stepped back to admire his handiwork. "For a guy who's been shot and strangled in the same night, you don't look half bad," he announced.

"I'll take that as a compliment," Corso said.

Downs helped Corso into his jacket, then went around brushing and picking the coat free of debris. "You're going home, right?"

"I'd hate to have to lie to my doctor," Corso said, patting himself down. He found his other sock in the outside pocket and dropped it to the floor on top of his shirt. In one inside pocket, he found the pages from Accounts Payable, soaked nearly through, but readable. From the other inside pocket he pulled his phone. He wiped the damp plastic on the side of the coat and pushed the power button with his thumb. It worked. He started to switch hands, thought better of it, and set the phone on the bed before he dialed.

"Send a cab to the Edgewater Hotel," he said. He turned to Robert Downs. "Thanks for taking care of me."

Downs shrugged. "Makes us even, I guess."

Corso grudgingly nodded.

"You should get some rest," Downs said.

Corso almost smiled. "Thank you, doctor."

"I'm serious."

"Gotta see a lady about some buttermilk," Corso said.

38

Monday, October 23 11:23 p.m.

One blue eye. Three brass chains. "It's late," she whispered through the crack in the door. "I've got a midterm tomorrow. I can't—"

"I'll just be a minute," Corso said.

"Is this about Donald?"

"Yes."

She heaved an audible sigh. "That's my past. I don't want to—"

"It's about you too," Corso said. "I think you better open the door."

Instead, the door closed. He waited a silent moment, wondering whether she'd gone back to bed before the first chain rattled.

Marie Hall wore one of those billowing flannel nightgowns favored by single women on cold nights—the white a little off from the washing machine, little shriveled roses around the edges—that and a pair of bright blue Road Runner socks. She closed the door behind Corso and stood with her hands on her hips.

"This may be the middle of the afternoon to you famous writer types, Mr. Corso, but I work for a living, so if you don't mind let's get to whatever it is you think is so important as to show up here at this time of night."

"I want you to tell me the truth."

Her foot began to tap. "You're starting to piss me off, you know that? I shared my private life with you. I answered your questions. And now you see fit to invade my privacy in the middle of the night and insult me!" She pulled the door open. "So—if you'll excuse me." She gestured toward the opening. Corso wandered farther into the apartment.

"I don't think you'll want your neighbors to hear this," he said.

"Get out."

"I need to know about the money," Corso said.

"Do I have to call the police?"

"I'm betting the police would find the scenario real interesting."

She pushed the door closed and started for the phone on the kitchen wall. Corso kept talking. "About how your husband, Donald, was a member of the second Balagula jury." She stood with the phone poised in the air, a foot from her ear. "About how he sold his ass to Nicholas Balagula for something like a hundred thousand bucks and about how you somehow managed to screw him out of half the money."

"Money? There was no money," she scoffed, pushing a button on the phone. She looked over as if to give Corso one last chance to leave.

"If you push that second one, Marie, the cops are coming. No matter what. There's no calling it off." Her finger wavered.

"You know what I'm betting?" Corso said. She didn't answer. "I'm betting if I were to run a serious financial check on you, I'd find you've got a little nest egg tucked away somewhere. A little something you can draw on for college tuition or"—he swept his hand around the room—"for a coupla nice pieces of furniture maybe." She started to protest, but Corso waved her off. "Probably got it squirreled away in some nice safe mutual fund or something like that."

"Don't be—"

"I'm betting that if I were to go down to where you work and ask around, I'd find out that for most of last summer you didn't take the bus to work like you usually did. I'm betting you drove a yellow pickup truck."

"You're crazy, you know that?" The tone was right, the gaze stony. Her lower lip, however, was not cooperating.

"Donald didn't need the truck. He was locked up in a downtown hotel." Corso reached into his inside coat pocket. Pulled out the list of jury expenses and threw it on the coffee table. "Ordering T-bone steaks and drinking buttermilk every night with his dinner."

"Get out," she said.

Corso turned on his heel and started for the door. Stopped with his hand on the knob. "I'll leave," he said. "I'm not in the business of terrifying people. But we need to get something straight here." She seemed to be paying attention, so he went on. "A couple of innocent people are dead because you sold your silence." He waved a finger at the woman. "So I'm putting you on notice, Marie Hall. As of tomorrow morning, I'm aiming every information source I own at you. In a week, I'm going to know things about you and your life even *you* probably don't remember. I'm going to be more intimate with you than your parents or your lovers." He waggled the finger again. "And if I find out you had anything to do, directly or indirectly, with letting Nicholas Balagula go free? I'm not only going to go public with it, I'm also going directly to the authorities with whatever I have."

He made a good show of it, closing the door with a bang and stomping down the stairs. He'd just arrived at the lower landing when the upstairs door opened.

"Please," she said, in a strangled voice. "I have so little."

She began to hiccup and then to sob. Before Corso could process the data, she disappeared into the apartment, leaving the door wide open.

Corso stood at the bottom of the stairs. He recognized the feeling, the odd mixture of triumph and revulsion he always felt at moments like this, when he'd managed to poke a hole in the nest of truths, half-truths, and outright lies that we all, over time, come to swear is the story of our lives.

He took his time walking back up. Stepped into the apartment and looked around.

She hadn't gotten the bathroom door closed. At the far end, she knelt in front of the toilet. The sound of her retching scratched the air like sandpaper.

Corso wandered into the living room, moving over by the stereo, where she was no longer visible. The sound followed him like a stray dog. He picked among her CDs. Heart. Barry Manilow. Barbra Streisand. All kinds of easy listening. Ricky Martin was in the player, Sarah McLachlan nearby.

When he looked up, she was standing in the hall with a towel pressed to her mouth.

"Tell me what happened," Corso said.

"It wasn't me!" she blubbered.

"I know. Just tell me what happened."

"They came one night. Maybe two days into the trial."

Corso stopped her. "You sure it was that early?"

"Positive," she said. "It was the first Wednesday night."

"Who came?"

"Three men."

"What did they look like?"

She described all three men. An older guy with a European accent and a couple of Hispanic guys. One tall, one short. Older European guy giving the orders. From the descriptions, Corso figured it had to be Mikhail Ivanov, accompanied by the dear departed Gerardo Limón and Ramón Javier.

"So what happened?"

"They pushed their way in." She was starting to blubber again.

"Take it easy," Corso said. "Just tell me the story."

She stuck her face into the towel and wept for several moments.

"They made me call Donald at the hotel," she said, when she'd recovered.

"You could call your husband?"

"Every night between seven-thirty and eight-thirty."

"Directly?"

"Oh, no. You had to go through a policeman first, who made sure who was calling. They had caller ID, and after a while—you know—you kind of got to know them and they kind of got to know you."

"So you called your husband. What happened then?"

She looked like she was going to cry again. "I don't know," she said, her lip trembling. "They put a gun to my head. They took me in the bedroom while the older guy talked to Donald."

"Then what?"

"After a while, the guy came in and said Donald wanted to talk to me." She wiped her mouth with the towel and then threw it over the back of a chair. "Donald said I shouldn't tell anybody that the men had come. Said it was super important. Said our whole lives depended on it."

"And you went along for the ride?"

She nodded miserably.

"It was probably for the best," Corso said.

Big tears ran down her cheeks. "I should have—"

"If either you or Donald had refused, they'd have killed you right there and then. Donald had never seen them. You were the only eyewitness. They had nothing to lose. If Donald goes to the cops, they get a mistrial and somebody finds your body."

"I don't understand," she said.

"If you're right about the date, they had the list of potential jurors from the very beginning. They went looking for a weak link, and Donald was it. He was a fanatic about his son's education. He was behind in his payments to Harvard. They were making noises about asking the kid to leave. He'd applied for a loan and been turned down. Donald was exactly what they were looking for."

"About a month later, I found the receipt in the mail."

"From?"

"Harvard." She looked sheepish. "I steamed it open."

“He’d paid it all.”

“Forty-two thousand dollars.”

“And you put two and two together.”

She squared her shoulders. “N
might think, Mr. Corso, I’m not s
ured it out.” She stared at Corso
agree. “You know what he tried to tell
wait for a reply. “He tried to tell me the money he sent
to Harvard was all of it. That he was broke again.”

“And you said?”

“I said the bill to Harvard was for forty-two thousand and the bill for my silence was going to be the same.”

“And he ponied up?”

“I should have asked for more.”

“You ever find out exactly how much he got?”

She shook her head and began to cry again. “What’s going to happen to me?” she said between sniffles. “I’m going to go to jail, aren’t I?”

“You’re an accessory before and after the fact in both bribery and jury tampering. They want to get nasty, they can charge you with interfering with a murder investigation and filing a false statement.”

“It’s not fair!” she cried. “I earned every dime of that money! Living with him all those years, doing without. I had a right. . . . I only took what was mine.”

“You’ll get off a lot lighter than Donald did.”

She looked up from her self-pity party. “I don’t understand. It was all over. Why did they kill Donald after everything was all done?”

“I think he was killed because he tried to go to the well again.”

“What do you mean?”

eded money to go into private practice. ver be able to prove it, but I think Don- d up one day and saw that Balagula was ttle for another trial and decided to in." Corso shook his head sadly. Balagula was a very, very bad

steeled herself. "I won't testify," she said, in a voice that made Corso a believer. "I'm not going to spend the rest of my life in fear, looking back over my shoulder, waiting for something to strike. I couldn't stand that. I'll go to jail first."

It took everything Corso had not to smile. It was like Renee Rogers said. First you scare the shit out of them and then you offer them a way out.

"What if I told you there was a way you could avoid testifying against Balagula and maybe stay out of jail at the same time?"

Hope flickered on and off in her eyes. "Oh, please," she sobbed.

"You'll have to do what I tell you."

"I will."

"You'll have to be a good actress."

She sat up straight like she was in school. Straightened her nightgown. "What do I have to do? Just tell me. I can do it."

"All you have to do is make one phone call," Corso said with a smile.

Tuesday, October 24 9:11 a.m.

The pages fluttered slightly as the book arched across the room and hit Corso in the chest. "Who told you to pay my bill?" Dougherty demanded. She was sitting up in bed wearing scrubs, makeup, and a frown. Joe Bocco slid down in the chair, hiding a smile behind his hand.

"Goddammit, Corso, if I want your help I'll ask for it." She looked around for something else to throw but couldn't find anything that wasn't connected to the bed.

Corso bent and picked up the book. "Any good?" he inquired.

"Dark," she said, then pointed a long manicured finger. "Don't change the subject."

Bocco got to his feet. "You kids don't mind," he said with a smirk, "I'll wait out in the hall while you work this out."

He crossed to the door, pulled it open, and allowed himself a final shake of the head before disappearing from view.

ed over to the bed and dropped the
. "You seem to be feeling quite a bit

ne until I inquired about the state
next thing I know they send in
who gives me a smarmy little
everything is taken care of."

Edward Crispin," Corso corrected.

"Whatever." She reached for the book again.

Corso took a step back. "I didn't want to lose you," Corso said.

"What did you say?"

"I said I didn't want to lose you."

"I don't need a goddamn sugar daddy. I'm a functioning, self-supporting adult. If I want—" She stopped. The frown disappeared. "Oh, Jesus, Corso, don't get soupy on me here. You'll ruin your image."

"It's only money," he said.

"You've got no respect for money, Corso."

"Money's not important unless you don't have any."

"That's easy for you to say."

"I felt the same way when I was broke. Nothing was ever about the money." He waved a hand. "Way I see it, I'm just a conduit through which money passes."

The movement of his right hand in the air pulled her eyes to his left hand, which was pushed deep into his pants pocket. "What's with the hand in the pocket?" she asked.

"What? A guy can't stand with his hand in his pocket?"

"That's not Frank Corso body language at all," she said. "What's the deal?" Corso didn't answer. "And that fruity shirt. You look like a bad foreign film."

With great care, Corso slid the ban[illegible]
his pocket. "I had a little cooking acc[illegible]

"A cooking accident," she repea[illegible]

"Yeah."

"Come here," she ordered[illegible]
on," she prodded.

This time, Corso wandered over [illegible]
looked him over, then reached up and pulled the turtleneck aside. She winced. "Damn, Corso. That's nasty.
Looks like whatever you were cooking tried to cook
you back."

"I'm taking Joe with me when I go," he said.

She eased the material back over the welt. "Looks
like you need him more than I do."

"Yeah."

"So you're going to stop over in finance and tell
Crispy Critters the bill is on me, right?"

"Sure."

She looked him over. "You liar. You've got no intention of doing any such thing, do you?"

"Nope."

"Get out of here, then," she said. "If you're not
going to show me any respect, you can leave."

Corso eased his damaged hand into his jacket pocket
and silently left the room. Joe Bocco leaned against the
wall in the corridor. "You kids get your spat worked
out?"

Corso ignored him. "I don't need you here anymore," he said.

"So our friends . . ."

"Won't be back," Corso finished.

Corso watched the wheels turning in Bocco's head.
"Then, way I figure it, I owe you a refund of—"

eed you tonight. Marvin too."

?"

or him.

y's a pro?"

e could use an extra pair of

ou got a pair in mind?"

"Got a woman I worked with a few times. She'll make good cover."

"Get her."

"What time?"

"I'm thinking we'll schedule the drop for eleven."

"If this guy's careful, we're going to need to be in place early."

"This guy's very careful," Corso said. "And very dangerous."

"This is gonna cost ya," Joe Bocco said.

"What else is new?"

Tuesday, October 24 9:22 a.m.

Mikhail Ivanov took a deep breath and coughed into his hand. His voice must not betray him. He knew it would be a mistake to underestimate Ramón and Gerardo. They complemented one another well. The strengths of one masked the weaknesses of the other. Ramón was smart but a bit too introspective for a man in his line of work. Whatever Gerardo lacked in intelligence and sophistication, he made up for with the kind of animal instinct that senses earthquakes days in advance.

He'd thought it over earlier and
final disposition of Gerardo and R
place after they returned to the
today's contact a mere holdin
ing them for services rende
suitable scenario for their p

He dialed. The phone began
Ivanov stood with the phone pressed to
full two minutes, before using his thumb to break the connection. He couldn't recall a time when they hadn't answered their phone. Thinking he must have misdialed, he tried again and got the same result.

Mikhail Ivanov was troubled as he pulled open the door and stepped out into the hall. The sight that greeted him did little to lift the pall.

The guy was there in the hallway, the sex peddler. Sixty feet away, knocking on Nico's door. "May I help you?" Ivanov asked the man evenly, as he started up the corridor toward him.

"Goddamn right," the man blurted.

Ivanov's practiced eye noticed how his right arm was tense, as if holding a great weight. Ivanov moved that way, approaching the man obliquely. "What can I do for you?"

The craggy, creased face was more haggard than usual. He looked as if he hadn't slept for a couple of days. "He messed the boy up."

"You've been paid for your services," Ivanov offered.

"Inside," the guy said. "He's all screwed up."

"You better go," Ivanov said.

The guy's face flushed. "Didn't you hear me, motherfucker? The docs are telling me—"

to pull his hand from his pocket, as ready. He clamped an iron grip sed the man's own momentum to e air. A silver stiletto flashed the man looked up at his once in the balls and then, y, again in the face. In an instant, ler was on his back in the hotel corridor while Ivanov stood above him, patting his suit back into place and inspecting the knife.

Between gasps, the flesh peddler tried to speak. "I'll get you . . . I'll . . ."

Ivanov dropped one knee onto the man's chest, driving the air from his body. As the man watched in horror, he slipped the blade of the knife between the man's lips, into his mouth. "What you are going to do, my friend, is ride that elevator back to the lobby and then run, just as fast as your little legs will carry you, back to whatever rat-infested sty a piece of shit like you lives in, and when you get there"—he rattled the knife blade around the guy's teeth—"you will give thanks that I let you leave here alive."

Ivanov's wrist twitched twice. The man emitted a piteous howl. Ivanov got to his feet. The guy sounded like he was gargling as he brought his hands to his mouth. He stared at his bloody palms for a disbelieving moment and then clamped them back over his ruined mouth. As he struggled to his feet, droplets of blood from the sliced corners of his mouth fell onto the thick wine-red carpet and disappeared.

Blood seeped between his fingers, as he waited for an elevator to arrive. He was rocking on his feet now,

emitting a low keening wail and
forth, as if dancing to a rhythm unh

Ivanov carefully wiped the knif
and stuck it in his pocket. Wh
hall toward the elevator, the fl

Tuesday, October 24

The sky was layered gray: lighter to the west out over Elliott Bay, where Bainbridge Island was little more than a smudge on the mist; darker and more menacing to the east as it tightened its coils around the buildings on Beacon Hill.

Corso stood on the corner of Second Avenue and Royal Brougham Way. He'd chosen the spot because it was directly in between Safeco Field and the new football palace that Microsoft billionaire Paul Allen was building out of pocket, two blocks to the north. In this neighborhood, limos were commonplace, twenty-four/seven.

When the gleaming Cadillac slid soundlessly to a stop a foot from his shins, the door seemed to open on its own. Renee Rogers sat in the jump seat, facing the rear, her briefcase clutched in her lap, her expression bland and ultraprofessional.

Corso got in and closed the door. At the other end of the opulent brocade seat sat the Attorney General of the United States. She looked more like a kindly aunt or a small-town librarian than the chief law enforcement officer for the most powerful nation in the world. The car started up Royal Brougham Way.

rso over. "I saw you once on *Good*
I didn't realize you were so tall."
w what to say, so he merely nod-

versation. Do you understand?"

gers. "Ms. Rogers tells me you
a scenario by which we might be able
to salvage our present untenable position."

"I believe so, yes," Corso said.

"Let's hear it."

"It goes back to the second trial," Corso began.

The Attorney General raised an eyebrow. "If Ms. Rogers can stand the mention of it, I guess I can too."

"It starts with a man named Donald Barth. He was a juror at the second trial."

She looked at him over her glasses. "And how would you come to that conclusion, Mr. Corso? The identities of those jurors have been destroyed."

He told her about Balagula having the master list of jurors from the beginning. About Berkley Marketing, Allied Investigations, and Henderson, Bates & May. And finally about Marie Hall's admissions. "I'll be damned," she said. "Go on."

As he talked, she took a lens-cleaning kit from the storage area in the door and began to clean her glasses. She looked older without the thick lenses magnifying her eyes. She didn't speak again until he'd finished and had settled back in the seat.

She adjusted the glasses on her nose and sighed. "When I told your publisher, Noel Crossman, that I'd allow you to sit in on the trial, I was hoping for a sense of closure to this whole thing."

She allowed silence to settle in th

"There can be only one answer, o
a glance at Renee Rogers and t
"This scenario that you envisio
as planned"—she shrugged
would have to be part of an
fice to finally bring Mr. Nichol

"Of course," Corso said.

"And if something were to go awry?" She flattened her generous lips. "Then—" She looked over at Corso with a flat, emotionless expression.

"Then the secretary will disavow any knowledge of our actions," Corso finished for her.

She cocked her head at him and smiled. "Where's that line from?" she asked.

"The original *Mission Impossible*. The voice on the tape recording always said that right before it caught fire."

The smile disappeared. "That is precisely what the secretary will do," she said.

"Ms. Rogers is going to need the authority to make a deal. She's going to have to be able to offer—"

The Attorney General held up a hand. "If the matter reaches a successful conclusion, Ms. Rogers's actions will be regarded as part of the overall plan and her authority to make legal concessions will have been granted directly through me."

"And if it doesn't?" Corso asked.

"Then she will have substantially exceeded her authority and any agreement into which she may have entered will necessarily be null and void." She waved a hand. "At best . . ." She hesitated for effect. "Even if it works out exactly as you envision, Mr. Corso, major

onstituency are going to have their
ape." Corso began to speak, but the
t him off. "They prefer their jus-
win, bad guys lose. This one is
s." She sat for a time having
We never had this conver-
a moment. She resettled herself
stared out the window.

They rode without speaking. "Understood?" she asked, finally.

They said it was. She must have had a signal arranged with the driver or a hidden button that she pushed. Ten seconds later, the car slid to a stop at the curb, directly across Royal Brougham Way from where they'd picked him up, twenty minutes earlier. The car door opened. "If you two will excuse me," the Attorney General said. "I have a press conference at eleven-thirty."

Corso stepped out into the rain, leaned down, and offered Rogers a hand. She took hold and joined him on the sidewalk. They stood side by side in the steady drizzle and watched the big black car disappear into the mist.

Tuesday, October 24 2:51 p.m.

Marie Hall read through the script again. "I don't know if I can do this." She brought a hand to her throat. "I'm so nervous."

"That's good," Corso said. "You ought to be nervous. You'll sound authentic."

"What if he—"

"Just follow the script."

Corso attached the microphone

checked the tape recorder volu

are," he said.

She took a deep breath

moment, a cheerful voice s

"Room Twenty-three fifty," s

"Thank you," the voice said.

The phone rang twice. "Yes."

"Mr. Ivanov?"

Silence.

"I saw your picture in the paper today."

"Who is this?"

"You came to my house."

"I'm hanging up now."

"You put a gun to my head."

"I don't know what you're talking about."

"You and those other two men. Last year. You made me call my husband at the hotel." She waited a minute. "You remember. I know you do."

"What do you want?"

"The paper says you and that baby killer are gonna get off."

"What do you want," Mikhail Ivanov said again.

"I want a hundred thousand dollars," she said, "and I want it tonight."

"You must be crazy."

"Crazy," she said, nearly in a whisper. "I'll show you crazy when I tell the goddamn cops. You hear me? I'll go right now. Don't you think I won't."

Ten seconds of silence ensued before Ivanov said, "Perhaps we can reach an area of accommodation."

"We better," she said.

ber 24 3:09 p.m.

pped a ten-dollar bill onto the
the waiter rolled it toward the
the man muttered. Ivanov
door open. The waiter
disappeared.

Balagula generally napped right after lunch, so Ivanov's presence in his room at this time of day was unusual. Balagula wiped the corners of his mouth with a linen napkin. "So?"

"We have a serious problem."

"Oh?"

"The woman whose husband—the one who became unburied."

"His wife."

"Yes."

"What about her?"

"She called. She says she saw my picture in the newspaper. Says she recognized me from when the Cubans and I went to her house."

"And?"

"She's demanding one hundred thousand dollars for her silence. She wants it today or she says she'll go to the authorities."

"The timing is awkward," Balagula said.

"Couldn't be worse."

Balagula shook his head. "What makes these people think they can hold me up?"

"Greed seems to run in this woman's family."

"She takes no lesson from the Barth fellow?"

"Apparently not."

"She cannot be allowed to interfere," Balagula said.

"This farce ends tomorrow." He looke
shrugged. "Set something up. Send

"That's also a problem."

"What problem is that?"

"I can't reach our Cuba
their phone."

"Since when?"

"This morning. An hour ago, I ha
hotel check the room. They didn't sleep in their be
last night. I also had the bellman check the parking lot for the car."

"Not there."

"No."

Balagula rose from the chair and paced around the room. "The problem must be handled," he said, after a minute. "We've come too far to allow anything to interfere."

"I know."

Nicholas Balagula stopped pacing and shrugged. "It appears, Mikhail, that you're going to be forced out of retirement."

"Yes . . . it does."

"She'll be alone," Balagula said.

"You think?"

"If she's foolish enough to try to hold me up, she's foolish enough to want to keep the money for herself. If she brings anyone, she'll have to split the money. No, she'll be alone."

"She said she'd call back tonight with where she wants to meet."

Nicholas Balagula thought it over. "Get the money. If the situation allows, kill her. If not, pay her and we'll send the Cubans for her later."

40

Tuesday, October 24 11:03 p.m.

Mikhail Ivanov recognized her from half a block away. She'd gained a bit of weight, but even under the streetlights she still had those narrow blue eyes like his mother's. He recalled the look of terror in those eyes when Gerardo put the gun to her head and led her into the bedroom, and how she couldn't stop crying as she listened to her husband's voice on the phone. He'd never have guessed she had the nerve for this.

She'd chosen her ground poorly: some sort of open-air church monument, three fluted stone columns standing at the edge of a bum-infested park. He'd been nearby for an hour and a half and, while the car traffic was unrelenting, the foot traffic was spotty. Those who did walk down Pine Street favored the opposite side of the street, where they did not have to cross freeway on-ramps. He was confident his task could be accomplished.

The bum was the only problem. Curled up asleep on the bench closest to Pine Street, he'd be no more than thirty feet from where Mikhail Ivanov envisioned making his move. During the past hour and a half, the tramp had risen three times: twice, early on, to stumble down into the park and relieve himself, and finally, half an hour back, to cross the street to the market and buy three tall cans of what appeared to be malt liquor. Since downing the contents of the cans, he had been snoring contentedly away. Perhaps if all went according to plan, he would awaken to find a bloody knife in his hand.

She wandered into the far corner of the park and looked around. Silhouetted against the black sky, she appeared to stand in some ancient ruin, left to rot amid the urban squalor. Mikhail Ivanov shifted the black athletic bag to his left hand and started forward, only to have a baby stroller nearly run over his feet. "Sorry," he mumbled to the thickset woman who acknowledged his apology with a smile and a nod. Watching her swinging her hips for a moment as she moved downhill, he breathed deeply and collected his wits. Satisfied with his state of composure, he waited for a lull in the traffic and then started across the street.

She was walking in small circles, staying just where he wanted her, on the Pine Street side, where it was dark and the traffic sparse. The half dozen cars, trucks, and vans along the curb had all been in place when he'd arrived and were probably parked for the night. Even better, Nico was right. She'd come alone. His right hand fondled the flesh peddler's stiletto in his overcoat pocket.

As he stepped up onto the sidewalk he began to visualize the move, the embrace of death he'd learned so long ago in the prison yard, so smooth and easy that, under the proper conditions, the victim could be leaned against a wall or a fence, standing up, stone dead.

As he passed the sleeping bum, he hesitated, leaned over, and looked down into the filthy face. A tiny piece of pink tongue hung from the side of the mouth. He was snoring quietly. Satisfied, Mikhail Ivanov strode across the uneven stones toward the woman moving among the columns at the far side.

He saw her eyes widen as she recognized him in the darkness. Saw her search her soul for courage as he came close. A final peek over his shoulder revealed the bum still unconscious on the bench. Across Pine Street, the woman had stopped walking and was making adjustments to the baby. On the Boren Avenue side, the sidewalks were bare.

He lengthened his stride, walked right up in front of her and set the bag on the bench. As he'd hoped, so much money, so close, was too much for her to ignore. She reached down and grabbed the bag's handle, at which point he slipped his arm under hers and drew her tight against his chest. His left hand was now on the back of her head, forcing her face hard against his coat, muffling her cries, as he brought the stiletto forward and up in a motion designed to eviscerate. She grunted from the force of the knife's impact. Had he not been holding her, she would have dropped to her knees. And yet . . . something was wrong. He could feel it.

He felt the knife penetrate the coat, but that was all. The sudden lessening of tension when a knife penetrates the body's outside wall, when the hand can feel the blade, wet and at large in the innards . . . it wasn't there. The point had somehow been deflected.

He drew the knife back and plunged again with all his might. Again she grunted. Again her legs buckled. Again the knife was deflected by something beneath her coat. Then he heard the scrape of a shoe, followed by the sound of a door sliding open, and before his eyes the street came alive around him. With all his strength, he tried to pull the blade upward.

A hand grabbed his wrist: the bum. The bum's other hand grabbed him around the waist and began pulling him backward. From the corner of his eye, he could see the woman with the stroller sprinting his way with a gun in her hand. He released his victim and turned to face the tramp. He lashed out once with the blade, heard a wail, and dropped the knife on the stones. His hand was on the automatic in his pocket when he felt the kiss of cold steel on the side of his face.

"Don't move a fucking muscle," the voice said. Ivanov shifted his eyes toward the sound. The man had thinning black hair and a scar running the length of his left cheek. He also had a sawed-off shotgun pressed to the side of Ivanov's head.

"Fucker cut me," the bum wailed. Marie Hall's mouth hung open as she struggled to her feet. She walked unsteadily over to the bum, pulled the scarf from her head, and began to wind it around his damaged wrist.

"Goddamn it. Goddamn it," the bum chanted.

Another hand grabbed Ivanov's arm and began to pull it from his coat pocket.

"Better be clean when it comes out of that pocket, buddy," Shotgun said. Ivanov relaxed his hand and allowed it to be pulled from his pocket. He felt fingers slide into his pocket and remove his gun and then felt the steel bracelet snap around his wrist. The shotgun ground harder into his temple as his other hand was forced behind his back and cuffed. "Go over him good," Shotgun said.

The woman dropped to one knee and began to frisk her way up to his groin. Took her five seconds to find the Beretta strapped to his left ankle. She set it on the uneven stones and completed her search.

"I want to see an attorney," Ivanov said.

In the darkness, someone laughed. Ivanov turned toward the sound. Frank Corso stepped out from behind the nearest pillar. "He's clean," the woman pronounced.

"Let's go," Corso said, picking up the athletic bag.

The shotgun was pulled away. The woman grabbed his shackled wrists and pushed him forward, toward the red minivan sitting at the curb with its sliding door agape. Behind him, he heard Corso's voice.

"Mary Anne, you and Marie take Marvin to Harborview." When Ivanov tried to turn and look, Shotgun grabbed him by the arm and forced him forward, causing him to stumble on the rough stones and nearly fall.

Shotgun got in first, all the way back in the third row of seats. The woman helped Ivanov up onto the big bench seat and then rolled the door closed. Outside in the park, the tramp cradled his arm like an infant. Marie Hall had shed her coat and was in the process of removing a Kevlar vest. The yawning barrel of the shotgun rested icily on the back of Ivanov's neck as Corso climbed into the passenger seat. A capped figure at the wheel put the van in DRIVE.

41

Tuesday, October 24 11:17 p.m.

The driver pulled the van to a halt.

"What's this?" Ivanov demanded.

The street was deserted. Corso swiveled the passenger seat around to face him. "This, Mr. Ivanov, is the proverbial offer you can't refuse." He gestured with his head. "That building across the street is the King County Jail." He held up a video camera. "I've got your attempt to murder Marie Hall on tape." The camera dropped from view and was replaced by a small gray tape recorder. Corso pushed the button. Marie Hall's voice said, *I'll show you crazy when I tell the goddamn cops. You hear me? I'll go right now. Don't you think I won't.*

Ten seconds of hissing silence, and then Ivanov's voice: *Perhaps we can reach an area of accommodation.*

We better.

It will be difficult to obtain that much money at this time of day.

Don't start with me. I'll go right to the damn cops.

I didn't say it couldn't be done, merely that it will be difficult. Perhaps if—

Corso snapped it off. "Sounds a lot like you, to me."

"What do you want?"

"Nicholas Balagula," Corso answered.

Were it not for the barrel pressing against the back of his neck, Mikhail Ivanov would have thrown his head back and laughed. "Be serious."

"You've taken the fall for him twice before. You gonna do it again?"

Corso turned to the driver, who until that moment had neither turned Ivanov's way nor spoken.

"He's looking at how much for jury tampering and attempted murder?" Corso asked.

The driver reached up and removed the blue baseball cap, sending a wave of brown hair cascading down onto her shoulders. She turned and looked directly into Mikhail Ivanov's eyes. "They'll call it twenty to life. He'll serve a minimum of sixteen years in a federal facility," Renee Rogers said. "Minimum."

"You'll be nearly eighty when you get out," Corso said. "That going to work for you, Mr. Ivanov? We combine what we've got on tape with Ms. Hall's testimony, and this is a slam dunk. You willing to spend the rest of the time you've got left behind bars to protect Nicholas Balagula?"

Ivanov was visibly shaken by the sight of Renee Rogers. "You can't," he stammered. "This isn't . . ."

"I can and I will, Mr. Ivanov," she snapped. "I'm not playing by the rules anymore. If this is what it takes to bring Nicholas Balagula to justice, that's the way it's gonna have to be."

"So make up your mind," Corso said. "You're either

going to help us nail your boss or we're going across the street right now and deliver you to the local authorities on charges of jury tampering and attempted murder."

"It's up to you, Mr. Ivanov," Rogers added.

Ivanov turned his head and looked out the side window for a moment. "Go to hell," he said finally.

"Okay," said Rogers. "Let's take him in."

Corso stepped out into the street and pulled open the sliding door. He took Ivanov by the elbow and started to pull him out onto the pavement. Suddenly Ivanov jerked his arm free and said, "Wait." He looked from Corso to Rogers and back. "And you—what—cut me some sort of deal? A plea bargain?"

"You disappear," said Rogers.

Ivanov's lips twisted into a sneer. "Into your silly Witness Protection Program?" He made a rude noise with his lips. "I think not."

"You walk," Rogers said. "On your own. You gather up whatever you have and you disappear."

Ivanov's eyes narrowed. "Just like that?"

"Just like that," Rogers repeated.

A garbage truck roared to a stop across the street. Amid the clatter of a pair of emptying Dumpsters, Ivanov said, "Since we were boys. . . ."

"What?" Rogers said.

"We've been together since we were boys," Ivanov said sadly.

"And in all that time," Corso said, "if there were risks to be taken, you took them. If somebody had to go to jail, you were the one."

"I was—"

"Has he ever, even once, stepped into the breach? Come forward and taken the beating for you? Ever?"

" 'Cause he's certainly not going to do it now," Rogers added. "He's going to walk out of that courtroom tomorrow a free man, and he's going to disappear before we think of anything else to charge him with, leaving you rotting in jail."

Ivanov took several deep breaths. "You want me to say what?"

"We want you to testify that you were present when the scheme to fake the concrete samples was implemented," Rogers said quickly. Before Ivanov could reply, she went on. "We also want you to confess to arranging the murders of Donald Barth, Joseph Ball, Brian Swanson, and Joshua Harmon."

Ivanov nearly smiled. "I clean up all your loose ends at once for you, eh?"

"One more thing," Corso said.

Ivanov turned his face away, shaking his head in disgust.

"You also confess to having personally killed Gerardo Limón and Ramón Javier, in an attempt to clean up your own loose ends."

"All at Mr. Balagula's behest, of course," Renee Rogers added.

Slowly, Ivanov swiveled his head around until he was staring Corso in the face.

A look of admiration swept over his features. "Really," he said. He nodded twice, as if agreeing with himself. "I told Nico you were a dangerous man. But I had no idea—"

"Well?" Rogers prodded. "What'll it be?"

"But I didn't—" Ivanov began.

"We don't care," Rogers said. "When you walk out

of that courtroom tomorrow morning, you have seven days to leave the country. We will keep your murder confessions confidential. But if you ever show up again on our radar screens, we'll prosecute you for three murders. Other than that, we will formally agree not to seek your extradition from whatever country you might choose to live in."

Ivanov shifted his gaze to Rogers. "You have the authority?"

"I do," Rogers lied.

"In writing?"

"Yes."

"Comes a time a man needs to look out for himself," Corso added.

Across the street, the garbage truck roared off, swirling diesel fumes and bits of airborne refuse in the night air. "You know what the joke is?" Ivanov asked.

"What's that?" said Corso.

"The hospital wasn't our fault. All we did was reduce the concrete by ten percent. We've done it a hundred times before." He shook his head sadly. "It was those two inspectors, Harmon and Swanson." He looked up at Corso. "They took out another ten percent of their own. Next thing you know they're driving sports cars and buying houses in Marin County."

"Greed's a terrible thing, isn't it, Mr. Ivanov?" Corso gibed.

Ivanov didn't answer, merely looked away.

"You agree to our terms?" Rogers said.

Ivanov dropped his chin to his chest. "Yes," he said.

Renee Rogers slid out of the driver's seat and stood in the street, pushing the buttons on her cell phone.

Then she spoke, first identifying herself and then demanding, "Two U.S. marshals to the corner of Fourth and Cherry. Pronto."

Joe Bocco pushed the jump seat forward, stepped out of the van, dropped to one knee, and jacked three rounds out onto the pavement. After pocketing the ammunition, he slid the sawed-off shotgun into a sleeve sewn into the lining of his raincoat and got to his feet. "If you guys don't mind, I think I'll pass on the marshals." He nodded toward the van. "He ain't going anywhere."

"I'll call you tomorrow," Corso said.

"Thank you, Mr. Bocco," Renee Rogers said.

He gave her a silent two-fingered salute and walked off. Corso and Rogers stood together in the street, watching until Joe Bocco rounded the corner on Spring Street and disappeared from view.

She put her hands on her hips and sighed. "This doesn't feel nearly as good as I imagined it would."

"How come?"

She looked toward the van and Ivanov. "I can't believe we're letting this slimeball go. He's every bit as responsible." She shook her head. "It's just not right."

"What's right got to do with it?"

"I like to think it has everything to do with it."

"You gotta stop confusing justice and the law."

"Oh, pleeeease—"

"Lawyers . . . the courts . . . you guys . . . you dispense the law. Justice is dispensed on the ends of piers and in back alleys."

Her eyes narrowed. "That's what the cliché says, isn't it?"

"It got to be a cliché by being true."

The muscles along the edge of her jaw rippled. She gave a grudging nod and jammed her hands into her pockets.

"I think this is where I came in," Corso said.

She swept her eyes over his face. "You're not coming to court tomorrow?"

"I'll catch it on the news."

They stood uneasily for a moment before Renee Rogers stepped forward and gave him a hug. He hesitated and then slowly wrapped his arms around her.

"Thank you again for saving my life," she said, and let him go.

"I told you—" he began.

She reached up and put two fingers over his lips. "I know, Mr. Hard Guy was just saving himself." She held his gaze. "I had my eye on you that night, you know."

"Things got a little out of hand," Corso said with a shrug.

Her eyes crinkled into a smile. "At least I was wearing my good underwear."

"Your mother would be proud," Corso said.

She managed a tight smile and turned toward the van and Ivanov.

"See ya," Corso said, and strode off up the street. He walked about twenty feet and then stopped and turned aroud.

"Hey."

She looked over her shoulder. "Hey what?"

"You know what Ivanov was saying about Harmon and Swanson buying themselves houses in Marin County?"

"Yeah."

"I had a guy say the same thing to me about the Joe Ball character. About how he and his wife just bought a house. Seems like every place we go people are buying real estate after they get involved with Balagula and Ivanov here."

Her spine stiffened. "So?"

"When you get Ivanov spilling his guts, ask him about how they got the jury list from the last trial. I'll bet you dollars to doughnuts the name Ray Butler gets bandied about."

She was silent for a long moment. "Sometimes I'm not sure I like you," she said.

"Join the club."

42

Wednesday, October 25 10:04 a.m.

Judge Fulton Howell took his time getting situated behind the bench. Satisfied that his chair was in exactly the right place and that the drape of his robe was correct, he turned his frowning visage toward the nearly empty courtroom. *Bang*.

"In light of the testimony of Victor Lebow—" he began.

Renee Rogers got to her feet. "Your Honor."

Out of habit, the judge looked over at Warren Klein, who sat stonefaced behind the prosecution table. When Klein failed to meet his gaze, he turned his attention back to Renee Rogers. "Ms. Rogers," he said.

"The prosecution would like to call a final witness."

The judge folded his arms over his chest and leaned back in the chair. "I was under the impression that Mr. Lebow was to be the state's final witness."

"Yes, Your Honor. As of Monday afternoon, it was our intention to have Mr. Lebow be the final witness for the prosecution."

"And?" the judge prompted.

"New developments in the case have provided the state with additional information that we believe, in the interests of justice, should be introduced in this court."

"In the interests of justice?"

"Yes, Your Honor."

"As I recall, Mr. Lebow's last-minute testimony was allowed on much the same supposed basis."

"Yes, Your Honor."

The judge looked over at the defense table. For the first time, Bruce Elkins sat with his hands steepled beneath his chin. Nicholas Balagula had abandoned his day-at-the-beach slouch and was now sitting bolt-upright in his chair.

"Mr. Elkins?"

"It was my impression that the state had rested its case."

"No, Your Honor, the state had not," Rogers said.

Fulton Howell deepened his scowl and called for the court reporter, who walked over, put her head together with the court clerk's, and returned to the bench with several pages of trial transcript. After a moment, the judge looked up and addressed himself to Bruce Elkins. "Apparently your impression was faulty, Mr. Elkins. The prosecution never rested its case prior to my call for an adjournment."

Elkins shrugged. "As previously stated, Your Honor, the defense does not wish to dignify these spurious proceedings. We remain confident that the jury will see through the web of innuendo which the state calls a case and will reach the judicious conclusion."

"I take it, then, you have no objection, Mr. Elkins."

"None," Elkins said, with a wave of the hand.

Fulton Howell's distaste for the tactic was evident

on his face. He swiveled his head back to face Renee Rogers. "Before I rule on this matter, Ms. Rogers, let me make it clear that any semblance of yesterday's travesty of justice will not be tolerated."

"Yes, Your Honor," she said.

His voice began to rise. "I will not permit this court to become any more of a laughingstock than it has already become. Whatever testimony this witness may offer had better be both verifiable and germane to this case. Am I making myself clear?"

Renee Rogers lifted her chin a notch. "The testimony is of sufficient magnitude and is sufficiently verifiable to have led to the investigation of one of our own staff members, Your Honor."

The judge looked from Klein to Rogers and back. "Would that explain the absence of Mr. Butler from today's proceedings?"

"Yes, it would, Your Honor."

He now turned his attention to the defense table. "And Mr. Ivanov?" he inquired.

Elkins spread his hands. "I have no knowledge as to the whereabouts of Mr. Ivanov."

"Mr. Balagula?"

"Mr. Ivanov is indisposed."

"Indisposed?"

"Yes."

"Indisposed in what manner?"

Renee Rogers broke in. "Your Honor."

"If you don't mind, counselor." His voice dripped acid.

"Your Honor," she said again, "with the court's forbearance, Mr. Ivanov will be the state's next and final witness."

Silence settled over the room like new-fallen snow. Judge Fulton Howell moved his gaze from table to table as if watching a tennis match replayed at half speed.

"Do something," Nicholas Balagula said to his attorney. He reached out and prodded Elkins in the back: once, twice. Hard. "Do something, goddammit!" he demanded. When he received no response, he jumped to his feet and started up the aisle. He made it about halfway to the door before a pair of U.S. marshals came out of the woodwork, blocked his path, and then, when he tried to force his way through, wrestled him to the floor, where he was handcuffed and subsequently pulled to his feet.

Most of those in the room at the time believed Bruce Elkins buried his face in his hands in a show of frustration. Truth was, the move was designed to hide his lips, which despite his best efforts seemed intent on arranging themselves into a smile.

43

Wednesday, October 25 10:14 a.m.

While hope springs eternal and charity begins at home, faith apparently requires the assistance of iron bars. The Ming Ya Buddhist Foundation of Seattle sat on Martin Luther King Way South, wedged between a derelict steel yard and an Arco gas station. The red-rimmed windows of the bottom two floors were protected by wrought-iron security bars, whose decorative loops and whirls were more reminiscent of New Orleans than of New Delhi.

Corso parked on the side street. On this side, a set of wooden stairs led up to a porch. Above the narrow door, a dozen gold Chinese characters glittered. At each end of the landing, a red lantern waved its tassels in the breeze.

Corso walked down the slight incline to the front of the temple, where, high up under the eaves, a pair of golden dragons flanked a molten sun.

Corso knocked on the red metal door. Nothing. He knocked again, harder this time, and waited. Still nothing. He had turned and started back the way he'd come when he heard the scrape of the door.

The boy was somewhere between twelve and fourteen. Bald and barefoot, he took Corso in from head to toe. He held the door open with his back and inclined his head, as if to question. "I need to talk to someone," Corso said.

Without hesitation, the boy leaned back into the door and pushed it all the way open. Corso stepped inside. The boy's feet pattered on the bare floor as he hurried around Corso. He pointed at Corso's shoes and then at a reed mat to the right of the door, where a pair of Nike sandals rested.

Corso dropped to one knee and then the other as he removed his shoes and placed them beside the sandals. The kid was off down the hall like a rabbit. Halfway down he stopped short, slid back a screen, and disappeared from view. Corso stood still. He could hear muted voices. After a moment, the boy stepped back into the hall and stood with his hands at his sides, not moving. Corso walked toward him, bending low under the doorway. A Buddhist monk sat cross-legged on the floor. At the sight of Corso, he adjusted the saffron-colored robe on his shoulder and smiled. His broad brown hand gestured to his left. Corso heard the door slide shut behind him.

He padded across the room, sat on the floor, and forced his legs across one another. Rice-paper screens covered the windows. The air was filled with the pleasant odor of incense. The room was dominated by a life-sized Buddha. Gold and gleaming, it sat between a pair of low tables, draped with red silk. Candles flickered on the tables.

"How can I help you, Mr. . . ."

"Corso."

"Ah."

"I have a few questions."

"Ah," the monk said again.

"About a woman named Lily Pov."

"A tragedy."

"Yes."

"And you are seeking what?"

"Understanding."

"Of what?"

Corso told him.

* * *

"I could not expect you to understand, Mr. Corso," the monk said.

"Try me."

"You spoke of a funeral for Lily Pov. Here at the temple."

"Yes."

He shrugged his smooth brown shoulders. "In the Buddhist tradition, there is no such thing. What would usually happen would be that the family and friends would go to the Pov home. They would bring an envelope with money to help pay for the funeral expenses. There would be an *ahjar sar*."

"A what?"

"Perhaps, in the Christian tradition, a deacon."

"Sort of a middleman between the sacred and the secular."

"Yes. The *ahjar sar* would bless the gifts and the mourners. Food would be served. This would go on all day."

"So if this is something that usually happens at home, why was Lily Pov's"—Corso searched for a word—"*bereavement* held here at the temple?"

"Mr. Pov has many friends in the local Khmer community, far too many for his house. We offered the temple as a courtesy."

"You know that she killed herself."

"So I was told."

"Any idea why?"

"We are not like Catholic priests. We do not hear confessions."

"Surely there must have been talk."

"There is seldom a shortage of talk."

"Hypothetically . . ." Corso began.

"Hypothetically," the monk repeated.

"Why would a woman who had waited nearly ten years to come to this country, who was engaged to a Cambodian man—"

"Engaged?"

"Promised in marriage."

"Ah."

"A woman who had the support of her elder brother and, as you say, the entire Cambodian community—why would a woman such as this choose to kill herself?"

He gave a serene shrug. "Who can say? Perhaps it was her duty."

"Her duty?" Corso considered this comment. "What if the prospective husband changed his mind and decided he didn't want her for a wife?"

"For no reason?"

"Yes."

"Then it is more likely that Mr. Pov would have

killed the prospective husband. In the Cambodian tradition, he would be within his rights to do so."

"What if . . . before the wedding . . . she became involved with another man?"

The question seemed to startle the monk. "Then the man to whom she was promised might be well within his rights to kill her. As would her brother. It would then be her duty to save them the trouble and take matters into her own hands." He read Corso's expression. "I'm sure this all sounds rather quaint and bloodthirsty to your ears, Mr. Corso, but as I told you earlier, our customs are often seen as odd by outsiders."

"People change their minds all the time."

"In your tradition, Mr. Corso, not in ours."

"Till death do us part."

"Hmmm," was all the monk said.

44

Wednesday, October 25 11:01 a.m.

On the far side of the marsh, three white vans were parked along the top of the levee, doors open, orange lights pulsing. Corso watched as a pair of men in bright yellow jackets wheeled a gurney to the rear of one of the vans and lifted a slack, black bundle inside. He pulled his eyes back across the surface of the water, his gaze floating from the rushes, whose brown tops leaked white into the fall wind, to the matted grassy hillocks cowering a foot above the waterline, to the rotten stumps and the lace of lilies, spread here and there across the wavering surface. And finally to the near shore, where the little man stood, stiff and straight at the water's edge, his fingers laced behind his back, his elbows touching.

Corso crossed the grass and stood silently at his side.

"The birds have all gone," Nhim Pov said, after a moment. "They have no tolerance for the noise and the engines and the lights."

"They'll be back," Corso said.

Nhim Pov pointed at the vans with his chin. "They've been here all morning. Ever since it was light enough to see."

"Tomorrow they'll be somewhere else."

Nhim Pov inclined his head. "Certainly, there is no shortage of death and misery."

"No . . . there never is."

"The son of Mr. Barth. He called. Said he's going back to Boston. Asked me to distribute what was left of his father's things."

"It's time for him to get on with his life."

Nhim Pov nodded. "One must go forward. Time never looks back." He brought his hands out from behind his back and heaved a sigh. For the first time, he looked at Corso. "So, you are still working on your story?"

"The story's over," Corso said. "This morning, a man confessed to the murder of Donald Barth."

Nhim Pov averted his eyes. "What is that saying you Americans have? Confession is something for the soul."

"Tonic," Corso said. "Confession is tonic for the soul."

"Yes."

"He will go to trial?"

"No," Corso said. "The confession was part of a plea agreement. The matter is closed."

"For all time?"

"Yes."

"Do you imagine he feels better now that he has unburdened his soul?"

Corso watched the wind plow furrows in the marsh water as he thought it over.

"I think . . . like most of us, he just did what he felt he had to do."

"Sometimes that is all that remains."

"Or so it seems at the time."

Nhim Pov emitted a dry laugh. "There are no mistakes, Mr. Corso. In the final act, everything comes to the end for which it was intended. If this man killed Donald Barth, I'm sure he had a good reason."

"And if it was another man who actually killed Mr. Barth?"

"Why would the first man have confessed if he was not guilty?"

"Perhaps he was *induced* to do so."

Nhim Pov smiled. "Forced by outside influences."

"Yes."

"Then I must assume the real killer had an equally good reason for his deed. Everything is done for a reason."

"What would be a good enough reason to kill another man?"

"Honor," Nhim Pov said immediately.

"Whose honor, the killer or the killed?"

"Both," Nhim Pov snapped. "To live without honor is to be no more than a beast of the field. To die without honor—" He broke off, his eyes locked on Corso's. The two men stood in silent conversation for what seemed an eternity.

"What about fear?" Corso asked. "What of a man who kills from fear?"

Nhim Pov sighed. "What is more universal than fear? What would make him more human than fear? A man without fear is not a man at all."

Half a mile away, the three white vans were moving,

turning around one by one, and heading back toward the road, lights flashing like orange pinwheels.

The two men stood in the quiet, watching the procession bounce out into the road and head north toward the freeway. Corso turned to leave. Nhim Pov's hand on his elbow stopped him. Pov started to speak but stopped himself. Corso pointed.

Above the tree line a dozen canvasback ducks veered across the sky, wheeled once around the marsh, and then splashed into the water, where, amid impatient quacks and airborne feathers, they began to feed.

45

Wednesday, October 25 1:19 p.m.

The Attorney General of the United States stood behind the bank of microphones, her short hair rippling in the breeze. "And I am pleased that the jury has so quickly and unequivocally brought this matter to an end, so that the long-suffering victims of Nicholas Balagula's criminal empire can finally find some sense of closure and some measure of peace in this tragedy," she concluded. The press began to fire questions but she ignored them. Smiling and waving like the queen, she turned and walked away from the podium.

"How long was the jury out?" Corso asked.

"Twenty-eight minutes. Guilty on all sixty-three counts."

Meg Dougherty pushed the button on the remote control. The screen went black.

"Am I crazy or did that woman just take credit for the whole thing?"

"Only the winning part," Corso said.

"So you've finally got an ending for your book."

Corso couldn't help himself. He laughed out loud.

"Guess what?" Dougherty said.

"I'll bite."

"The *Times*'s insurance company is picking up my hospital bill. Since I was working for them when it happened, they figured it was only fair."

"Not to mention good publicity."

"There's that."

Corso wandered over to the window and pushed the curtain aside. The morning sun poured itself onto the floor. As Corso stood looking down on Ninth Avenue, Meg Dougherty asked, "You okay?"

Without turning her way, he said, "I suppose."

"Want to tell me about it?"

He shook his head.

"It's that bad?"

"It's that something," he said. He released the curtain and ambled toward the bed, then stopped in the middle of the floor and shrugged. "One of my oldest movies up and changed its ending on me."

She tilted her head on the pillow. "What movie is that?"

"The Western. The one where the intrepid sheriff"—he patted his chest—"faces down the lawless gang." He waved a hand. "All alone." He read her puzzled expression. "You know," he said. "Sun directly overhead, lots of dust, guy with a star on his chest. That kind of thing."

"*High Noon*?"

"More or less."

"So?"

He hesitated, seeming to listen to some inner voice, and then said, "So maybe I didn't turn out to be as brave and intrepid as I'd always imagined."

"How so?"

He winced. "It was much more ambiguous than I figured. It was hard to tell the good guys from the bad guys. There didn't seem to be any moral high ground. More like we all just got down in the swamp together and rolled around in the muck."

"And you *do* love the moral high ground."

He nodded sadly but did not speak. The streaming sunlight highlighted flecks of airborne dust, filling the room with a glittering curtain of mist. Corso eased his right hand into the shimmering shaft of light, turning it this way and that until, satisfied that the sun had touched it all, he returned it to his pocket.

"When are they going to let you out of here?" he said finally.

"Two weeks," she said.

"Ought to take me about that long to put an ending on the Balagula book," he said. "After that I could use some help on—"

She waved him off. "Thanks," she said, "but I've still got a lot to process. A lot of healing to do."

She almost smiled as he tried to speak with boyish enthusiasm.

"Maybe we could . . . you know . . . after you've had time to—"

"We'll see," she said, turning her face away.

Corso hesitated and then wandered over to the bedside, where he stood looking down at her. He bent over the rail and kissed her once on the cheek, lingering a moment before straightening and making for the door.

"Corso."

He stopped and looked back over his shoulder. She had tears in her eyes.

"You're the best friend I ever had," she said.

She couldn't tell whether the movement of his head was a nod or a tremor. Either way, he grabbed the door handle, slid through the narrow crack, and disappeared.

It's getting worse."

She was right. No more fluff floating down from the dome of the sky. Now it was a torrent of ice slanting onto the metal skin of the Ford Explorer, hissing like static and rocking the big car on its springs. Despite the full-blast roar of the heater, snow had collected at the extremities of the windshield, leaving only a pair of crescents through which they could peer at the deserted freeway ahead.

"How far have we gone," she asked.

Corso checked the odometer. "A hundred and fifty-three miles."

"We should have driven out of it by now."

"Presuming your friend Jerry was right."

She shifted in her seat and bared her teeth. "Don't start with me, Corso. This fiasco was *your* idea, remember? As I recall . . ."

The recollection lodged in her throat as a violent gust of wind buffeted the car, throwing it out of the solitary set of tire tracks they'd been following for the past hour, sending the rear wheels skittering back and forth across the icy surface. Dougherty grabbed the overhead handle.

"What was that?"

"The wind," Corso said, as the Ford wiggled back into the ruts.

She tapped a long red fingernail on the dashboard. "You noticed the outside temperature gauge?"

Corso flicked his eyes down to the green digital readout. What had, in Chicago, read twenty-four degrees Fahrenheit was now registering minus three.

"We should have turned around when the snowplow did," she said, for what Corso reckoned to be the eighth time.

He grunted. As much as it pained him, she was right. For the past hour, the freeway had been deserted. Service areas closed. Snowed-over cars and trucks abandoned along the shoulders of the road. Seemed like the whole state of Illinois had decided to sit this one out in front of the fire.

"When the snowplow gives up and turns around . . . you know . . . I know this sounds crazy to you, Corso, but maybe we should have taken the hint. . . . Maybe we should have showed a modicum of . . . of . . ."

Corso wiped the inside of the windshield with his sleeve. "Exactly where are we?" he interrupted.

"In the middle of a goddamn blizzard is where we are."

"I mean like on the planet," he said. "Where's the map?"

Dougherty was feeling around on the floor beneath her seat when Corso feathered the brakes several times and brought the Ford to a halt.

Her dark eyebrows merged as she looked up at Corso.

"What?"

Corso inclined his head toward the windshield. She sat up and looked out. Whoever they'd been following for the past hour was gone. While the eastbound lanes of I-90 were a maze of ruts and tracks, the westbound lanes ahead were an unbroken ribbon of drifted snow.

"Where the hell did he go?"

"Beats me."

"What are we gonna do?" Dougherty asked, as much to herself as to Corso.

"Depends on where we are," he said.

She started to reach for the floor.

"I think you put it in the door thingee," Corso said.

He watched as she retrieved the map and snapped on the overhead light. "Presuming the odometer is right, we should be somewhere along the Illinois-Wisconsin border."

She checked the map again. "There should be a town named Avalon somewhere up ahead." Corso clicked on the high beams, but the extra wattage only made visibility worse. Looked like they were inside a Christmas paperweight.

"This was really dumb."

"We'll get off at the next exit," Corso said. "Spend the night in Avalon."

"How long has it been since we passed anybody?"

"Maybe an hour," Corso said, easing his foot off the brake, allowing the car to creep forward.

"You know why that is?" she demanded.

"No . . . but I've got a feeling you're going to enlighten me."

"It's because we're the only people on the planet

rat's-ass dumb enough to be out driving around on a night like this . . . that's why."

Corso pressed his lips tighter and gave the Ford gas.

They rode in silence. A mile and they passed a trio of cars, snowed over and abandoned on the shoulder. Then two more cars and an abandoned bus before Dougherty pointed and said, "Stop."

Corso eased the Ford to a halt. Twenty yards ahead, covered with snow, a road sign rocked in the wind. Dougherty popped the door open. The interior was immediately filled with swirling snow. "I'll be right back," she said, slamming the door.

He watched as the wind propelled her to the snowed-over sign on the shoulder of the highway. Her cape was pressed tight around her body as she used the flat of her hand to smack the sign, sending a wall of snow slipping to the ground around her boots.

Avalon 2 miles. She used her hands to clean off several smaller signs mounted lower on the post. Blue and white symbols. Gas, food, and lodging.

Leaning into the wind with her cape flapping wildly, she trudged back to the car and climbed in.

Her eyelashes were a solid line of snow. Her lower jaw chattered as she spoke.

"Daaamn, it's c-c-c-cold out there."

"You okay?"

When she nodded, the snow in her hair dropped into her lap.

"Let's get out of here," she said, brushing snow down onto the floor.

"Avalon, here we come," Corso said, easing the car forward.

She shuddered. Tried to turn up the heater but found

it was already running full bore and then sat back and refastened her seat belt.

"There's the exit," she said.

Corso tapped the brakes several times as they rolled down the exit ramp and skidded to a stop. "Icy," Corso said.

On the far side of the road, the gas, food, and lodging symbols were accompanied by a blue and white arrow, pointing to the right.

They both leaned forward and peered down the tree-lined road.

Dougherty rubbed at the inside of the windshield with her sleeve.

"I don't see a thing."

"Town's probably just up around the corner," Corso offered.

Fifty yards and, without warning, the road got steep. The Ford skidded several times as the two-lane road wound down into the valley below. Corso wrestled the wheel.

"Town's probably down at the bottom of the hill," she said in a low voice.

"It better be," said Corso. " 'cause there's no way we're getting back up this thing until the snow melts."

"A problem we wouldn't have if you had just—"

"Give it a fucking rest, will you?" he snapped.

Suddenly her tone matched the weather. "Is that my employer speaking? Am I being ordered to just take my imaginary photographs on demand and otherwise keep my mouth shut so as not to annoy the famous writer?"

Corso sighed. "No . . . it's your friend Frank Corso speaking, and he's telling you that we're in this together. Maybe trying to drive to Madison wasn't the brightest idea I ever had, but we're stuck with it now . . . so we might just as well not act like . . ." Uncharacteristically, he fumbled for a word and then gave up.

"I see. You're not telling me what I can and can't say. You're just telling me to stop being such a bitch."

Corso searched his mouth for a denial, but "Something like that" came out.

Her face said she should have known. "How quick they forget."

"What's that supposed to mean?"

"Whatever you want it to."

"Isn't this conversation just a joy to be part of on a wintry night?"

"I can remember a time when you thought so."

"That was then." He took a hand off the steering wheel. "We were . . . you know . . . then." Waved it. "You know what I mean. It was different then."

She put on her astonished face. "I most certainly don't know any such thing. Why doesn't the famous on-the-lam crime writer enlighten me."

"When you're . . . you know . . ."

"Doing the nasty."

"Yeah."

"Go on."

"When you're . . . you know . . . involved like that . . . the rules are different. You put up with a little more shit than you otherwise might."

She sat in silence for a moment and then emitted a dry laugh. "So what you're saying is that when you're getting laid, you'll listen to a lot more bullshit than you will when you're not."

He thought it over. "Makes complete sense to me," he said finally.

She looked at him for a long moment. "Amazing," she said. "Guys are absolutely amazing." When he didn't respond, she folded her arms across her chest, sat back in the seat, and said, "You'll be sure to let me know when I'm allowed to speak again, won't you?"

The muscles along the side of Corso's jaw tightened. Ahead, a bright yellow sign announced a 20 percent grade. Corso worked the brakes. Gritting his teeth as the Ford slid around a corner, Corso turned his head toward Dougherty.

She sat stiffly in the seat, staring through the windshield, wearing her most disinterested gaze.

"Why don't we just . . ." he began.

He watched as her eyes opened wide. "Corso!" she bellowed.

He snapped his eyes back to the road. It took a moment before his brain was able to register and categorize what his eyes were seeing.

Ahead, a snow-encrusted pickup truck lay on its side, blocking both lanes, passenger door open and pointing at the sky. When he tapped the brakes, the Ford surrendered the last of its traction and began to accelerate down the steep incline.

"Do something!" Dougherty screamed as the hill pulled them faster and faster toward the wreck. Corso stood on the brakes, but the Ford was out of control now, gaining speed, turning a lazy circle before plowing headfirst into the wreck.

Inside the Ford, Dougherty's face was a mask of fear. The last image she processed was the bottom half of Corso's face covered with blood. And then the Ford began to pinwheel along the undercarriage of the pickup truck, the scream of tearing metal filling the air, in the instant before they bounced over the guardrail and became airborne.

First time Corso opened his eyes, all he could see were flames dancing across a stained ceiling. The only sound to reach his ears was the groan and crackle of the fire. Unable to raise his head, he experienced a moment of doubt, wondering if perhaps he hadn't died and gone to hell. He was still pondering this possibility and trying to move his extremities when the ebony wings folded around him and again the world turned black.

Second time he opened his eyes, he sat straight up and winced as a brain-tumor headache nearly threw him back to the floor. The fallen snow reflected halogen bright through the side windows, and then he remembered it all. How Dougherty saved his life. He looked around. She lay at the other end of the fireplace, huddled in a heap beneath her cape. He remembered how she'd used the lighter he'd found to make her way through the deserted house looking for something to burn. How she'd found long empty drawers in the kitchen still lined with fancy paper. How she'd leaned the drawers up against the hearth and stomped them to splinters with her boots. He could see the violent shaking of her hands as she lit the crumpled paper and waited for the splinters to catch fire. And then the larger pieces of the drawers and then the kitchen cabinet doors, and then it started to get warm. And how he'd tried to get up but couldn't and her soothing voice telling him to stay on the floor. How they were going to be all right. After that, things got spotty.

One segment at a time, Corso levered himself from the floor, until he stood unsteadily.

At his feet, Dougherty stirred but did not waken. Corso made his way around the corner into the kitchen, where it was noticeably colder. His breath swirled about his head as he looked around. She'd burned everything that could be torn loose and fed to the fire. All that remained was the frame of what had once been a modest set of kitchen drawers and cabinets along the north wall.

Sliding his hand along the countertop, he crossed the kitchen to the back door. His reflection in the wavy glass upper panel of the door stopped him in his tracks. He didn't recognize the face that peered back at him. A seeping green bruise ran completely across his forehead like a bloody headband. His eyes were blackened and nearly swollen shut. Everything below his nose was a solid sheet of thick coagulated blood. He rested his forearms on the countertop and bowed his head, breathing deeply, somewhere between sleep and wakefulness, until a voice from the other room startled him. "Corso," it called.

He had to clear his throat three times before he could rasp, "In here."

"You need to lie down."

"I'm okay," he said.

"You're nowhere in the vicinity of okay," she insisted.

As if to prove her wrong, Corso pushed himself off the countertop and staggered back into the front room. She was kneeling on the floor with pain in her eyes. Corso sat on the hearth, bringing his face close to hers. "You okay?" he asked.

She nodded, without meaning it. "Except for my hands," she said, bringing them out from under the folds of her cape. Her hands looked like they'd been boiled. "I froze them last night. They burn like hell."

"Keep them warm" was all Corso could think to say.

"You should see yourself," she said through her teeth as she slipped her hands back under the cape.

"I have."

She started to get up, but Corso put a firm hand on her shoulder.

"You saved my ass," he said.

"All I did was start a fire and keep it going."

As if on signal, the fire in the hearth collapsed upon itself with a rush of sparks. "Where'd you get the boards?" Corso asked.

"There's a barn outside." She shrugged her shoulders. "There was nothing left in here to burn, so I decided to try out there. I fell through the floor. That's when I froze my hands. Ripping up the old floorboards and dragging them inside."

Corso got to his feet. "We gotta keep the fire going. That's how somebody's gonna find us."

Dougherty began to protest and get to her feet.

"Stay still," Corso said. "I'm a little fuzzy, but I'm okay."

He brought one hand to the top of his head, as if to keep it in place, and then eased across the room and pulled open the door. The bright white reduced his eyes to slits. He stood in the doorway gulping the frigid air. The storm had passed, leaving behind a wind-whipped blanket of white reaching nearly to the tops of the fence posts lining the driveway. He stepped out onto the porch and drew the door closed.

It was more of a shed than a barn. No more than a dozen feet across. Listing heavily to starboard. A rusted split rim and a broken rake hung from the right-hand wall.

She'd burned almost half the floor. Corso stepped inside and grabbed the broken end of one of the boards. The rotting wood crumbled in his hand as he forced it upward, pried it loose from its ancient nails, and then tossed it out into the trampled snow.

Wasn't until he tried to kick the nearest full board loose that he realized the other half of the floor was nearer. No dry rot here. Just solid lumber nailed on two-foot centers along its length.

Corso stepped carefully over the exposed floor joints, reached up over his head, and grabbed the rusted split-rim hanging from the wall. With a grunt he raised the rim above his head and brought it down on the nearest board. The board broke in two. Corso stepped to his right, repeating the process as he moved along, breaking the wood into two-foot lengths.

He dropped the rim to the floor and was bent at the waist, waiting for his vision to clear, when he first heard the sound. An engine.

Carefully he picked his way across the maze of broken floor and made his way outside. Shading his eyes from the glare, he scanned the horizon. Nothing. He stood still and listened, but the sound did not repeat itself.

After several moments he heaved a sigh, stepped back inside the shed, and continued tearing up the shattered pieces of wood, throwing them outside onto the pile. While the far side of the floor had covered nothing but dirt, this side was lined with black plastic.

As he worked his way toward the front of the shed, he began to realize that the black plastic was not a single sheet of material but instead a large folded package held together by long lengths of silver duct tape.

Curious now, he used the flat of his hand to press down on the upper layer. Beneath the black, something brittle shifted. Instinctively Corso pulled his hand back. Then he heard the noise again.

This time he was positive. The sound of a diesel engine at work sent him hurrying back outside. Out on the road, a bright yellow road grader sent a black plume into the sky as it moved along, pushing the snow before it.

Corso began to wave his arms, trying to catch the driver's attention. A full minute of frenzied waving sent Corso to his knees in the snow. And then the blat of the horn, and when he looked up, one of the side windows of the road grader was open and a hand was waving.

He stayed on his knees as the huge machine backed up, turned its front wheels, and started down the driveway toward him. Above the roar of the machine, he heard Dougherty's voice cry, "Yahoo!" He looked to his right. She was standing in the open doorway. She opened her mouth to speak, but by then Corso was already back inside the shed, finding the end of the duct tape and peeling it off. Corso reached down and yanked the top of the plastic apart.

The sight sent him reeling backward, tripping over one of the floor joists and falling heavily to the dirt. The roar of the diesel was closer now. Dougherty was shouting something into the wind. He climbed to his feet. His head throbbed as he shuffled back across the floor. He peeked. Quickly. Out of the corner of his eye. There it was. The ivory grin. The tufts of brown hair still stuck to the skull. The empty eye sockets starting back at him. He brought a hand to his mouth and turned away as his stomach turned over.

He moved carefully, making his way outside. The machine was right in his face now, idling as the driver popped open the door and began to climb down. One look at Corso stopped his descent. Then, without a word, he climbed back into his seat. He stuck his head out the side window. "You don't look so good, buddy," he yelled. Corso nodded his agreement. "I'll send an aide car right out," the driver promised. "You just take it easy till they get here."

"Better send the cops too," Corso shouted. "There's something in the shed they ought to see."